TROUBLE
IN THE FLOATING CITY

MICHAEL CICCARELLI-WALSH

Trouble in the Floating City

Book One in The Zoboros Series

Cover designed by Momir Borocki

Table of Contents

For Mom and Dad, who taught me that the greatest joy in life is doing what you love.

Prologue

"We're out of time!" cried Azral, the floorboards creaking beneath her feet as she ran. She rounded the door to her bedroom, skidding to a stop before her thin frame collided with her equally thin, equally frantic husband, his arms shaking from either his own nerves or the weight of their combined luggage.

"Is Hendricks on his way?" he asked quickly. Clothes exploded out of one of his suitcases and his eyes bugged out of his head as if he had just made the mistake that would get them killed.

"We have two minutes…" she answered, rolling her eyes as she collected their clothes. *Next time I'll do the packing*, she noted, swiftly refolding everything until it all fit properly into their beat-up leather suitcase. Despite Jeslow's formidable intelligence, simple tasks still seemed to elude her husband.

They're almost here. She had seen them through the window coming up the lane, silhouettes against the setting Sun, hundreds of them. All she could think about was what would happen when they arrived. *Focus on the moment*, Hendricks echoed in her head, *don't let the fear paralyze you.* She tried to shake the dark thoughts away, but more came rushing in, memories of a vicious war and the evil part they played in it…

She looked into Jeslow's eyes and saw the same fear staring back at her. She felt his calloused hands wrap around her own. She pressed closer to him, feeling his warmth against the bitter cold seeping into their shanty home.

"Who told them?" she whispered.

"I don't know, but it doesn't matter. What matters is that we get him out of here."

Azral took a deep breath. "Get our things upstairs. I'll get him."

"Hurry," he whispered. Suddenly he was gone, his feet pattering up the stairs. She felt cold again.

Something echoed from the distance. A pop.

Gunfire…

They were closing in on the house. She slipped into the darkness of an adjacent bedroom, her only ally a single shred of sunlight retreating beneath the blinds. She tiptoed across the wooden floor, careful to dodge the toys littering it as she made her way to a crib on the far side. She peeked over its rubber edge and found a pair of gleaming blue eyes staring back at her, sensing the coming danger.

"Come on, sweetie," she whispered, scooping him in her arms, "it's time to…"

The window exploded into shards. She dove behind the crib, the baby tucked beneath her as it cried. Bullets arced along the walls. The toys shook and rattled against the floor. Then, as soon as it had started, the gunfire ceased, replaced only by the baby's cries. And yet the toys around them still shook…

"Shhhh, shhhh, everything's okay," she whispered, stroking the tiny wisps of hair on his round head. She drew a triangular necklace from beneath her shirt and dangled it in front of him. His eyes fixed on it like a magnet, lost in its shining golden edges. He reached a tiny hand up and poked at the center where three arrows met, so entranced he forgot the concept of crying.

The shaking stopped.

Azral sighed with relief. She crawled past the window, one hand cradling the baby against her chest while the other dodged the shards beneath her, then hopped to her feet and ran the rest of the way to the stairs, where Jeslow was rushing down to meet them.

"Are you alright?!" he cried, his face pale and his eyes wide.

"Are you?!" she blurted back.

Glass shattered somewhere in the house.

"Hurry!" said Jeslow.

Azral rushed up the stairs while Jeslow locked the door at the bottom, the one Hendricks had installed for just such an occasion.

The occasion she had prayed would never come.

Azral slowed as she reached the top, making her movements more careful and calculated as she approached the balcony door. Even with the blinds drawn, she feared the gunmen might somehow spot her. She knelt beside the door and peeked between the blinds, scanning the sky first.

Nothing. Just the last oranges and purples reflecting off the clouds as the Sun set on this forsaken planet. Beneath it, a sea of villagers had formed around their home, each face angrier than the last. She recognized them all: Kolanto, the fisherman she always bought from, and Gaisen, the Nurrano carpenter who had built their shanty home just a few months before. She even spotted Kieves, the doctor who had delivered her son, loading his machine gun as he pushed toward the front of the crowd.

Something else caught her attention. Amongst the guns and blazing torches stood a little girl, no more than seven cycles old, climbing up a rundown hovertruck that sat abandoned across the dusty road. A flag of blue and white was draped over her shoulders like a cape, fluttering in the breeze. As the girl turned to face the house, Azral saw a fire in her eyes. The girl wrenched the flag from her neck, raised it up high and screamed.

"KILL THE TRAITORS!"

The mob answered her with a deafening roar. They started chanting her cry at the house, louder and louder, their venom sinking deeper and deeper beneath Azral's skin.

Azral looked to the skies. Still nothing.

The crowd began to turn their backs on the house and face the little girl instead, reciting her chant as if she was their new champion. Azral's eyes locked on the little girl outside, somehow more frightened of her than all the gunmen.

Is this the world my child will inherit? she asked herself, stroking her baby's soft cheeks. *No. It'll be a different world entirely…but only if we survive tonight.*

Suddenly, all was quiet. The chanters just stood there with their backs to her. She noticed the little girl was staring at the crowd, too, equally confused.

A gust of wind tore the flag from the girl's hands and swept it into the crowd. She turned and immediately froze as a stealth ship swept overhead.

Azral burst into tears. *Hendricks.* The ship stopped in front of the balcony, its flat twin engines purring almost inaudibly on each of its long, razor-thin wings; its sleek, silvery belly reflecting the villagers' angry faces back at them as it hovered in place. It spun around seamlessly, its rear liftgate opening for the reception.

The mob protested with bullets. They pinged off the ship's curved face and up into the twilit sky without leaving a scratch. The ship answered by flashing a series of high-powered lights: first three, then two, then three again, forcing the villagers to shield their eyes from its sting.

Azral felt a hand on her shoulder. "That's the signal. Are you ready?" asked Jeslow.

She stared through the open liftgate and into the dark belly of the ship. It was so close, and yet seemed so terribly far away. All she could think about were the guns aiming at them from below…one for every awful thing that led them here. She shook her head. There would be another time to figure out how they had been discovered; right now they had to move. And fast.

Jeslow kicked the door open and Azral raced across the balcony with the baby in her arms, the warmth of the ship's engines hugging her as she leaped into the cargo hold.

She turned, watching Jeslow scoop up their luggage and run for the ship. The crowd had been caught by surprise when she ran, but now they were ready. Bullets peppered the balcony, smashing flowerpots and splintering wood while Jeslow ducked as low as he could.

"HURRY!" she screamed, her heart racing. With a great heave Jeslow tossed their suitcases into the cargo hold and dove in after them, tumbling across the cold metal floor until Azral caught him in her arms, her hands already searching for bullet wounds.

"I'm alright," he groaned, lifting himself slowly to his knees. He reached out a hand and stroked the baby's head. "Is he okay?"

"Yes," she whispered. She offered him their child, but Jeslow didn't take it. His attention was on something else. She followed his eyeline over her shoulder and down a dark corridor, where a dim light glowed off a control monitor. Behind it sat the silhouette of their pilot: two broad shoulders on either side of a wide, black chair.

"Thank you, Hendricks," said Azral. The silhouette didn't move, didn't speak. An uncomfortable silence filled the ship.

"Where's he taking us?" whispered Jeslow.

"He has an assignment for us. It's somewhere more remote than this, somewhere the two of us can be safe."

"The *two* of us?" Jeslow spat back.

Azral bit her lip. She hadn't planned to have this conversation here.

"Azral, I'm not abandoning our son!"

"Then he'll die!" she fired back. "We'll be recognized anywhere we go. The longer we keep him, the harder his life will be."

"His life will be hard regardless," said Jeslow. "Do you realize what people will do to someone like him after everything that's happened?"

"Hendricks has a family who will take him in," she answered, her eyes on her son, who stared wistfully back at her. "They have experience with children like him. They can teach him, guide him, *protect* him."

Jeslow drew his breath to protest, then sighed it away. Azral couldn't blame him for being angry. They had gotten used to these narrow escapes over the past few cycles, but it was different now. The galaxy was different now. And they were no longer the only two in danger.

Jeslow turned to their muted pilot, frustrated. "Where are you taking Kano?!" he demanded, his voice echoing down the shaft.

Hendricks turned his head, the glow of the control console revealing a scar that dredged just below his left eye all the way down to his lip.

"Home," he answered.

Chapter 1

A Secret Meeting

The wind carried a chill with it. Kano felt it cut through his clothes and dig under his skin as he stood atop the mountain. He folded his arms in tight to hold whatever warmth they could, realizing then that he had nothing to protect himself, no jacket to warm him nor communicator with which to call for help. It was just him and this mountain, its slick black rocks sticking out of the ground like daggers in all directions, its base concealed beneath a layer of swirling clouds that flashed with lightning and roared with thunder. All this made Kano ask himself one very important question:

How did I get here?

Two figures appeared in the distance. They stood among the jagged rocks, staring at him. He couldn't make out their faces so he waited for them to approach. They didn't.

A third figure emerged between them. This one drew closer, slow, limping, its face concealed beneath a blood red cloak.

Kano stepped back, but there was nothing to step on. He teetered on the edge, glancing down at the sharp drop into the storm clouds, imagining how the rocks below would skewer him – if the lightning didn't catch him first.

He threw his weight forward and stumbled into the pale, veined hands of the person beneath the cloak. Its body felt so thin, yet as firm as the rocks it stood on. It felt warm, too, and getting warmer. He smelled smoke…

Kano scrambled back as flames singed away the cloak. The figure stood there, the fire consuming its body, yet it didn't flinch. It just stared back at him, a silhouette beneath a layer of orange and red.

"Who are you?" Kano heard himself say. As if to answer, the figure reached out a burning hand. Kano stepped back, only this time he felt his weight slip again, and the next thing he knew he was falling through howling wind and pouring rain, watching the fire shrink as he plummeted into the clouds…

Kano leaped out of his sheets. He looked every direction, expecting to see the figure standing there, but found his bedroom empty of anything except the usual junk.

Again? He rubbed his forehead. It was damp. He had had this dream more times than he could count, though it had never played out like this before. It always came to him in flashes – a mountain that he had never been to, a man that he had never met. This was the first time he had actually *been* there.

He shook his head. Nightmares were the last thing he needed right now. Tomorrow was Shantima, the one time of the cycle when the city would be filled with fun and fireworks and food…so much food. He needed sleep if he hoped to get any fried aivin before the lines got too long, but that wouldn't come with his heart pounding like this.

He treaded softly down the hall to the bathroom sink and splashed some cool water on his face. *It was just a dream,* he reminded himself as he glanced up at the mirror.

Fire. Fire everywhere.

He stumbled back, rubbing his eyes. When he opened them again the room was dark. Empty. Safe. His blue eyes stared back at him, back at the matted clump of black hair hanging over his forehead and ears, at the bony shoulders…they were beginning to broaden, he noticed, though it still looked as if a sharp breeze could send him toppling over. He sighed, glancing at the rot forming in the low ceiling. At least in this apartment he could feel tall.

He felt a rumbling creep into his hand, powerful and unnatural, that seemed to pulse with the heavy beating of his heart. It wanted to come out.

Deep breaths. He shut his eyes and retreated into his exercises. *Keep control.* He clasped both hands together. With each breath the shaking slowed, the urge trickling away until it disappeared into a void.

He opened his eyes and stared at his hands. These…episodes used to be few and far between. Now they came at least once a week, some mild like this one, others so strong that he feared the energy would burst from his hands and crush anything in its path. He had seen it happen…*allowed* it to happen only a few times in his life, and each time he had been lucky there had been no one nearby to get hurt.

...Or report me.

A shadow danced in the corner of his eye. He jumped back, another rumbling rising through his right hand. He balled it into a fist and drew another deep breath, waiting for the energy to subside.

"Makoto, is that you?" he hissed.

His alien brother rose from the shadows like a phantom. He was humanoid in shape, but his Nurrano skin weaved into an argyle pattern of red and black. Like all Nurranos, he was hairless, the top of his head reflecting the light that peeked through the seam of the kitchen door. He wore long sleeves and thick, woolen pants. Strange choice for the summertime, but given the temperature of his home-world, the summer weather here probably felt like a blizzard.

Even in darkness, Kano could see a grin spreading on Makoto's face. He hated that grin; it meant his little brother was up to something. Makoto raised a finger to his black lips as he reached for the kitchen door. Light poured into the hall as it opened, but Makoto remained in the shadow of the door, still smiling.

Whispers leaked into the hallway. Kano recognized Yuchi's voice, shrill and stern even when hushed. *What's she doing up?* Makoto's mother always made it a point to be in bed promptly at nine o'clock. Kano hadn't bothered to check the time when he got up, but he was pretty sure it was closer to dawn than it was to her bedtime.

And who is she talking to?

He crept toward the door, his curiosity piqued. Makoto motioned for him to get down low. Together they crawled across the kitchen floor, the tile cold against his hands, and probably like ice for Makoto. They pressed up against the cabinets beneath the countertop and listened to the voices whispering on the other side of it. There were two. The second voice sounded familiar, though it was hard to place. It had a rasp to it, like smoke had grinded the windpipe into sawdust. He glanced at Makoto, who shrugged.

The whispers stopped. They heard footsteps. *Did she hear us come in?* The footsteps treaded on, *tap tap tap*, but they seemed to be getting quieter, more distant. Makoto poked his head up to see where they were going.

Makoto motioned for him to stand up as well. When he did, he saw the mysterious man sitting in the rocking chair with his back towards them…Makoto's father's rocking chair. No one else ever sat in that chair.

Kano looked to Yuchi. She stood by the window with her back to everyone, the reflection of her red and black face darkening as it tilted toward the ground, her black eyes covered in shadows and her arms wrapped tight around her yellow bathrobe. Whoever this visitor was had arrived unannounced, for Yuchi always dressed her best for company.

"Is he dead?" she asked.

"Worse. Missing."

"How long do we have?" Her words came out choked.

The man rose. He seemed to triple in size, his head practically scraping the ceiling. The rest of him was cloaked in a large, black overcoat that swayed as he joined her by the window. In his reflection, Kano saw a grim look on his long, rugged face, one that made the night surrounding them seem somehow darker. The stubble on his chin had a hint of gray, some of the hairs separated by a deep scar running down the left cheek.

"*That's the Chief of Police,*" he whispered to Makoto.

"Shhhh!" Makoto pulled him down behind the counter as the man turned. They crouched on all fours, neither daring to breathe.

Kano couldn't believe it. Chief Hendricks, *here*. He had only ever seen the man on TV, and briefly at that. The chief was famous for keeping his speeches short and his answers shorter. He struck Kano as someone who hated conversation, which only reinforced the question: why had he stopped to chat in their little apartment this late at night?

"I can't promise you much time," he continued, his voice like grinded chalk. "This creature has broken some of my best, and my best don't break. I'm making arrangements as we speak. For now, stay low, keep your family close. When I call tomorrow, be ready."

Kano heard the whoosh of the overcoat and the creak of the front door.

"When it comes," said Yuchi, her voice suddenly restored to its usual sternness, "will you be able to stop it?"

There was a long pause. "No...but I can slow it down."

The door shut. A thousand questions swirled through Kano's mind. *What creature? Who was missing? And what arrangements was he making?*

He felt Makoto tug on his shirt, realizing then that Yuchi's footsteps were drawing nearer. They scurried across the floor, not stopping until they had safely slipped into Makoto's bedroom and sealed the door behind them.

"What was *that* about?" blurted Makoto.

"I don't know," said Kano, "but I don't like it."

"Do you think it has something to do with Dad?"

Kano hadn't thought of that. Makoto's father had been on business for the past few weeks. Could he be the one missing? Kano felt a heavy weight sink into his stomach at the thought. Makoto's father and mother had watched over him for as long as he could remember. They were family…they were everything…

There was a knock at the door.

"Hide!" Makoto hissed, scrambling to open his closet. "If she sees you, she'll know we were listening!"

Kano dove into the closet, landing in a pile of jackets and pants that reeked of sweat and neglect. The door shut behind him, sealing him in with the stench. He held his nose and watched through the breaks in the wood paneling as his alien brother snatched up a book and opened the door for Yuchi.

"Mother," he said through a fake yawn, "I was just catching up on some reading." Kano noted that he was holding the book upside down. He suspected that Yuchi noted it too.

"I thought you'd be up," she said, allowing herself in and seating herself on the bed.

Makoto sat beside her, marking the page he had been pretending to read.

"Makoto, you may hear in the news tomorrow about a bombing on Darraden. It was small, but…"

"Was Dad there? Was he hurt?!"

"No. No, if your father was on Darraden we would have an entirely different problem."

Kano stifled a chuckle. Darraden was a thieves' den, a planet full of vices that no spouse would ever approve of.

"What I'm worried about is the two of you. Darraden is too close for me to sleep easy at night. For all this to happen right before Shantima is…"

"Mom, don't say what I think you're saying."

"I know how much you boys wanted to go, but the bomber is still out there, and frankly a festival with thousands of people presents the perfect target."

Kano felt like the wind had been knocked out of him. *She can't do this.* In a few hours, everyone would be piling into Downtown. What were they supposed to do, watch it on TV instead? *You can't taste the food on TV!*

"But Mom," pleaded Makoto, "that attack happened on Darraden. This is *Famora*. It's a peace festival, for goodness sake."

"I know sweetheart, I know, but the people behind the attack don't care about that. They'll strike wherever the damage will be greatest. I'm doing this to protect you, and to protect Kano too. I have a promise to keep." She stroked his bald head, but he pushed away. "I'll talk to Kano in the morning. I'm sorry, sweetheart."

Kano got a creeping feeling as he watched Yuchi leave. The gears in his head began to turn. *The visit. The warning.* Something much bigger was going on here, he could feel it. Makoto didn't seem to be catching on as he sulked on the bed, but Kano knew better. There was a reason the chief of police had come tonight, a reason he had warned them to stay close. Yuchi hadn't cancelled their plans because there might be an attack on the festival tomorrow. She did it because there *would* be one.

Kano hardly got any sleep after that. When the Sun finally rose, he was already up, letting the morning breeze flutter through the open window to rustle his unmade sheets. He sat in the windowsill with one leg dangling over a twenty-story drop. Heights like this were nothing to him, nor to anyone else who had grown up in the floating city. He imagined the mountain peaks on the planet's surface, hidden beneath a pink layer of clouds that floated under the city like a never-ending ocean.

He stared up the long line of buildings before him, each one floating freely on its own platform. Hundreds of them, climbing up for several miles, and then back down in the distance to form a giant horseshoe. City Hall stood proudly at the top where the two halves met, its banners waving to the thousands of Famorans below. It looked like a speck from down here, constantly disappearing as buildings bobbed into his line of sight. An orange sky surrounded it, glowing with the rising Sun, the silhouettes of hundreds of hovercars trailing through it on their way east toward Shantima.

Boom.

The explosion echoed up the street like a clap of thunder. Kano jolted, gripping the windowsill before his own panic could send him toppling over. *It's happening.* He craned his head out as far as he could, gazing around the building toward the East Side, where sparks of yellow, red, and green rained down on the tallest and grandest buildings in all of Famora.

Fireworks. He leaned back and clutched his racing heart. *Just fireworks.* Time had crawled by all night as he awaited the inevitable, terrible news. He was already trying to guess at tomorrow's headlines: maybe *Shantima Attacked.* Or *Explosion at the Crossing.* No, wait: *Ironic Twist at the Peace Festival*—that was a sure winner. Feeling dizzy, he hauled himself back into his bedroom and shut the window.

Why is this festival happening at all? he wondered. *If the police chief knows what's coming, why didn't he cancel it? Why didn't he warn anyone…except Yuchi?*

The realization struck him. *She knows something.*

Kano marched from his room and followed the enticing scent of bacon to the kitchen, where Yuchi was flipping the juicy strips one by one on the pan. They sizzled and popped, something that would normally stir his empty belly, but today he couldn't find his appetite. Makoto, who would by now be pacing the kitchen for a taste, seemed to be suffering the same affliction. He sat on the couch, his eyes staring blankly into their only television set.

Kano turned to Yuchi. She looked lost in her cooking, the same way her son was lost in the TV. No doubt she was preparing the same speech she had given Makoto the night before, only this time she was using a gourmet breakfast to soften the blow. Clear desperation. And probably a bad time to press her with questions. Deciding it could wait until she was finished, he left the kitchen and joined his brother on the couch.

Makoto didn't even acknowledge his arrival. Kano could feel the anger steaming off him, as it often did when Makoto didn't get his way. Knowing he was better off letting his brother simmer for a bit, he turned his attention to the TV, where the festival was just getting into full swing. Thousands of people were already lining the walkways, with thousands more surely on the way. The bubbly reporter on screen was bouncing from person to person, asking them silly questions that they answered with an alarming amount of excitement – excitement no one on this couch would get to experience today.

"Why don't we change the channel?" he asked.

Makoto offered something of a grunt, which Kano took for a yes.

One click and a spaceship filled the screen, its jet-black body seeming to stretch infinitely into the darkness of space. *What show is this?* he wondered, leaning in. Two rudders stuck out beneath a curved face of glass like fangs on a great beast, and a pair of wings arced high over the top of the ship like it was a bird swooping in for the kill. Each side of the ship was lined with spikes that could tear the wings off a star cruiser, and where there weren't spikes, there were cannons, or turrets, or other horrible mechanisms that Kano didn't even have a name for. All he knew was that there was only one place that could create a ship this deadly.

"For three hundred cycles, the *Derelict* terrorized the known galaxy," the narrator intoned, ominously. "Sailors claimed that sightings of this ship were a bad omen, for wherever it appeared, they believed that the Poterian fleet would soon follow." The screen showed a field of fire and rubble beneath the lights of a thousand fierce ships.

Kano felt a chill. He had heard stories of the Poterian blitzes. They came in the night and burned everything to a crisp. He had been fortunate enough to grow up after their defeat, but the adults remembered the war all too well, especially Yuchi. Kano always avoided mentioning it, to save her the tears.

"The last confirmed sighting occurred at the great Battle of Mogaddu. Many believed the ship was destroyed there along with the rest of the fleet, but no trace of it has ever been found. Now, twenty-one cycles later, new theories and modern science have helped us recreate the battle and finally uncover the location of the long-lost ship."

A sizzling plate of bacon landed in front of him, with eggs soaked in bacon oil. Yuchi was really going the extra mile on this one. Another plate landed in front of Makoto, but he didn't stir.

"Kano," she began, "there's no easy way to put this, but—"

"I know," interrupted Kano. "Makoto told me earlier." His brother shot him a quick glance, then returned to the program. "I'm fine, really. I wouldn't want to go after hearing that news."

That should lower her defenses. Kano readied his first question: *Why are we in danger?* A good start; it wouldn't give away that he had been eavesdropping last night. When he looked at Yuchi, though, something seemed off. Her usual energy was gone, her warm presence was chilled, and judging from the bags under her eyes, she hadn't had a moment of sleep since their surprise visit last night. He opened his mouth, but something inside him wouldn't let the words come out. He felt as though each question would only upset her more. He quickly took a bite of a juicy bacon strip instead.

Yuchi gave a small smile. "Would you like some toast, too? I have butter and jam, I could—"

"*He said he's fine!*" snapped Makoto.

Yuchi cast a sharp look at her son. For a moment she was coiled to snap back, but instead whirled around and returned to the kitchen without another word.

Kano let out the breath he hadn't realized he'd been holding. Fights between the two of them were the stuff of legend, two overly sensitive people with overly loud voices. He was getting a headache just thinking about it. There was no telling if Yuchi would double-back and go on the attack. Kano racked his brain for any excuse to remove himself from the line of fire.

"I should let Jaden know we're not coming," he said, rising from the couch.

"I already told him," said Makoto, his eyes still glued to the screen. "He says he's going with or without us, and that he'll leave if the fireworks get too scary for him."

Kano froze halfway off the couch, his bottom hovering uncertainly over the cushions. Clearly, his brother still wasn't catching on to what was happening. "You heard the police chief last night," he whispered. "Something bad is coming."

"You seriously believe that?" Makoto checked for his mother, who was busy buttering toast, then hushed his voice. "The police chief is a nut. Everyone knows that." He leaned closer. "I heard he had auto-turrets installed around his house just in case of Poterians."

"I doubt that," Kano lied. Chief Hendricks was a notoriously secretive man. A war veteran, he carried a certain militaristic air, as if a new war could start at a moment's notice. Some politicians had once tried to oust him from office, claiming his "paranoia" was affecting his mental state.

"You can doubt it all you want," replied Makoto. "But I'll believe one of those stupid fairytales that old witch in the Dockyards used to tell us before I believe whatever conspiracy garbage Hendricks is spewing."

"And what if it's true?" pressed Kano. "What if something *is* coming?"

"Well then I guess we're screwed anyway." A platter of buttered toast landed between them, with some jam on the side. Makoto grabbed his plate, threw some toast on it, and marched off to his room. Yuchi sighed and retreated to her own room, leaving Kano alone with the TV.

"Original reports believe the *Derelict* sat here at the front of the formation, but recent models suggest that it was actually placed nearer to the center, where…"

Kano grabbed the remote. He wasn't in the mood to learn about Poterians and their scary ships. He flipped the channel and smoldering ruins filled the screen. *Oh, much better.* Candles swayed along the circumference of the wreckage, casting a glow on the piles of rubble and shattered stone that towered over the onlookers. A young reporter stood there while flashing lights hovered in and out of sight behind her.

Darraden, he realized, raising the volume.

"…where thousands gather to mourn the twenty-three lives lost in the embassy attack yesterday. As authorities continue to search for those missing, that number is expected to rise…"

An embassy? No wonder the chief had been so rattled. If the attackers were willing to strike there, then anything on Famora would be fair game.

"IDF officials have identified the terrorist known as Taranis as the bomber." An image appeared, and suddenly Kano felt the whole world go cold. Tall and thin, the bomber stood shrouded in a black cloak that made him look more demon than man – or whatever species he was. Kano couldn't say for sure; the bomber's face was hidden beneath a metal mask. There was something haunting about that mask, perhaps because it was shaped like a skull, or perhaps it was the strange markings etched into its metal.

"He has been linked to a string of bombings throughout the Outer Territories, though his motives remain unknown. This would mark his first attack on a Central System."

Kano stirred in his seat. He could picture it: this *thing* standing in the middle of the festival, just waiting to blow all those people up…

Jaden. By now their friend was probably already there. He had to warn him.

Kano raced down the hall and grabbed his communicator. The thing was so worn it could barely clamp around his wrist anymore, and the metal was so chipped that it had lost most of its original gray color. He tapped the screen at its center. Despite all the cracks and scratches on it, it miraculously came to life. He began dialing the numbers when something flashed past his window. Something shiny. Something orange.

Oh no. He rushed to the window as the hovercar paraded by, its sleek coat of polish making its obnoxious color even more pronounced, its phantom engine purring with blue energy as it positioned itself a few feet away. A mane of over-gelled blond hair was slicked back over the driver's seat and two pale, skinny arms drummed anxiously against the steering wheel. Just when Kano was about to open his window and shout to Jaden, a flash of red and black leaped into the backseat, and a moment later the hovercar was gone, rocketing off toward the East Side.

Makoto! Kano slammed his fist against the wall and felt the thunder rise into his hand. He took a deep breath, his arm shaking. *How could he be so stupid?* He could feel his hand pulsing now. *Deep breaths.*

He had to tell Yuchi. He raced back into the living room, but when he did, he saw it again on the TV. The mask, with those markings that twisted together into a face of death. *He's here. Yuchi knows it, and now I know it.* She couldn't help now: she had no hovercar to pursue them with. Telling her would only make her more frightened. He would have to bring Makoto back himself.

Chapter 2

The Golden Aivin

Kano grabbed a few coins off the counter and burst out the backdoor, bounding down the fire escape two steps at a time. He dialed Jaden's number; it rang unanswered all the way to the bottom of the stairs.

Typical. He raced up a rickety walkway that hung between two buildings, ignoring the pink clouds that hovered menacingly beneath his feet. A group of kids lounged on the railings on either side of him. He stuffed his hands in his pockets as he brushed past, keeping a careful count of his coins. Fourteen before, fourteen after. Good. He would need them where he was going.

The walkway forked left along the edge of the city. From here he could see Downtown on the other end of the horseshoe, its buildings tall enough to scrape the sky if they weren't already a part of it. Multicolored lights danced from building to building in quick flashes while fireworks popped and fizzled above them, encapsulating the whole show in an umbrella of sparks. From here the festival looked so small, as if he could scoop the whole thing in his palm and place it somewhere safe, somewhere Taranis couldn't touch it. But he was just one kid, separated from it by a sea of clouds.

In the distance, he spotted the orange speck racing toward the lights. *I'm gonna kill them.* He entered a docking station along the edge, one that reeked of diesel and possibly urine. Speeder bikes hummed in a line, each long and thin with two fat hoverpads on either end to keep them floating a few inches off the ground. There were still traces of white paint on them, but rust had turned them mostly to varying shades of red and brown.

"Ah, if it isn't *Kano*!" boomed a voice from across the station.

Kano winced. *Ragar.* When he looked across the way, he saw four large crab legs scuttling toward him. Sagging over them was a red-scaled Bolani, his gray mechanic's uniform barely able to contain his gut. All four of his arms were spread out in greeting, each one dotted with grease stains. He had a puffy face with three eyes spread across it, the middle of which was able to move apart from the other two. That, or it was just a lazy eye, Kano wasn't sure. He had never met another Bolani to compare him to.

Ragar looked winded by the time he reached Kano. He gave him a once-over with his middle eye, seeming to sense the urgency. "You late for a date or somethin'?"

"Something like that," said Kano as he inspected the speeders. They ranged from broken to possibly usable. He knew as much about speeders as he did about Bolanis, and he knew Ragar knew that too, much to his dismay. "I need something fast, Ragar, and something that doesn't look like it needs to be taped together."

Ragar clapped his two pairs of hands together. "Ahhhh, you'll be wanting the Ditari XII then." He pointed to a model slightly less rusted than all the others. "Just came in."

"You sure about that?"

"Swear on my mother's grave."

Kano rolled his eyes and started to walk out of the station. It wasn't long before the crab legs came pattering after him. "Look, I don't give my best models out to just any driver, but because you seem to always bring my speeders back in one piece—"

"When they're not already falling apart," interrupted Kano.

"I'll let you rent the Ditari for…twenty cyos."

"Twenty?" spat Kano. "Your rentals are always twelve even!"

"Yeah, but the tourists don't know that," whispered Ragar.

"Do you want them to find out?"

Ragar folded his arms. "Eighteen cyos and you can keep it for the whole day."

"Ten and I'll have it back to you in an hour for your next tourist."

"Fourteen."

"Deal." Kano tossed him all the coins he had and hopped on board. He twisted the throttle. The engine answered with a cough, and before he knew it, he was flying over the edge of the platform and across the field of clouds, the speeder shaking between his legs.

Will this thing really get me to the other side? He checked the fuel gauge. Only half-full (surprise, surprise), but still plenty to get him there and back, as long as the engine didn't give out, which was becoming increasingly likely with each pitiful cough of exhaust.

He saw the orange speck descending between the towers. He twisted the throttle as far as it would go, but it wasn't fast enough: Makoto and Jaden were already disappearing into the swarms of hovercars all converging on Downtown. Kano flew straight into the mix, dipping and weaving through traffic. Horns blared at him, but he didn't care; he needed to find his brother before it was too late.

Soon the towers began rushing by in great flashes of glittering windows and shimmering metal. He had made it past the clouds, but the orange eyesore of a hovercar was nowhere in sight. That was okay though; if he wanted to catch Jaden, he just needed to find the valets.

A few minutes of frantic maneuvering and he spotted them, little red dots scurrying across a crowded platform. Sure enough, the orange hovercar was there among the thousands of others, its valet steering it to the very front of the platform. No doubt Jaden had bribed him for a prime spot to put his cherished hovercar on display. It was no skin off Jaden's bones; all that money came from his family. They owned some big company on Vasilia, so Kano had heard, but Jaden never seemed to want to talk about them or their money – despite Makoto's constant questions.

Kano glided down to the hovercar just as the valet stepped out. He was a Braiman, short with folded, gray skin and two floppy tendrils for a mouth.

"Where's the driver?" he asked.

"Dien-floom," spat the Braiman, pointing a hooked finger down toward one of the many walkways that wound through the rifts between the floating buildings.

Kano gulped. The walkway was packed, the festival goers marching practically shoulder-to-shoulder in either direction: Humans, Nurranos, Sitchari, Gorvs, the crowd was as colorful as the fireworks bursting over their heads. He would never find Makoto or Jaden in this. Not unless he figured out where they were going.

He turned to the vendors' carts. They dotted the walkway like rocks anchored against a flowing stream. One of them was sure to catch Jaden's fat wallet. Kano brought the speeder down closer and caught a whiff of aivin frying inside one of the carts. His belly rumbled. *Oh, now you're hungry?* He sped on, knowing Jaden would never stop for peasant meat. He caught another scent, something musky and stifling. *Perfumes. Probably expensive.* This was more like it.

He touched down beside the cart, the nearby shoppers scrambling out of the way as the speeder's hoverpads blasted them with hot air. He turned to the shopkeeper, a large man dressed in uncomfortably tight silks, who stood before a shelf of brightly colored jars. Kano had no idea what the jars contained, but whatever it was, it was making his eyes water.

"Have you seen a guy with blond hair?!" he called over the sputter of his engine. "About this tall, had a Nurrano with him?"

The shopkeeper shrugged.

"HEY!" barked a familiar voice. He swiveled around. "You can't fly those down here. It's pedestrians only!"

Marcus. The cadet wore a light-green button-down uniform that was two sizes too large. He marched toward Kano with more bravado than his small frame could carry. In school, Marcus was just another Human in his class, but outside he was one of the many cadets training for the Hyb Academy, a military school as prestigious as it was pretentious.

"Have you seen Jaden?" Kano asked casually, as if he was talking to his classmate and not the authority figure Marcus was trying so desperately to be.

The cadet sneered. "Yeah, I saw him and your brother heading toward the fireworks show. Pray they don't blow it up."

"I'm not holding my breath," replied Kano, lifting off.

Whatever frustrations Jaden brought Kano (of which there were many), he inflicted ten times more on the cadets at school. Jaden had notoriously claimed the top rank in the class the moment he arrived in Famora three cycles ago, and since then had never let it go. He never seemed to care that he had it, though, unless the cadets were in earshot. "Oh, I can't wait to throw away my acceptance letter to Hyb," Kano had heard him say on more than one occasion, and every time he did so, the cadets turned a bright red against their green uniforms. They hated that a rich know-it-all who had never studied a day in his life could swoop in and steal their prize. Kano was pretty sure that Jaden had nothing against the cadets, he just took pleasure in annoying people, especially people not as smart as he was.

Kano followed the walkway to the Crossing, a spiraling ramp that looped hundreds of feet high around a wide, hollow center. It served as the intersection for hundreds of walkways that weaved their way through Downtown, which meant virtually everyone in attendance was converging on it. They had packed into an immovable mass, all pressed against the railings to watch as rockets screamed through the Crossing's center. Children reached out with glee, trying to touch the sparks, their parents too busy watching the fireworks explode overhead to notice. Not that it mattered: the fireworks were well out of reach of anyone, but that didn't stop the cadets from barking at anyone who tried.

At the bottom sat the Launchpad, a flat platform now covered in debris. Scorch marks had blackened the once polished surface, souvenirs of festivals past. Beneath it floated Lower Downtown, a collection of smaller, simpler buildings of brick and stone. It held mostly museums and libraries now, relics of the old Famora that existed before the boom. Kano had always found a charm to it; it was the perfect place to spend a quiet afternoon. Today would not be the day for quiet, unfortunately.

He set his sights on a ramp running between the Launchpad and the Crossing, along which city workers were scrambling back and forth with fresh fireworks for the show. If there was a place for Makoto and Jaden to cause trouble, that was it. He lowered his speeder and, sure enough, spotted a shiny blond head positioned at the bottom of the ramp. There was a cadet blocking his path, and a small line of workers forming behind him.

"For the last time, you're not getting through without a pass, Jaden!"

"Then I'll have to tell the City Council that you stopped me from making their approved modifications to the show," came Jaden's nasally voice.

"You'll make modifications over my dead body," said the cadet.

They stopped and turned at the sound of Kano's engine. He set the speeder to idle mode so they could hear him.

"What's going on here?" he called.

"This guy's holding up the show!" shouted a worker, his arms shaking beneath all the fireworks he was carrying.

"Kano! You decided to show up!" cheered Jaden, clapping his hands together in the customary Vasilian greeting. "Could you please tell her that I have special orders to work on the show?" He turned his head so the cadet wouldn't see him wink.

Kano rolled his eyes. The cadet blocking the Launchpad was at least a head taller than Jaden, with green eyes and auburn hair that came down in curls. He recognized her from school, not just by her hair, but by the grimace on her face, which he suspected – based on the way she carried it to class every day – was a permanent feature. Whatever game Jaden was playing, it wasn't going to work on her.

"Jaden, something's come up. You and Makoto need to come back with me right now."

"Leave? But we just got here! Besides, I've got work to do." Jaden stepped forward.

The cadet stepped in his path. "Don't even try it."

Jaden switched his approach with a carefully placed hand on her shoulder. "Come on Cass, we go way back, you and me."

"My name is Sandra."

Kano heard footsteps. He turned. A gang of five cadets had formed up behind Jaden, malicious smiles on each of their faces.

"You're blocking foot traffic," said a portly cadet at the front of the formation.

Jaden gave him a once-over. "I don't think I'm the one blocking people, mate."

"Choose your next words carefully," replied the cadet, grabbing Jaden's pressed, silk shirt in his sausage-like fingers, "or you'll be watching the rest of the show from a cell."

Jaden glanced over the cadet's shoulder and a smile flashed across his face. The cadets weren't quick enough to catch it, but Kano was. There was something else going on here. He followed Jaden's stare to a depot across from the ramp entrance, where thousands of fireworks were laid out across long rows of wooden tables, ready to be carried down to the Launchpad. They came in all shapes, sizes, and colors, but were all dwarfed by one near the back. Rings of mortars spiraled down its fat body, aimed in all directions so the whole thing resembled a giant bouquet of flowers – if a very dangerous one. Crowning it was the golden head of an aivin, its curved beak aimed proudly toward the sky. It was an odd sight, made even odder by the fact that it was somehow floating between the tables. Someone was carrying it…someone short…

"Hey, where do you think you're going with that?!" barked one of the workers.

The cadets spun around in unison, spotting the aivin as it gained some speed beneath its wings. Jaden took the opportunity to kick the portly cadet in the groin. The fat fingers loosed from his shirt, and Jaden leaped onto Kano's speeder.

"And for the record," said Jaden, smoothing the ruffles in his shirt while the cadet fell to his knees, "cadets can't make arrests, but if you wanna be a dear and call us in, I'll be happy to tell the police exactly why you'll be carrying an icepack around the barracks." He turned to Kano. "Well come on, man, take off!"

Kano stared at the scene, dumbfounded. Makoto was emerging from behind the tables, his smile wide, his short arms cradling the giant aivin, his long legs scrambling up the Crossing as the cadets rushed after him.

Kano felt a vein bulging from his forehead. *Of course watching the fireworks wasn't enough for Makoto. He had to go show off his Nurrano strength and steal one twice his size.* Kano jammed on the throttle and launched along Makoto's escape route with a cloud of exhaust.

"This was the best you could get from Ragar?!" Jaden shouted in his ear, fanning away the smell of diesel.

"I'd say this one's pretty good by his standards," answered Kano. "And I didn't have time to be picky; you guys ran off before I could warn you about the attack."

"Attack? What do mean…?" Jaden thumped him on the back of the head. "Ah jeez, man, you've been watching too much TV again."

"No, I mean it. Last night we saw Yuchi talking to the police chief, and…"

"*Really?*" interrupted Jaden. "Because last night I saw a fairy princess that farts flowers and bakes cookies through the power of friendship. Look, as far as I'm concerned, if you can get me the hell away from here, I'm all for your delusions. But you gotta get Makoto and that firework on this speeder *first*."

Kano saw the aivin's head weaving through the crowd, so nimble it could pass for a ballet dancer, while a horde of green-shirted cadets barged their way through the crowd in pursuit, their batons raised.

"Where's he going?" asked Kano.

Jaden laughed.

"You guys are completely winging this, aren't you?"

"I prefer the term 'improvising,' but if you wanna get technical, then wing us that way." Jaden pointed to the railing Makoto was so gracefully climbing onto.

Kano swung them beside Makoto, a narrow strip of open air between them and the Crossing with nothing but the pink clouds below. Makoto tossed the firework effortlessly to Jaden, who grunted as if the thing had punched the wind out of him. The speeder dipped from the added weight, and again when Makoto hopped onto the back. *Hold together*, thought Kano, clutching tight to the handlebars. He jammed on the throttle and soon they were gliding away from the Crossing and toward the edge of Downtown, but at only half the speed they were moving before.

"Nice moves, Makoto," said Jaden, beaming at the crown jewel towering over his head.

"I make my people proud," replied Makoto, spinning around so he could swing his tired legs over the back of the speeder.

"Tell that to Yuchi when we get back," snapped Kano. "You'll be lucky if you haven't already given her a heart attack."

"Well technically, Nurranos have two hearts, so it's not really as big a deal as you're making it out to—"

"Shut up, Jaden!" Kano felt the energy pulse through his hands. He took a deep breath, speaking now between clenched teeth. "Now why did you guys need to steal this…thing?"

"This *thing* is a Golden Aivin," corrected Makoto, "and it is the greatest firework ever forged by man."

"Braiman, actually," corrected Jaden. "Pyromaniacs, all of them. Only they could create something so beautifully evil."

"And tell me, then," continued Kano, "why you want to set off something so beautifully evil when it was gonna go off during the show *anyway?*"

"Set it off?" spat Jaden, offended at the thought. "No, no, no. Something this magnificent should be put on display."

Kano felt a headache coming on. *How is this moron top rank in the class?* "You can't put something stolen on display, that's how people find it and take it back!"

"Guys…" started Makoto.

"What Makoto? Can't you see Kano is busy complaining?"

"Guys…the leader…"

"The leader of what?"

Kano heard it just before it zoomed by. A speeder, longer and bulkier than his, its frame jet-black and polished with love. The twin exhaust pipes glowed blue from the phantom engine purring inside it. It spun around to face them. Atop the beautiful work of machinery was a rider clad in a dark-green uniform, its chest lined with silver medals and its head cocooned within a black helmet, its visor reflecting their frightened faces back at them.

"Guys, I can't outrun him on this thing," said Kano, his hands trembling against the feeble handlebars.

The rider drew a baton from its belt. At the push of a button the tip pulsed with electricity. A moment later the rider was charging for them.

"Then outmaneuver him!" shouted Jaden. "*Dive, dive, dive!*"

Kano dipped them into a nosedive, jamming the throttle as far forward as it would go. Tower windows rushed past him in a blur. The wind howled in his ears, yet he could still hear the other speeder thundering after them, growing louder and louder as it closed the distance. He shifted gear and swung them out of their nosedive, propelling them around one of the towers and straight toward a wall of oncoming traffic.

"Wooo! Here we *goooo*!" cheered Makoto.

Horns blared as Kano weaved between hovercars, relying on his instincts to get them out of this alive. A part of him wished he had left Makoto and Jaden to the terrorist (they would have probably been safer), but that opportunity was gone. Now the best he could do was steer them higher, to where the traffic was lightest.

"Get us back to my hovercar!" shouted Jaden. "We can outrun him in that!"

"One thing at a time!" screamed Kano, dipping down as a hoverbus roared overhead. Then he heard it: the crackle of electricity. He went into another dive, glancing up as the rider rocketed over them.

"Nicely done, Kano!" cheered Jaden, soaking in their new bird's eye view of the Crossing.

Kano smiled, but when he hit the shift, that smile faded. The shift wouldn't move.

"You can stop diving now…" said Makoto.

"I can't, it's locked!" Kano tugged at the handlebars, but they wouldn't budge. The speeder kept plummeting toward the center of the Crossing.

"Oh boy…" mumbled Jaden.

A rocket screamed past them and exploded overhead. Sparks rained down and singed their clothes while the railings began rushing past, the people on them pointing and screaming.

"Why did you drag me into this?!" Kano screamed, the sparks biting at his back. He glanced over his shoulder and spotted the jet-black speeder diving after them.

"Get us out of this nosedive before he catches us!" screamed Makoto.

"I can't!" cried Kano, tugging helplessly at the shift.

Jaden rolled his eyes and drew a match from his pocket.

"Hold her steady, Makoto!" he shouted, passing the Golden Aivin over his shoulder. Makoto excitedly aimed it up at their target. "Keep us moving straight!" he shouted back at Kano.

"That won't be a problem!" Kano shouted back, watching the frightened faces of the crowd whiz by.

"Brace yourself!" Jaden lit the fuse. It vanished in a puff of sparks that snaked past Makoto's hand and up the majestic firework.

"My whole life has led to this moment," whispered Makoto, close to tears with joy.

By the time the rider realized what was happening, it was too late. The aivin's mortars flushed with red flares that swirled round and round, climbing higher and higher up the Crossing in a vortex. Then the aivin's head burst off. Golden sparks exploded out of it, forming into the shape of a giant aivin. It flapped its golden wings as it soared through the tunnel of red flares, its beak aimed straight at the rider.

The rider shielded himself with his hands as the great bird exploded. The red flares burst in unison, forming a glorious orchestra of fire. There must have been a thousand explosions in total, and just as many colors that rained down for thousands of cheering people.

Makoto roared with maniacal laughter. *"That was incredible!"*

Kano felt the tension release from the handlebars. *Just in time.* The speeder began to level out as they reached the Launchpad. That was when Makoto shouted something.

"What was that?" he turned around just as the rider collided with them, speederless. Kano felt a hand clench tight around his shoulder, and before he knew it, he was out of his seat and tumbling across the platform. The rider was tumbling with him, keeping his grip as they spilled out over the edge. Kano clung to the edge with both hands, his feet dangling above a sea of pink. The rider grabbed his leg. It felt like a ton of bricks had just been tied to him. *He's much bigger up close,* he thought, his fingers slipping, the weight sucking him down. He tried to pull himself up but it was no use. His arms ached; he could barely breathe. He saw the workers scrambling toward him but it was too late. He slipped from the edge, gasping in the air as it rushed to meet him, the cool vapor of the clouds patting his face. He saw the rider for a moment, staring at him through the black helmet, before vanishing into the clouds.

No one ever told me how dark it was down here, he thought. With every moment he fell, the clouds seemed to choke more and more sunlight away. He spun himself upright and away from the wind, his heart pounding, just in time to see the last wisps of sunlight disappear. All he could think was *Please don't die, please don't die, please don't die*. No one had ever died falling off Famora, but knowing his luck, he might just be the first.

A blue light flickered in the distance. It grew brighter and brighter, almost angelic, and suddenly it was upon him, bursting through the clouds and wrapping him in its energy. His momentum slowed. He felt weightless. A blue bubble began forming around him. He pressed his hand to it. It hummed against his skin and shuddered at his touch, but never allowed his hand to pass through. He had seen these a million times before: people fell off platforms every day…but never him. He had never seen the appeal of free-falling, and after this experience, he hoped to never try it again.

The sunlight was returning. Though he couldn't feel it in the weightlessness, the bubble was pulling him up. Soon the clouds cleared away and Famora returned to him, its buildings towering hundreds of feet overhead. The bubble didn't take him back to the Crossing, though. Instead, it carried him to a low-lying platform among the brick and mortar of Lower Downtown. He saw Jaden and Makoto waiting there in his borrowed speeder. Jaden's mouth was moving, but Kano couldn't hear him through the bubble. He found that to be a pleasant improvement.

The bubble lowered onto the platform and popped on contact, sending Kano stumbling into his friends.

"Nicely done team," said Jaden. "Now let's get back to my hovercar before that other guy shows up."

Kano nodded, scanning the platform for another blue bubble, but not seeing one yet. All he saw were children racing toward the edge, laughing as they dove off for another free-fall.

"First time on the Trampoline?" asked Makoto.

"But certainly not yours," replied Kano, watching the last child disappear over the edge. Makoto chuckled.

Kano sat down at the controls and hit the throttle, but this time the speeder answered with only a cough, more pitiful than any he had heard before.

"Are you out of gas?" asked Makoto.

"That's impossible," said Kano. "It says here we have half a tank." He tapped the fuel gauge and the meter dropped from the center all the way to E. *Dammit Ragar...*

The speeder dropped with a crash, throwing all three of them off. When Kano stood back up, he could see speeders descending from the Crossing.

"Cadets..." grumbled Makoto, spitting on the ground in disgust.

"This way, hurry!" said Jaden. He rushed across the platform and toward a wide, round building of marble that looked wholly out of place among the brick. A bulbous glass dome topped it off, reflecting the sky and towers above in a swirling aura of blue and silver.

"No, please, anywhere but there," pleaded Makoto.

"There's no time!" Jaden shouted back, pointing to the speeders circling like vultures.

"He's right," said Kano, following Jaden up the stairs. He could hear Makoto grumbling behind him, but unlike his brother, he could care less about what lay inside, so long as it kept them safe from the cadets.

He reached the top and faced a pair of glass-paned doors. Golden-red light reflected off the panes, giving the whole thing an enchanted look, as though the doors led into another world, another time. There was no time to stand around wondering about it; Jaden had already plowed through them. He and Makoto raced in after him, neither aware of the blue bubble floating over the platform behind them.

Chapter 3

The Archives

Their mad rush inside came to an immediate halt. A hundred pairs of eyes, most with bags under them, were peering up at them from computer screens or glancing over at them from behind shelves. The only sound was the glass-paned doors creaking shut behind them. Slowly, the watchers returned to their business, leaving Kano, Makoto, and Jaden standing awkwardly in place.

"Well, we better start acting like we belong here," mumbled Jaden, leading the way.

Wherever 'here' is, thought Kano. He craned his neck for a look at the glass dome arcing high overhead like a second sky. Sunlight filtered through it, casting a yellowish glow over everything, including the dust that choked the already stuffy air. He had expected this place to be broken up into floors and sections, but instead it was one giant, circular room with computer stations rounding its edge. The center of the room was taken up by a labyrinth of shelves that towered almost as high as the dome. Blue datacubes lined each shelf, each one small enough to fit in his palm. There must have been over a million of them, most far out of reach of the people below. Little bots zipped up and down the shelves, their hoverpad bases humming so softly they gave the room a certain melodic ambience. Kano watched one of the bots scoop a datacube in its wiry arms and fly it down to one of the students. The bot hovered there, its single red eye focused on the student. It wasn't until the student took the cube that the bot flew away for its next delivery.

"Where are we?" asked Kano, his eyes lost in the swarms of other bots flying from shelf to shelf.

"Only the most boring place in the entire city…" said Makoto.

"It is not!" said Jaden, loud enough to make some scraggly students glance up angrily from their screens. He hushed his voice. "This is the Archives, a one-stop shop for anything and everything that you could ever want to know."

"And where Jaden spends most of his weekends," whispered Makoto so only Kano could hear.

"You can find a lot of great stuff here," continued Jaden, claiming an open computer station. "Histories, biographies, records, blueprints. If it happened in the galaxy, there's probably a datacube for it."

"I'll try to contain my joy," said Makoto.

Jaden tutted. "You're missing the opportunity here." He typed something. A few moments later, a bot was floating beside him, cube in hand. He took the cube and placed it on a flat console beside the computer screen. The cube began to glow. Files exploded onto the screen, hundreds just waiting to be clicked on.

"What are you looking for?" asked Kano.

"Common cadet drills," he answered. "Tactics, formations, field notes, everything they use in their training. We can find whatever search strategy they're using and figure out a way to slip through it."

"Are we even allowed to look at this?" asked Kano, a knot forming in his stomach.

"It's public record," assured Jaden. "If it wasn't, then the bots would've locked it up in the Classified Section."

Classified Section. Kano looked around anxiously. If there were classified documents here, then no doubt the building was under careful watch. He even *felt* like he was being watched. He didn't see any green uniforms, but he did see plenty of bots, their red eyes darting every which way. Surely one of them was focused on him. He spied one on its descent to a nearby station. The bot handed its cube off to a blue creature and flew away without as much as a glance in his direction.

The blue creature, however, was watching him intently.

It had two black eyes the size of apples and a face so wide it looked like someone had grabbed its cheeks and stretched them out as far as they would go. Its teeth looked more like needles than actual teeth, packed together in two long, terrifying rows. It hopped out of its chair, its bare feet landing with a plop. It was much shorter than he expected, barely taller than the chair it had been sitting in, with a faded gray poncho covering most of its little body, and two unnaturally long arms hanging down almost to its feet. Kano had never seen a species like this before, and he had the horrible feeling it might be the last thing he ever would see.

A bot floated down between them, cutting off his view. When it rose again, the creature was gone. Kano blinked. *How could he just disappear?* He looked everywhere, but the only blue he saw came from the cubes glowing on their consoles. *Am I going crazy?*

A cool rush of wind stirred the otherwise stagnant air. Kano turned. In the doorway stood a towering figure, the Sun blazing behind it. Its helmet was singed, its dark-green uniform in tatters. Kano remembered the rider wearing gloves, too, but they were gone now, likely destroyed by the fireworks. In their place were two clenched Human fists.

Kano realized he wasn't the only one staring; all the students had stopped what they were doing to watch. Even Jaden and Makoto had frozen. No one made a sound. All they could hear were the echoes of the rider's boots as it marched into the building and removed its helmet.

They have the same face, Kano realized. It was the face he had seen the night before, in his own living room, only this one was unwrinkled and unscarred, with the hair buzzed so short it was hard to tell its actual color. His neck was thicker too, with veins sticking out in places Kano didn't even know Humans had them. There was one other difference between the rider and the chief, the most jarring of all: instead of brown eyes, the rider's were a bright orange, blazing like fire as they surveyed the scene.

"Leave it to Junior to ruin the fun," mumbled Jaden, dipping into a nook underneath the computer station. Kano and Makoto packed in on either side of him before Junior could look in their direction.

"You know him?" whispered Kano.

"Oh, we've bumped shoulders a few times," said Jaden, "and I gotta say, he's not one to let things go."

Perfect. Kano knew Junior only by reputation. Highest marks in the school (besides Jaden) and voted most likely to get accepted to the Hyb. He had also been voted least likely to lose in a fight, making the thump of his boots suddenly more terrifying.

The boots stopped right in front of their station, so close Kano could have reached out and touched them. He held his breath, his heart pounding.

They treaded on. *Oh thank goodness.* Kano eased back, and his head bumped against the back of the station.

Oh no.

Two burly hands lunged under the station. One grabbed him by the collar, the other Jaden. A moment later they were hovering in midair, mere paperweights as they stared into those orange eyes.

"Long time, no see!" said Jaden. "How's the family?"

"Shut up," said Junior. "Tell your Nurrano buddy to come out too."

"I'm pretty comfortable down here, thank you."

Junior swung a savage kick underneath the station. There was a yelp, and Makoto came crawling out, clutching his shin.

"You three are coming with me," said Junior, releasing Kano and Jaden. He drew his baton and thumped it against his palm. "Any questions?"

Kano glanced at Jaden, just in time to catch him wink at Makoto.

Please, not again.

"As a matter of fact," began Makoto, "I'd like to see a lawyer about my leg."

"I'm sure you'll survive," Junior mumbled back.

"Yeah, maybe you're right…" he said, placing the bruised leg tenderly on the ground. He squealed and collapsed.

Junior rolled his eyes and bent over to pick him up.

Kano heard typing. He turned to Jaden, who was leaned up against the station, his hands hidden behind his back as he typed. Jaden smiled at him as if to say, 'Get ready.'

Somehow, Kano didn't feel ready.

Junior hoisted Makoto to his feet. The Nurrano stood half his height, though he looked even smaller with the end of the baton digging into his chest.

"Don't make me use this," said Junior.

"I wouldn't dream of it," said Makoto.

Something beeped. Junior turned. A single red eye stared back at him, hovering there with a datacube in hand.

Junior shook his head and returned to his prisoners. "Alright, hands over your heads, I don't want any—"

A thin finger tapped his shoulder. He turned again. A second bot hovered beside the first. It placed a datacube in his hand without his asking.

"The hell?" He tossed the cube away just as another bot floated in and replaced the cube in his hand.

"*ENOUGH!*" He brought his fist back, ready to drive it through the bot's big, glowing eye, when a wiry hand pried his fingers open and crammed another cube into it.

Kano looked up. A swarm of bots were raining down on Junior, each one fighting to hand him the next cube.

Kano felt a tug at his shoulder. Jaden was pulling him into the maze of shelves, Makoto right at their heels. They disappeared just as he heard Junior cry, "*I DON'T WANT YOUR DAMN CUBES!*"

"Which way?" he asked, spotting a fork in their path.

"Through here," answered Jaden, leading them right, then left, then right again. Thousands of datacubes rushed by with every turn. The maze went on forever – or Jaden was just leading them in circles, it was hard to tell. When they finally stopped, their path forked into five possible directions: four were other passages, the fifth a set of stairs that sank beneath the building. At the bottom of it was a sealed metal vault.

"Is that the way out?" asked Makoto.

"No…" said Jaden, turning to each of the other four paths that snaked into the unknown.

"You're lost, aren't you?" said Kano as the clop of boots echoed down the passageway.

"Temporarily inconvenienced," answered Jaden. He bolted down the steps, his fingers tapping on his shiny communicator.

"What's down here?" asked Makoto, he and Kano chasing close behind.

"Storage," Jaden answered quickly, stopping at a panel beside the vault.

Kano stared at the shimmering metal of the vault, then at the panel. They would need a card to swipe in, and not just any card. A vault like that required special clearance of some kind. *Very special clearance.*

"This isn't storage," he realized. "It's the *Classified Section!*"

"Same thing!" said Jaden, ripping the cover off the panel and plugging his communicator into one of the exposed wires.

"But we're not allowed in there!" Kano protested.

"Neither is Junior," said Jaden, "which is good enough for me."

Kano watched the symbols flash across the screen of Jaden's communicator. "Jaden, we could go to jail for this!"

"Do you have a better idea?" whispered Makoto.

"Well I can't think of a worse one…"

The vault door clicked open. They heard footsteps thumping over their heads.

"It's now or never, gentlemen," said Jaden. He tugged at the door, but his frail arms didn't stand a chance against solid metal. Makoto joined him, their combined strength enough to get the door inching forward.

This is it. This was where he drew the line. He had helped them steal from the festival, taken a fall off Famora, but if Jaden and Makoto wanted to break into a classified room, then they could face the consequences themselves. If anything, they deserved it after everything they had put him through today.

He started up the stairs, quietly, listening to them struggle with the door. Suddenly, a shadow fell over him. A silhouette stood atop the stairs, staring down at him with fiery eyes.

Junior. Though the cadet seemed so much shorter up there, and skinnier too…

And on fire.

Kano bolted back to the vault. He grabbed hold of the door and pulled with all his might. They slipped inside, one by one, Kano going last. He looked back just before the vault closed, but the man on fire was gone.

All the light was gone, too.

"I don't like this," said Makoto.

A blue light flickered in front of them, illuminating the console beneath it. It wasn't just any light, though; it was a hologram – a man, about the size of a shoe, standing atop the console with a smile on his face.

"Access codes please," he chimed.

Jaden stepped forward. He plugged his communicator into the console and began typing. Kano was about to protest when the blue man disappeared, shrouding them in darkness once more.

"Good going," he mumbled. "Now that little guy is gonna call security."

"Relax," said Jaden, "he's just rebooting."

The lights came on. They found the room around them was empty, save for the console, and barely wide enough to fit the three of them. A tall glass wall stood behind the console. The lights beyond it flipped on, one row at a time, illuminating a succession of shelves lined with datacubes that were caked in dust and cobwebs.

The blue man materialized with the same joyful grin. "Hello," he said, "my name is Clarence. How may I assist you?"

Jaden turned to Kano, looking much too satisfied with himself.

"What should we ask him first?!" said Makoto.

Jaden smirked. "Tell us about Taranis. Is he really that bad?"

"Taranis," repeated Clarence. A bot emerged in the distance and scurried between the rows of datacubes. It snatched one and zipped back to a console on the other side of the glass, setting the datacube down gently with its wiry fingers.

"Identity unknown," continued Clarence. "Location unknown. Earliest sightings date back seven months ago to the planet Camini."

"Can you show us all of the planets he's been seen?" asked Jaden.

The lights dimmed. A giant circle appeared on the glass wall – a map, dotted by thousands of planets and stars and systems all slowly spinning clockwise. *It's the whole galaxy,* Kano realized, *or at least most of it.* The map was incomplete. There was a long, gray blur where the Rift lay, and the uncharted space beyond where it was said the Poterian Empire was hidden.

Red dots appeared along the charted edges of the map like sores, all scattered without rhyme or reason.

"See," said Jaden, "Taranis never hits more than one planet in a system. Fat chance he'll break that streak with half the Republic on his tail."

Kano shook his head. "Hendricks knows things that we don't. Clarence, can you tell us why Taranis is attacking these planets?"

"No motive is known at this time," stated Clarence cheerily.

Kano folded his arms. Not even classified records knew anything about this terrorist. He would have to try another angle. "Clarence, what can you tell us about…Yuchi Sasaki?"

"One moment please." The bot scurried off again and returned with another datacube, this one trailing with cobwebs. When it deposited the cube, at least a thousand files burst across the glass, arranging themselves into a timeline. "Yuchi Sasaki, born in cycle 5795. Enlisted in the Interplanetary Defense Force at the age of eighteen cycles. Became a transportation officer, moving supplies between IDF outposts in the Outer Territories."

"Hendricks was a pilot too," said Jaden.

"Did she serve under Chief Hendricks?" asked Kano.

"No," answered Clarence. "But Yuchi Sasaki and Aaron Hendricks Senior did serve together under Admiral Carmichael."

"*The* Admiral Carmichael?" blurted Makoto. That name was the stuff of legend. It was said that the admiral had faced down the entire Poterian fleet with a force a fraction of its size – and destroyed it. To this day, no one knew what he had done to win the battle; there were no survivors.

"What was she transporting for Admiral Carmichael?" asked Kano.

"Level Ten clearance required," stated Clarence.

Kano glanced at Jaden. "I'm on it," Jaden replied, typing away on his communicator.

"Tell us about her son, Makoto!" blurted Makoto eagerly.

Kano shot him an annoyed look. "What?"

"Makoto Sasaki. Born 5828 in Famora. Nurrano. Son of Yuchi and Yamamoto Sasaki."

"Now do Kano! Kano Sasaki!" cheered Makoto, far too amused with himself.

"Kano Sasaki," continued Clarence. "Adopted. Born 5825 on Darraden. Human."

Kano froze. *Darraden?* "That's not true," he stammered, "I was…*Kano* was born here."

"Brought to Famora in 5826. Adopted by Yuchi and Yamamoto Sasaki."

5826? That left him on Darraden for a whole cycle – a whole cycle that he never knew about. *A whole cycle I spent with Mom and Dad.* He had tried a million times, but to this day he couldn't recall their faces. He didn't even know their names. Yuchi never told him anything about them, no matter how much he pleaded. All she would say was "just know that they loved you very much," a sentiment that became less comforting every time he heard it. If they really loved him, why weren't they here? Why hadn't they tried contacting him sometime in the last sixteen…fifteen cycles? He had so many questions…and a machine that could give him all the answers.

"Clarence," he began, "who were my…Kano's parents?"

"Parents Azral and Jeslow," said Clarence. "Chief scientists in the Republic's Interplanetary Defense Force."

Azral and Jeslow. Things were off to a great start. "Where are they now?" he blurted, leaning up against the console.

"Current location unknown. Last confirmed sighting on Sitcharen in cycle 5825."

Not the answer he wanted, but if he could find out why they disappeared in the first place…

"You said they were scientists. What did they study?"

"Quantum physics."

"What were physicists doing for the IDF during the war?"

"Classified," replied Clarence.

"Classified?" spat Kano. "The whole section is classified! Where did they go?"

"Current location unknown."

"No, during the war, dammit!" His hands began to vibrate, but he didn't care. He had never had a chance like this before, and he wasn't about to let the blue man stop him now.

"Level Ten clearance required."

"Hang on," said Jaden as he typed. "I'm almost there…"

"Hurry," said Kano, his eyes wide, his fists shaking.

"Kano, you need to take a deep breath," said Makoto.

"I'm breathing just fine!" he snapped. The room rattled around him.

"Minor tremor detected," said Clarence. "Activating lockdown."

"No, wait!" shouted Kano. The room was flooded in red light. The bot pulled the cube from the console and rushed it back to its place on the shelf. "*Come back!*" he cried, pounding his fist on the glass over and over again. "My family is on that cube!"

An unnatural energy began to swirl around his fist, weaving between his fingers in angelic wisps. Jaden stared at it, horrified, as Kano drew his fist back.

"Kano, *wait!*" he cried.

Kano struck the glass again. This time the energy exploded from his fist and tossed him away like a rag doll. He crashed into Makoto and together they tumbled onto the floor.

"Whoa," said Jaden.

Makoto rose first, rubbing the back of his bald head. "Well I don't see how this could get any worse," he grumbled.

"Authorities have been alerted to the disturbance," said Clarence jauntily.

"Thanks, Clarence."

Kano rose in a daze. *What was that?* He stared up the glass wall. A giant crack ran up from where he had struck it. He had never felt that amount of power before. It was like the whole world had concentrated itself into the palm of his hand. It was incredible, exhilarating…

"*Heavy,*" groaned Jaden, struggling to push the vault door open.

Suddenly remembering where they were, Kano raced to Jaden's side and helped him push, the red lights flashing in his eyes. Soon they had a sliver of an opening, and Makoto shot through it first.

"Last one out buys lunch!" he shouted, bolting up the stairs.

"You only said that because you're a Nurrano!" shouted Jaden, his skinny legs chasing Makoto at half the speed.

Kano raced up two steps at a time, passing Jaden easily and following Makoto into the maze of shelves. Something felt different, though. The place seemed quieter than before, stiller. The bots hovered above him, frozen, their red eyes blinking. When he reached the edge of the maze, Kano found the computer stations were all abandoned, not a soul in sight save for Makoto, and not a sound other than their own footsteps.

"Guys, we made it!" Makoto shouted back to him.

Kano saw it: the glass-paned doors growing in the distance.

"*Guys!*" called Jaden.

Kano glanced over his shoulder. Jaden was a little further back. Behind him, just emerging from the maze, was the behemoth of a cadet beneath the tattered uniform, barreling down the passageway.

"Keep going, Jaden!" Kano called back. He was almost at the doors, Makoto already through them. He could hear the boots gaining on them. He kicked his feet up faster, swung his arms harder, the datacubes whirring by him in a blue blur as he ran.

He shoved through the doors and into the sunlight, so bright off the stone steps he didn't see Makoto standing in front of him. He slammed into his brother and fell back against the stone.

"Why did you stop?!" he asked, brushing the bits of rock from his elbow. As his eyes adjusted, he found his answer.

An army of cadets covered the steps below, their batons drawn, while a crowd of students stood impatiently behind them, waiting to be let back inside. In front of them all stood a man dressed in a blue and white officer's uniform, its plastic plating reflecting the sunlight. A thin trim of gray hair surrounded his bald head, which also reflected the sunlight quite well. He had a long, narrow face with a large nose and pointed chin. His thin lips stretched into neither a smile nor frown, and sunglasses covered his eyes to conceal any trace of emotion.

"It's alright boys," he called, his voice more stern than conciliatory. "Just walk down quietly with your hands raised. No one's gonna hurt you." He glared at a portly cadet beside him, who mumbled something to himself as he stuffed his baton into his belt.

"Colonel Novak," said Jaden, emerging from the Archives with Junior right behind him, the cadet's baton pressed against his neck. "Today just keeps getting better."

"I said quietly, Upton," said Novak, all emotion still absent from his face.

Kano looked to the Crossing, where thousands more were staring down at him, oblivious to the fireworks bursting over their heads. *Exactly how much trouble are we in?* he wondered anxiously.

Junior waited until he reached Novak to release Jaden. "Colonel," he said with a two-armed salute, "these three were caught stealing government property. When I pursued, they broke into the Classified Section."

"I'm sure I would've done the same if you were the one chasing me, Junior," replied Novak, the slightest smirk crossing his lips.

Kano was stunned. Had the colonel just taken their side?

"Sir, the penalty for breaking into—"

"I know the penalty, Junior. You can stand down now."

"But sir—"

"You've done quite enough getting everyone riled up over a firework. Now *stand down.*"

Kano could feel the white-hot anger bubbling off Junior. The cadet shoved his baton into his belt and stormed off without a word, the other cadets stepping well out of his way.

"You three, with me," ordered Novak. "Everyone else, back to your posts. We've still got a festival to maintain, and I'm sure the early birds are already boozed up for trouble."

The cadets dispersed. Kano caught a few exchanging funny looks as they passed. Even he was perplexed. First the police chief showed up at their house, and now the chief's second-in-command showed up here to reprimand them over a firework. Kano wasn't one to believe in coincidences.

Novak escorted them to his hovercar: a two-seater, blue with a white stripe running down the middle. Similar to most police cruisers, but smaller and sleeker, fit for the pleasure of someone in command.

He sat on the hood and stared at the boys for a moment. "Do you know why my hovercar is so shiny?" he asked.

"Because you use Slixu wax to get the extra—"

"No Jaden," he interrupted. "It's because I don't get called into the field very often. Hell, I rarely wear this stupid thing." He shook the armored plating, getting as close to a frown as his lips dared to go. "No, I came as a favor to the chief. I believe you two had a brush with him recently."

Kano and Makoto glanced at each other. It was Kano who spoke. "I don't know what you're talking about."

"You should leave the lying to your brother," said Novak. "I understand he's the more proficient at it.

Anyway, Hendricks had hoped that what you overheard would have been enough to keep you both out of trouble. Now I see that it's quite the opposite."

Hendricks knew. He knew the whole time.

Novak continued in a hushed voice. "Whatever you three were digging for in the Archives, you won't find it. Level Ten requires clearance the likes of which is held by only a handful of people in the entire galaxy. Trying to crack into it is enough to put you three in jail for a long, long time – something I'm sure would thrill my cadets." He gave Jaden a harsh look before continuing. "But every now and then I do enjoy disappointing them. Hendricks ordered me to give you these." He drew three metal bracelets from his belt, each lined with blinking red lights. He grabbed Kano's arm and clamped one on before he had time to react. The lights on it turned green. When Kano tugged at it, the bracelet wouldn't budge.

"These will give us your location at all times," continued Novak, clamping one onto a pouty Makoto. "Upton, you are to drive the Sasakis home right away. Their mother has already been informed that they're coming, and what they've been up to."

Kano gulped. *I'm dead. We're dead.* The only thing he had left to look forward to in life was finding out how Yuchi would end them.

"Would it be alright if we stopped at my place first?" asked Jaden as the final bracelet clamped around his wrist.

"I don't care," mumbled Novak, climbing into his two-seater. "Just get it done." He slammed his door and rolled down the window as he took off. "And if you do anything stupid, I'll know!"

Kano noticed the smile on Jaden's face – the smile that said this was exactly what Jaden planned to do.

Chapter 4

Missing

"What are you up to?" asked Kano, watching Jaden's reflection scramble back and forth around the dining room.

"You'll see," said Jaden for the tenth time, running wires across a dusty dining table set for a nonexistent family.

Kano continued to stare out the window, though to call it a window was an understatement. The entire wall was made of glass, overlooking many of the towers of Downtown as they bobbed in the sky. He could see the fireworks exploding in the distance, the swaths of onlookers marching toward them like an army of ants along the walkways. A picture-perfect view, yet he kept finding himself staring at his hand instead, at the dried blood on his knuckles from where the power had struck. He could still feel it, its energy, tickling up his fingers, coursing through his veins.

It wants to come out again.

He had thought the urge would wear off after a few minutes, like it always did. Instead, it was getting worse.

His hands kept shaking. He had to make a conscious effort just to control his breathing. Something wasn't right. Whatever barrier had kept his powers at bay had broken the moment he struck that glass. Now he had no idea when or where his powers would strike.

Something bumped his back. He jolted; his hands shuddered. He tucked them into his pockets, taking deep breaths to keep control. It was just Jaden, doing…whatever it was he was doing. Kano turned around. A web of wires covered the table now, trailing from four separate laptops. Three of the screens were spewing code faster than Kano's eyes could follow. Jaden was just activating the fourth, which showed a map of Famora, with three dots all blinking at the same location.

Their location.

"Oh no, no, no!" blurted Kano. "Do *not* mess with the bracelets."

"Oh I'm messing with the bracelets," said Jaden. "No way I'm letting the government spy on me that easily."

"Yeah, screw the government!" called Makoto. Kano turned to the mezzanine, where his brother stood poised in one of Jaden's silk suits, the sleeves drooping over his hands.

"Give it a few more cycles buddy," laughed Jaden, "and that one's all yours."

Makoto descended a spiral staircase, his oversized black loafers clicking with every step. His borrowed suit matched the rest of Jaden's apartment: fancy and far too big for its owner. The dining area alone was bigger than their entire West Side apartment. It was a massive, open-plan studio. Its ceiling rose fifteen feet high, its white walls covered in giant paintings that made it look more like a history museum than a home. The paintings showed scenes of soldiers charging over rolling hills and mighty warships racing into battle, the flash of their cannons illuminating the blackness of space. Jaden could name every army, every ship, and every bloodstained battlefield that graced his walls (and had recited them to Kano on several occasions). Kano never cared much for them; they were fun to look at, but those battles happened long ago and far away. Should a battle ever break out in the streets of Famora, he would find a painting of that much more interesting.

Makoto cracked open a bottle of Kono against the counter, its golden liquid bubbling up the neck and dripping onto the floor, filling the air with the stench of overpriced booze.

Kano snatched it before it could reach Makoto's lips. "Give it a few more cycles buddy, and that one's all yours," he recited.

Makoto frowned and walked away.

"I've got it!" cheered Jaden. "Quick, come over here!" He grabbed Kano by the arm and led him to a console wired to the laptops. Holding Kano's wrist over it, the bracelet beeped.

"What did you just do?" asked Kano.

"Watch." Jaden swiped his own bracelet, then led Kano to the screen with the map. He started typing, Kano watching anxiously over his shoulder. "Makoto, did you swipe yours yet?"

"Just did it, boss!" called Makoto.

"Perfect." Jaden punched the final key. Suddenly, their dots started moving across the screen, slowly, toward the West Side.

"Nice!" Makoto shouted right by Kano's ear.

Kano jumped, not expecting his brother to be standing so close. He took a deep breath, fighting the energy that was bubbling up in his hands. "This is dangerous," he said through clenched teeth. "If they find out we were tampering with—"

"No one's gonna find out we…" Jaden trailed off. His eyes widened.

"What's wrong?" asked Kano.

Jaden rushed past him to the computer. "No, no, no…" He started typing frantically.

Kano had to crane his neck to see what was happening on the screen. The dots had separated, each arcing onto its own path. They twisted and turned, weaving past each other on their elaborate trip to nowhere.

"*Jaden!*" he screamed, not caring that his hands were shaking much harder now.

"It's okay, I can fix this!" said Jaden, typing faster. Suddenly, the dots started splitting, multiplying into more and more dots that traveled in increasingly erratic patterns.

"Gahhh!" screamed Jaden, relinquishing control of his laptop. He took a deep breath. "Okay, good news and bad news. Good news: the cops can't track us, at least not for a while."

"And the bad news?" asked Makoto.

"This is the first place they'll come to look for us," answered Kano.

Jaden nodded as he threw on his coat.

"Where do we go?!" exclaimed Makoto.

"Anywhere else," said Jaden. "My hovercar makes an easy target, so we'll have to go on foot. Hendricks and his goons will be looking for groups of three, so I suggest we split up and try to blend into the crowd. Find somewhere safe, away from cadets and police and whatever the hell else Hendricks has in his arsenal. And whatever you do, *don't* go home!" He gave Kano a long, hard look before he made for the door.

"Where will you go?" asked Kano, though what he really meant was *Where should I go?*

"I'll figure something out," said Jaden. "And I'll come find you when things simmer down. I'll be heading north, so you should head south. Might be the perfect opportunity to visit that cute Nurrano girl you're always talking about – and her witch of a grandmother."

"She's not a—" Jaden slipped out the door before Kano could finish, "…witch."

Makoto drew a long, uncomfortable breath. "Well, I guess I'll make for the industrial district. They'll never notice one more Nurrano in that crowd. Have fun with the witch!"

"Wait I—" Kano gave up as the door shut behind Makoto. He was alone, at least for now. The police would likely be joining him shortly.

He grabbed one of Jaden's coats from a rack by the door. *She's not a witch*. Makoto's parents had hosted her and her granddaughter plenty of times for dinner; they were good people. The grandmother was just a bit…odd. She had loved telling them stories, when they were little, about ancient heroes and wizards and monsters. All a bunch of fairytales, but he liked them all the same, mainly because all the heroes had strange powers…

He glanced at his hand again, the power still tingling inside it. *If anyone knows what's happening to me, it's her.*

His communicator buzzed. It was Yuchi, calling for about the thirtieth time, no doubt wondering why they weren't back yet. He could call her back later. He already knew her diagnosis for whatever was happening to him: *Lie down while I make you some soup.* Though the soup was tempting, he knew he needed something more. He needed answers.

⊲◆⊳

"Right. Left. Left again. Good," Novak said over the pounding of Junior's fists.

Junior swung again and again, though he didn't see the pads that Novak was holding in front of him. On the left, he saw Jaden's face with that stupid smirk on it; on the right, he saw his father's grimace with those sharp, cold eyes that whispered, "*I let them get away with it.*"

He struck the pad and felt his knuckle split against the fabric. Blood trickled between his fingers, joining the torrent of sweat already streaming down his arms. He kept punching, splattering red onto the pad as if it were a canvas. Novak kept shouting orders, but Junior didn't hear him anymore; he just kept pounding the right pad, harder and harder, right in that stupid scar running down its cheek –

"ENOUGH!" yelled Novak.

Junior yielded. He stepped back as Novak threw down the pads and shook out his wrists.

"A few more of those and my whole arm would've sailed clean across the room," he said with the slightest grin. Junior didn't return the smile. He just stared at the gash in his knuckle, at the blood oozing down his hand.

"Why don't we get that cleaned up?" Novak pressed a hand against Junior's sweat-soaked back and led him into the barracks. They passed row after row of empty beds and sealed lockers, the fluorescent lights buzzing overhead. Normally, the barracks were crowded and rowdy, but today they were silent. Today every cadet had an assignment somewhere in the city. Every cadet except Junior.

He followed Novak to a kitchenette in the back of the barracks, his eyes locked on the gray tiles passing beneath his feet. Today was supposed to be his day, the day he led the cadets through a successful Shantima and proved to everyone that he was fit for command. Instead, three morons from the West Side had led him on a ridiculous chase and made a fool out of him in front of the entire Cadet Corps. He grinded his knuckles against his good hand, smothering it with blood. *If only Novak hadn't gotten there when he did. I had that little brat by the throat...*

"Hold out your hand," said Novak, drawing a bottle of halocine from a cabinet. He poured it over a rag. When he raised it to Junior, he paused. "This'll sting," he warned.

Junior snatched the rag from him and pressed it into the gash. He felt the chemical seep into his wound like lava through rock. His knuckle screamed, his eyes began to water, but his face never flinched. He just held the rag there until the pain faded into numbness.

Novak threw away the bloodstained rag and began wrapping the cadet's hand in a bandage, eying him carefully the entire time. Junior knew that look. It was the one he wore when he wanted to make a point.

"You know, Junior, there was a time when I would've done anything to look tough in front of my platoon. Put out a match on my bare chest, jump out of a moving hovercar, anything to make me stand out from the other boys in the barracks." Junior tapped his foot, hoping Novak would get to the point soon. "Then one day, another cadet showed up, big and tall and cocky as hell, and he could put out the whole ream of matches on his chest, and leap from one moving hovercar into another, and do just about everything else at least a little bit better than I could. I watched as all my friends gravitated towards him, and that's when I realized how valuable their admiration really was."

"And let me guess," said Junior, "this guy ended up being my father?"

"No, actually this guy wrecked his hovercar at the age of seventeen and now drinks his meals from a straw. My point, Junior, is that there's more to leading people than just running out in front of them."

"And what if I'm the fastest runner?"

Novak tightened the bandages. "Then heavens help you when you meet the opponent you can't outrun."

Junior rolled his eyes. If such an opponent existed, he wouldn't find it on this floating rock. Famora may have been a paradise for everyone else, but for him it was a personal hell. Day after day he sat through pointless classes and stood through pointless drills, just waiting…waiting for the day when they would finally send him somewhere that actually needed his help. He could be fighting crime lords in the Outer Territories, or insurgents in the Mid-Rim, or preparing for the next Poterian attack. Most people said they were gone, never to return. But he knew better.

"Could you follow me, Junior? I could use your help."

Junior blinked. Novak was already walking out of the barracks and into a hallway. He rushed to catch up. Normally, this would be considered following orders, but since Novak had relieved him of duty for the day, he was free to do as he pleased. It was his choice if he wanted to stay here and train. Boxing helped him clear his mind. Besides, where else would he go? Back to the festival with all its silly fireworks? No thank you. Back home to confront his father? Surely that could wait a bit longer…

He followed Novak down the hall to an office tucked in the back corner. The office itself looked more like an afterthought, with a flimsy wooden desk smothered in papers and an old, hardwired computer bolted to it.

Novak never seemed to mind. He had a real office in the Police Plaza with all the amenities, but he preferred this one, where he could work closely with the cadets instead of the grumps upstairs. Plus, if there was ever a job that he didn't want to do, all he had to say was "recommendation letter" and the cadets would come running.

"You know, those three you chased into the Archives left quite a mess," he said as he stacked some folders together.

"I'm aware." Junior watched as the stack grew taller.

"Apparently, they left a huge crack in the glass. From what I've heard, a Gorv with a sledgehammer couldn't do that kind of damage."

"Oh really?" replied Junior, only half-listening. His attention was instead on an old picture framed on the desk. It was Novak arm-in-arm with his father, their nylon flight suits glowing with the Republic's blue and white colors. It must have been taken early in the war, he could tell by his father's face: there was no scar there – and a smile.

"That cadet you were talking about earlier, was he anything like my father?"

Novak chuckled. "Your dad was always a little too focused on his work to cause any trouble." He glanced at the picture. "But he wasn't always so prickly, either. He enjoyed games and jokes as much as the rest of us in the barracks, but I think he had a better understanding of what we would face after training. We were all scared, don't get me wrong, but every night before lights out I would see your father writing in a journal. After a few weeks I finally asked him, 'What the hell are you scribbling about?' He told me that, if he survived, he wanted to remember this time. That didn't make much sense to me then, but now I see that your father was wiser than any cadet ever to pass through the Hyb."

"Were you there when he…?" Junior ran his finger down his cheek.

"No. But if I was, that fight would have gone very differently." Novak handed him the stack of folders. "Take these reports up to my upstairs office. I'll need them for our visitors this evening."

"Visitors?"

"Folks from the IDF. Part of the Taranis investigation. They want to make sure we're ready for an attack if one should happen. Personally, I think we're better off without them, but your dad thinks otherwise."

Junior nodded and left with the stack. *Taranis*. When he had first heard about the attack on Darraden, he hadn't been too concerned. Taranis had struck plenty of places before, and always at random. But then his father had left in the middle of the night wrapped in his overcoat, the black overcoat that always meant business of an unofficial nature. After that, his father spent the entire morning making calls and pacing the house instead of being here to coordinate his officers during the festival. Clearly he was hiding something, as usual.

But what could Taranis have to do with us? The maniac had no clear motive, though of course everyone had their theories. Some said he was a resistance fighter from the Mid-Rim or a surviving Poterian out for revenge, but Junior suspected differently. Not just any terrorist could put his father this on edge. No, whoever this Taranis was, he had some connection his father's secrets.

He climbed the stairs to the lobby of the Police Plaza. It was a stark contrast to the stuffy barracks hidden beneath the building. The lobby was wide and open, with ceilings that climbed five stories high and a grand staircase behind the information desk that led to the top, each floor another level in the pyramid. That staircase was Junior's target, but between him and it was a sea of officers and detectives shoving past each other to deliver their reports. Evidently, the rest of the police force was much more concerned about the IDF coming than Novak was.

Junior clutched the stack of reports tight to his chest as he marched into the fray. Being a head taller than most of the other officers made it a little easier to navigate, though all the shoving wasn't helping.

"It's not my fault! They're *lying* to you!" cried a voice from behind him. The smell of grease filled his nostrils, and suddenly something large slammed into his back. He fell to his knees, the reports spilling across the floor for the crowd to trample over.

He glanced over his shoulder, his fists clenched around the few reports he had managed to hang on to, to find a set of Bolani legs skittering past him, their owner struggling as two officers attempted to restrain all four of its arms. "That speeder was perfectly fine when she checked it out. If the engine died it was because of user error. *User error!*"

The officers dragged the Bolani down the stairs and out of sight, leaving Junior to scoop the crumpled reports off the ground. *Novak's gonna have plenty to say about this next time I see him,* he thought, piling the last of the papers into a disfigured stack. He spotted one more across the floor, a red folder that had been kicked away from the rest. He crawled over to it. Across the top was one word stamped in big, bold letters:

MISSING.

Who was missing? He opened the file. There was a picture of a Nurrano, with his last known sighting scribbled in the corner. The next page had a Galanad, and after that a Human. Over thirty people, all last seen within the past few months. He flipped to the last page. The picture wasn't a person. It was a mask. A mask with strange markings etched across it.

Chapter 5

Nobara's Point

Kano stood alone before the wooden door, rehearsing his introduction.

"I was just passing through and I thought— No, that sounds too casual. I missed you and— No, that just sounds pathetic. Long time, no see, I – no, no, no! Why is this so *hard*?!"

He glanced up the brick wall at the sign looming overhead. 'NOBARA'S POINT' glowed in red, flickering letters – mostly. Both of the O's had gone out, and the T looked about ready to die as well, but still it hung proudly to the weathered bricks.

From the distance, he heard the fireworks pop and the crowds cheer, but here in the Dockyards the walkways were empty. This was no place for the festival crowd. This was the haunt of sailors who reeked from weeks of space travel and wore long, oversized garb that made most Famorans raise an eyebrow. They came here to deliver the city its food, its water, and its precious tourists, but Famorans were never quick to thank them for it. The Dockyards sat fifty feet beneath the rest of the city, separated from Lower Downtown by a series of ramps and stairs so long and convoluted most sailors didn't bother to climb them. There was only one thing they would climb for, one thing at the halfway point between the Dockyards and Downtown that was worth the trip, and that was Nobara's.

Kano walked to the railing opposite the door and looked out at the vast sea of landing platforms floating below, bright orange rays cutting between them as the Sun began to set beneath the clouds. Transport shuttles were packed in tight rows on each platform, with many more circling above in search of an open landing space. Tourists poured out of them onto lines that snaked all the way to the very top of the climb, where police scanners waited to admit them into Downtown. *So Hendricks took precautions after all*, thought Kano, though he wondered if a police scanner was really enough to stop a terrorist as cunning as Taranis.

Kano had found himself worrying less and less about Taranis as the day wore on. No bombs had gone off, no throngs of frightened people had gone running through the streets. The day had certainly been dramatic, but not for the reasons he had expected. Still, the biggest crowds had yet to come, and the darkness of night would be ideal for a terrorist to make his escape.

He never visits more than one planet in a system, Jaden's words echoed in his head. He rubbed his palms together over the edge of the railing, hoping the cheers from Downtown would not turn to screams in the night.

The door creaked open and the roar of a hundred shouts and cackles rushed through to meet him. When he turned, two Malorans were stumbling out of Nobara's, their shirts stained with so much Kono and dirt it was hard to tell what color they had originally come in. The Malorans locked onto Kano with their yellow eyes, and he found himself instinctively pushing his wallet deeper into his pocket. They looked like giant, pale millipedes, slithering toward him on a hundred tiny legs, their abdomens bent upright so their faces were level with his, their crooked arms outstretched in greeting. *Now would be a good time to walk away.*

He had started off when he felt their clawed fingers clench around his shoulders and pinch his skin. The Maloran grip. He had heard somewhere that it was unbreakable. He tried wriggling his way out, but it was no use. They had him.

"Ah, this one smells of Famora," hissed one of the Malorans.

"Yesss," said the other, "that and…something else. You see this hair?" Kano felt its claws dredge across his scalp. He shuddered. "Do you think it's Poterian?"

The other gasped. "Oh, don't insult our new friend. It's handsome hair, certainly not the kind belonging to those evil warbirds."

Kano rolled his eyes. The Malorans had sided with the Poterians during the war, and the only reason they denounced their old allies now was to keep the charade alive. Yuchi had warned him of their routine. It would start with flattery and stories over drinks and end with them slithering away once the bill came due. He wriggled again, and felt their grips tighten.

"Come, come," hissed the one on his right. "Join us. We must know where you come from. Chances are we have a tale or two from whichever world it is."

If only I knew. He thought back to the Archives. *Why didn't anyone tell me I was from Darraden?*

He entered the tavern, the Malorans flanking him on either side. The air was thick with bareno smoke. It tasted bitter, and it made the sailors look like shadows beneath the dim, yellow lights. He passed a group that was rolling in their seats while a hairy Comora stood atop their table, weaving a tale about how he stole a ship with the help of its captain's daughter. Across from them, two squishy pink Galanads were tossing colored dice with their tentacles, screaming in their native tongue every time a die landed on the red side. In the corner, Kano spotted a Braiman propped up against a coatrack, its tendrils rolling up and back down in synch with its snoring.

The Comora laughed so hard he toppled off the table. Kano jolted, the power pulsing through his palm. He tucked his hands in his pockets while another sailor helped the Comora up.

"Oy, anybody seen my drink?" asked the Comora.

Kano stepped in something sticky. He looked down and, sure enough, there was the drink, its purple liquid pooling around him. He heard something sizzling. Smoke was rising from his shoes. He jumped back, the power pulsing again within his pocket. He needed to get out of this crowd.

One of the Malorans dove down to wipe the liquid away with a napkin while the other held him firmly in place. Kano started to feel hot under the ears. All the Maloran was achieving was to spread the acid around on his shoes. He wanted to scream at them, but he held his tongue, fearing too much emotion would cause the power to come blasting out.

The Maloran rose, gave a bow, and then continued leading Kano into the thicket of sailors. Kano struggled as he squeezed between sweat-soaked backs, hoping this would be his opportunity to slip away, but at no point did the Maloran grip loosen from his shoulders.

Just when he thought the sailors' stench would suffocate him, he popped out of the crowd and right into the counter. Wooden shelves lined the back wall, each packed with drinks in bottles of dark colors and odd rounded shapes. The Malorans slithered in on either side of him, goading him to order the first drink.

"You two, *scram*!" barked a voice from behind the counter.

Kano felt the weight release from his shoulders. When he looked back, the Malorans were gone.

"You should choose your friends more carefully," the voice jeered.

"Those aren't my friends," he replied, turning back to the bar. Staring back at him were two bright brown eyes. Li. For a moment he had forgotten how to breathe, his eyes lost in the diamond pattern on her skin that shimmered gray and gold. She leaned over the counter with both arms, her thin muscles skating up beneath the sleeves of her tunic. He realized now was the time to give the line he had been rehearsing. But which line had he decided to go with?

"I wasn't talking about the Malorans." She smirked, grabbing a handful of mugs from under the counter and lining them in front of her.

He was so flustered, it took him a moment to catch her meaning. She never had liked Jaden much. Not that he could blame her: the guy couldn't go more than thirty seconds without flirting with her.

"You three are the talk of the town, you know? Something about a speeder chase and fireworks?"

"It wasn't my idea," said Kano, watching as she filled the mugs with Kono in rapid succession. "I just got mixed up in it by accident, that's all…"

"A likely story!" She loaded the drinks onto a little wheeled bot. It zipped across the counter, its gears buzzing with excitement as sailors snatched the drinks off it and tossed down coins in their place. "So, how much trouble are you in?" she asked.

"Trouble?"

"Well, why else would you come to see her?"

"I didn't— I mean, I came to see you too…"

Li rolled her eyes. "Nama, Kano's here for you!"

Pots clattered in the kitchen. A few moments later, a short Nurrano woman emerged through the kitchen door wrapped in a red shawl, the gray and gold diamonds of her face misshapen by wrinkles.

"Kano, my child!" She hobbled around the counter as fast as her frail legs could carry her, her patrons stepping respectfully out of her path. She embraced him. "You've gotten so tall!"

He held her tight, all the memories of her visits rushing back to him. He was surprised to find so much strength still in her old bones.

When she finally released him, a Human sailor with a metal eye stepped forward and placed a barstool beside her. She sat down and gave the man a smile.

"Your name keeps coming up today. What were you three up to at Shantima? And don't go blaming Jaden for it. As far as I'm concerned, you are as guilty as he is!"

"It's a long story," he sighed. "But everything's settled now."

"Is it?" She glanced at the metal wristband. "And tell me, what do Hendricks and Novak have planned for you?"

"Nothing—" He caught her stare; it cut through him like a knife. "Well, technically I'm supposed to be home right now."

Nobara thumped him on the head. "Well you better get there before Yuchi has a heart attack!"

"Well, technically she has two hearts, so—"

Nobara gave him another thump on the head. "No time for jokes. This is our busiest day of the cycle. What do you need?"

"I...um..." He couldn't even form the words. This wasn't something he normally talked about, especially in a crowd. He needed to be careful how he phrased it, else others may catch his meaning. "I had...an incident at the Archives today." He waved his hand at her.

Her eyes widened. "Can you still feel it?"

He nodded.

Nobara waved her granddaughter over. "Li, fix our guest a drink, would you?"

Li placed an empty glass in front of Kano. She grabbed a bottle from beneath the counter and uncorked it.

"No dear, our guest requires something special – from the cellar."

Li's eyes darted to Kano. They could see right through him now. "Oh, silly me."

Kano watched her disappear into the kitchen, his gaze lingering on the empty doorway.

"How do you feel?" asked Nobara.

Kano snapped out of his trance. "I feel…off-balance." He looked down at his bloodied knuckles. "You once told me never to let anyone see—"

"Did anyone?"

"Just Jaden and Makoto. I don't think there were any cameras there."

"Where?"

"The Archives."

"The Classified Section?"

"You really do hear everything here, don't you?"

"It's my job, dear."

Kano leaned forward, an idea forming. "And what have you heard about Taranis?"

A few heads turned at the mention of the name, then slowly returned to their conversations. Nobara hushed her voice. "Not much beyond what they say in the news. This whole 'masked man on the loose' sounds a bit theatrical if you ask me. In fact, it reminds me of some of the characters we would see on the news back in the day…" She paused, thinking. "There is one thing I keep hearing, though I don't have much to back it up—"

"What is it? What?" Kano was on the edge of his seat now.

She hushed her voice. "The rumor is that wherever he strikes, people go missing. Don't ask me who or why; I don't know. What I do know is that he's not alone. Be cautious what you say and who you say it to, especially in a place like this. You never know who might be helping him."

Kano gulped. He hadn't thought of others conspiring with Taranis. Suddenly all the sailors around him seemed hostile, even the ones who were laughing. Could others be planting bombs for him?

A bottle slammed on the counter. Kano jumped, only to find Li standing over it. She unscrewed the lid and poured a greenish juice into a glass.

"Thank you?" he said, studying the strange liquid.

"Enjoy," she replied snidely, taking the bottle back through the door.

Kano took the glass in his shaking hand. *Whatever this stuff is, it had better help.* He tilted his head and knocked the drink back. His taste buds screamed. It was so *bitter*. He felt it bubbling down his throat, but it didn't settle. It kept moving, like a living animal was trapped inside him. He fell forward against the counter, his stomach twisting and aching. A rough, wrinkled hand rubbed his back. "It's almost done," he heard her say.

The churning slowed. He felt a warmth rise from his toes all the way to his fingertips, and just like that, his hands stopped shaking. The urge was gone. Erased. He felt free, but at the same time…empty.

"It only lasts about an hour," assured Nobara. "When it returns, it should be stable."

"What is this stuff?" he asked, waving the empty glass.

"An old recipe. I keep it around for Li, just in case. A little of this and that, but the key ingredient is the nectar from the fireflowers on Krios."

"You've been to Krios?!" exclaimed Kano. He often forgot that beneath this wrinkled skin was a young Nurrano who had experienced more of the galaxy than every sailor in the tavern combined.

"Yes, and it's a very long journey, so don't expect to come drinking my supply every time you're having a bad day." Her shawl shifted as she climbed out of her barstool. Something glittered around her neck. Something gold…something familiar…

"What is that?" he asked.

Nobara glanced down. "Oh, it's nothing," she said, quickly stuffing it back beneath her shawl.

Clearly not. He had no idea why it seemed so familiar, but for some reason it made him think about the Classified Section again.

"Nobara, could I ask you one last question?"

"Of course, but be quick. You need to go home, or have you forgotten?"

"I haven't, I just— Do the names Azral and Jeslow mean anything to you?"

Nobara froze. Suddenly, everyone got quiet. Kano looked around. All eyes, including the metal one, were on him.

Nobara let out an uncomfortable laugh. "Oh, silly child. You read all sorts of strange things in the Archives. Come now, it's getting late. Your *mother* will be worried sick."

Kano nodded, suddenly frightened by all the attention. Nobara took him by the hand and led him to the door, her grip surprisingly firm. Kano didn't resist. The patrons slowly began chattering again, but some gave him odd glances as he passed. He wondered what his parents could have done to merit such a response, but dared not ask out loud.

Nobara opened the door for him. "You never heard those names before, did you?" she whispered.

Kano shook his head.

She sighed and tugged the necklace from her neck with a quick snap, careful to keep it concealed as she pressed it into Kano's hand. "This was a gift from long ago. It has many meanings, but for now, know that if you see one like it, you are in the presence of a friend."

Kano nodded. He had come here hoping for answers, but realized now he would be leaving with more questions.

"Keep it hidden," she continued, "but always close. It's getting late now; come back another time, when we're closed. I can tell you more about them then."

Nobara shut the door in his face. Kano sighed. He had waited his whole life for information on his parents; he supposed he could wait a bit longer.

He opened his hand and stared at the golden triangle, rubbing his fingers along the arrows that pointed toward the center.

"You shouldn't be flashing that around in public," a snide voice remarked.

Kano looked up. Li sat on the hood of a parked hovertruck, chewing on a bay leaf.

"And why's that?"

She hopped off the hovertruck and waltzed toward him. "Because some people aren't too fond of it." She glanced down at the bloody cracks running through his knuckles. "You need to be more careful. Someone could have seen you."

"I'm aware." He tried to stuff his hand into his pocket, but Li took it in hers before he could. Her hand began to glow a bright white. Skin began visibly growing over the red rifts in his knuckles, and in moments the cuts had vanished.

Kano just stared, wide-eyed. "You— I've only ever seen you make plants grow. Like…tiny plants. This is…"

"Powers have more than one use, Kano. You would know if you put in the time to practice."

"I'm sure practicing is easy for you: your powers don't break windows and toss you halfway across the room."

"Are you speaking from experience?"

Kano blushed. He stared down at his hands. "I didn't ask for this."

"But you have it anyway, and the sooner you accept that, the sooner you can start using it." She rubbed her hands over his. "Yours are getting stronger too, aren't they?"

Kano nodded. "It used to be easy to control. Today was the first time when I…well, when I couldn't control it."

"Nama can help you – and not with elixir this time. Come in tomorrow morning before we open."

"And do what?"

She smiled. "You'll have to come over and find out."

A feeling came over Kano. *Kiss her*. She was just standing there, looking at him with those brown eyes. Now was the moment. He started to lean in, ever so slightly, when he felt a rush of hot, compressed air. He leaned back, faking a stretch, as a hovercar lowered beside them.

The passenger window rolled down. Jaden sat there in a trimmed suit and sunglasses, one elbow leaning out of the open window, a chauffeur beside him at the wheel. "Hop in Kano, we've got some place to be."

"You sure you should be out and about with the police looking for you?" asked Li, her arms crossed.

Jaden lowered his sunglasses. "Where's the fun in hiding? Besides, we've got room for one more, beautiful."

"I can think of a few better ways to spend my evening." She turned to Kano and winked. "I'll see you tomorrow, if you're not in jail by then." She went inside, leaving Kano with the sinking feeling that his entire night had been ruined by Jaden's timing.

"You two got a date or something?" asked Makoto from the backseat.

"Something like that." Kano climbed into the backseat, clutching the necklace tight as they took off for their unknown destination.

Chapter 6

VIP Access

The speeder thundered over Downtown, the towers whizzing by as Junior climbed higher and higher up the face of Famora. He twisted the throttle up to max, ignoring the honks of the hovercars he was weaving past. He didn't care. All that mattered was reading that Taranis file.

He hadn't dared read it within the Police Plaza, even in the safety of Novak's office, for fear of getting caught. Instead, he quickly photographed every page of it onto his communicator. Now all he had to do was blow up the images on his computer at home and he would have access to whatever secrets his father had uncovered.

Home. He could see it now, floating off the edge of the Upper District, detached from the city like a little island in a sea of pink. Just the way his father liked it. He never knew how his dad had gotten his own hoverpad, but he assumed it was one of the many perks of being a war hero.

The Hendricks Mansion slowly grew in the distance – though in Junior's opinion, it was about the saddest excuse for a mansion that he had ever seen. It looked more like something out of Lower Downtown, old-fashioned but sturdy, without much thought for aesthetics. Stone columns outlined two stories of plain, gray walls that spread into two wings. *Two wings for two people*, Junior thought bitterly.

The platform it stood on had no decorations, no fountains or fake grass or even a bench to sit on, just a dozen or so hovercars parked on it, all the latest and best models money could buy. Junior rolled his eyes. All these hovercars could only mean one thing: secret meeting. A bunch of pretty and polished people here to talk about things that he wasn't allowed to hear. They had come here often when he was a child, but less and less over the cycles. He couldn't even remember the last time he had seen them. Not that it mattered: he already knew they had no interest in seeing him.

He lowered his speeder into an open patch, his phantom engine spraying dust and dirt onto the nearest hovercars. A smile flicked across his face. He would make sure to keep his upstairs window open so he could hear them complaining when they left.

He glanced at the window of his father's study. The shades were drawn, but he saw shadows pacing back and forth against the orange firelight, wisps of bareno smoke rising from between their fingers. Good: they'd already started.

The foyer was empty when he entered. A collection of empty glasses sat on a console table beside an unfinished rubili cocktail. He licked his lips. Seafood was rarer than diamonds on Famora. He grabbed a handful and crunched into them all at once, tossing the tails back onto the plate as he chewed. He started up the stairs at the back of the room, his footsteps echoing through the halls.

He stopped.

Something came over him. He couldn't explain what, but before he knew it he was back down the stairs, tiptoeing toward his father's study. He grabbed one of the empty glasses off the table as he passed, his eyes set on the firelight flickering through the seam beneath the study door. Bareno smoke leaked into the hall, flavoring the air with the smell of cherry and must. He pressed the glass to the door and his ear to the glass, listening to the whispers that leaked through.

"What of the boy…Hendricks?" wheezed a man who sounded so old even speaking had become an exercise for him.

"I have my best man on him," answered a rasp that could only belong to his father. "I can ensure his safety as long as you uphold your end."

"Oversight of the…Dockyards has been a…challenge," replied the old man, pausing every few words to take another breath. "We have more tourists today…than any other day…in the cycle. Finding people we can…trust to screen them is…not as easy as it used to be…"

"It never was *easy*," added a woman with a harsh, matter-of-factly tone. "Which makes me wonder how we can trust this man you have tailing him, considering you haven't told us who he is?"

"I trust him with my life and then some," answered Hendricks. "That answer should suffice for now."

Tailing who? Junior wondered, pressing his ear closer.

"Hendricks Junior!" boomed a voice from down the hall.

Junior leaped to his feet, fumbling with the glass. When he turned, a familiar, eager gaze was waiting for him, though the young man behind it seemed much sharper than he used to be, sporting a blue silk suit with a matching blue tie and cufflinks. He was a little larger too; the blue buttons around his gut looked about ready to burst.

"Lieutenant Carmichael," said Junior, feigning enthusiasm as he stepped away from the door. *If I can just slip around this moron and up the stairs, they'll never know I was here.* "How…how have you been?"

"Actually, it's *captain* now, so very well, thank you!" The captain embraced him before he could slither away.

"Congratulations," he gasped, the cufflinks digging into his sides.

Carmichael released him and patted him on the chest. "What's your dad been feeding you? You must be as tall as he is by now!"

Taller, thought Junior, though he didn't say it. He didn't want to say anything that might extend this conversation. Even without his ear pressed to the door, he could tell the whispering inside had stopped.

Carmichael's eyes fell on the glass in his hand. He smiled. "At least one of us finds all this babble interesting. I've been walking in circles just trying to stay awake."

"Now I know who's been eating all the rubili," said Junior. He expected that might get a chuckle from Carmichael, but instead the captain roared, his belly jiggling as his laughter echoed through the house.

"It's…it's good to see you again," said the captain, trying to compose himself. "Wish I could say I was visiting on better circumstances. Terrible news on Darraden. The IDF sent me to conduct some investigations, and your father was kind enough to invite me in for a briefing."

"I'm sure he's happy to have you," Junior lied. Carmichael's father had once been his own father's commander and mentor, not to mention a war hero, but *this* Carmichael was a different story. This Carmichael had flunked out of the Hyb and only narrowly managed to scrounge his current position in the IDF, no doubt thanks to his surname. Hendricks made no secret of his disappointment in the young Carmichael. Junior suspected the only reason his father had invited Carmichael in the first place was to keep a close eye on him and his "investigations" on Famora.

"Anyway, it was good seeing you, Captain. I should probably get back to studying for—"

The door flew open and there stood his father, with a dozen pairs of eyes behind him, all focused on Junior.

Carmichael wrapped an arm around Junior, beaming. "Everyone, you remember this kid, don't you? Look how tall he's gotten!"

"Yes, hello Aaron," interrupted an older woman, her stern voice the same one Junior had heard a moment ago. She leaned back in her leather chair, weaving her fingers together, each nail long, red, and sharp. "I know you must be excited to attend your first meeting, Captain, but these are not social visits."

"Ah, but this is Hendricks's son, after all. Hell, if I'm somehow qualified for these meetings, then I'd say he deserves to be a part of the conversation, especially since it pertains to—"

"*Enough*, Carmichael," hissed the woman.

An uncomfortable silence fell over them, filled only by the crackle of the fire in the mantelpiece. It cast a red glow over their faces, highlighting the creases that age had worn into them. Junior noticed dark circles beneath some of their eyes. They must have traveled a long way on short notice.

Hendricks stepped in to break the silence. "Thank you, Carmichael. No harm done." He directed the captain back to his seat, a frail wooden bench in the corner of the room. "Put the glass away, Junior. We shouldn't be much longer." With that, he slammed the door.

Was he angry? Frankly, Junior didn't care. He had more important things to do. He climbed the stairs, wondering who the mysterious boy was that they were all so interested in.

⊲◆⊳

"Don't make me go in there!" Kano kicked and flailed as his friends dragged him out of the hovercar.

"Make this easy on yourself!" said Makoto. He pinned Kano's left arm to his side while Jaden came in to pin the other arm, and together they carried Kano into the crowd.

Kano tried to kick them, but the crowd gave him little room to maneuver. It kept getting tighter, shoulders bumping him from all sides. *There must be thousands of people here, and all of them heading in the same direction.*

"Did you *really* think we were going to get in on the busiest day of the cycle?" he asked.

"Don't worry, I have a plan!" said Jaden, a little too proudly.

Kano rolled his eyes. He had endured enough of Jaden's plans for one day.

His foot scraped against the metal walkway. He felt the beat of the music pulse through it. They were close. If only he could see over this crowd…

"We're almost there, can you smell it?!"

"Oh I smell something!" cheered Makoto.

That's probably all the cheap perfume, thought Kano.

Boom.

Kano felt the faintest pulse rush to his hand. *The elixir.* He saw green sparks falling from the twilit sky. Just a firework, though now it seemed he had bigger problems.

"Guys, we need to go back. Something's wrong."

"For the last time, there's no terrorist here," said Jaden. "And there's gonna be no complaining, either!"

"But—"

"No…complaining."

Kano took a deep breath to stifle his rage. His friends were leading him into easily the worst possible place to have an episode, and he couldn't even explain the situation to them, not with all these people around. He closed his eyes, trying to think up a way to get out of this, but his options seemed to be growing slimmer the deeper they marched into the crowd.

He slammed into something hard. When he opened his eyes, all he saw was black fabric. He tilted his head back, slowly, until he found the owner of the shirt: a Gorv, its red eyes peering down at him. He gulped. If ever there was a creature built for killing, it was a Gorv. It had gray skin that folded over itself like layers of impenetrable rock, and muscles that rose and cascaded along its arms like mountains. Beneath its scowl were rows of finely pointed teeth, said to be sharp enough to rip a man's arm off. Kano had no intention of finding out if that was true.

The Gorv's pointed ears angled down as it waited for them to explain exactly why they had pushed to the front of the line – an explanation Kano was just as eager to hear.

"Here you are," said Jaden, holding up a pin. It was no bigger than the tip of his finger, a white circle with a spear running across it, its edges trimmed with gold.

A pin? His plan is to get in with a stupid pin?

The Gorv snorted and stepped aside. Before Kano could process what had just happened, his friends were tugging him past the bouncer and along a far less crowded walkway.

"What was on that pin?" he asked, glancing back. There was at least a dozen other Gorvs all stationed at the edge of the crowd, ensuring no one passed without permission.

"It's called a Montiquo," said Jaden. "It can get you into just about any place on Vasilia. It's not well-known out in these territories, but a club as…esteemed as this one is sure to recognize it."

Esteemed was not the word that came to Kano's mind when he saw the giant sphere floating in front of them. *The* Sphere. It hovered at the edge of Downtown, casting a wide shadow over the Dockyards below. Colored lights pulsed across its surface to the beat of the music that pounded inside, ringing louder in Kano's ears with each step. Everything about this club was big, bright, and flashy, but none of that could hide the shadows lurking inside. It was no secret that this was a main attraction for gangsters, and not the low-level thugs hanging around side streets, but the real gangsters, the high rollers who had operations across dozens (if not hundreds) of planets, all stopping by Famora on "business." Just the place he wanted to be right now.

Their walkway fed into the center of the Sphere, where its open mouth consumed all those who had made it past the Gorv line. The other patrons looked much older and more distinguished than Kano's lot, wearing puffy suits of red or lavender and long, elegant dresses of yellow and turquoise, each one accessorized by flowers, jewels, exotic animal skins, or some combination of all those things.

"Couldn't you have at least brought me a change of clothes?" asked Kano, staring at his plain T-shirt and shorts.

"I did, but you were struggling too much to bother getting them on you," answered Jaden, adjusting his silk tie. "Consider this your punishment for being such a pain in the ass today."

"Jaden, the punishment is bringing me here. I'm telling you there's something wrong with me." He held out his hands. "Ever since the Archives, I haven't felt the same."

"You know, I had a funny feeling yesterday, too. Turns out it was indigestion."

"You know what I'm talking about," he said flatly.

They passed under the entrance. Kano shivered. Everything felt colder in here. And darker too. The colored lights were dimmed, lining the edges of the floor and walls instead of the ceiling, which loomed like a black void over their heads. Another rounded wall stood across the lobby, this one lined with doors. Each door was a different color, with different people lined up at each one.

"*Another* line!" whined Makoto.

"What color are we looking for?" asked Kano, though he really didn't care which.

"Blue," answered Jaden. He led them around the lobby, passing door after door and line after line until there was hardly anyone in sight. Kano was about to ask him if he knew where he was going when Makoto pointed.

"I see it!"

Sure enough, the blue door was coming up, though there were no other doors near it. There was no line, either.

"Jaden, what exactly did that Montiki get you?" asked Kano.

"*Montiquo*, and we get automatic VIP access."

"You're kidding!" blurted Makoto.

Perfect, thought Kano. That's where all the worst of the worst liked to hang out, or so he had been told. He could already picture it: a high-class version of Nobara's Point, where instead of sailors everyone was a trained killer with an equally deadly bodyguard accompanying them.

Jaden stopped at a panel beside the door. He held his pin to it and the door lifted open.

To Kano's surprise, the room was tiny, with a single, smiling attendant in a bright red vest. He was tall, with a thin black beard that came to a fine point on his chin. Beside him was a shiny metal box, and behind him another blue door.

"Gentlemen," said the attendant, giving Kano's outfit a once-over, "thank you for joining us tonight. To proceed, please remove your shoes."

Kano and Makoto glanced at each other, each raising an eyebrow.

Jaden's shoes landed in the metal box with a clang. Kano could see his friend was just trembling with excitement.

"Welcome back, Mr. Upton," sighed the attendant as he sealed the box. There was a whoosh from inside it, followed by another. When the attendant reopened it, a new, shiny pair of silver shoes were inside, each with a band of glowing red light lining the sole. Jaden tugged them on – a perfect fit.

"Rest assured, you will receive your original shoes once these are returned at the end of your visit," said the attendant, as if reading Kano's mind. Kano nodded and cautiously followed Jaden's example. Soon, he and Makoto both had fancy, fitted shoes.

"Alright gentlemen, a few rules before you enter the club." The attendant strapped himself to a harness beside the door. Kano and Makoto exchanged another confused look. "Please, no suspicious, reckless, or dangerous behavior while inside the Sphere." Jaden chuckled. "Please report any such behavior to a member of our security team, which are stationed throughout the interior and can be identified by their red vests, much like this one. Finally, and most importantly, *do not remove your shoes*. Understood?"

Kano nodded, though he had no idea what the last part was all about. The attendant seemed to know that, which made his grin all the wider.

"Good," said the attendant, placing his hand on a lever. "Enjoy your stay."

He pulled the lever. The door whooshed open and Kano felt a rush of air. A moment later he was airborne. He flew through the door and out into the open air, spinning through space while the colors swirled around him.

"What the hell is going on?!" he cried. His only answer came in the form of Jaden's whooping.

The red lining on his shoes turned green. Suddenly, he felt as though a great weight had been strapped to his feet. It tugged him gently down on top of the sealed door they had entered from. Jaden and Makoto landed on either side of him, but he didn't notice them. He just kept staring at the shoes.

"Ahem."

Kano looked up. An attendant stood before him in a bright red vest.

"Welcome to the Sphere," she began. "Please stand clear of the door so other guests may enter."

Kano nodded and walked away, his head still spinning. What kind of crazy house was this? Everywhere he looked, people were walking along the curved walls, some standing upside down high over his head as they moved between the dance floors and bars that dotted the walls – or floors, whatever they were. The Sphere seemed somehow bigger on the inside, as if someone had rolled up an entire city block and allowed it to combat the normal laws of physics. Off in the distance, at the center of all this madness, floated a green, humming orb – a gravity well. Kano watched the energy pulse around it, mesmerized.

"What do you guys think?!" asked Jaden.

"It's...it's..." began Kano, unable to form words.

"...gimmicky," Makoto concluded.

"You just like raining on my parade, don't you?"

"Always."

Jaden shook his head, chuckling. Kano hardly noticed their conversation; he was too focused on the VIP section. It was a narrow strip of red that wrapped itself around the entire circumference of the Sphere, elevated from the rest of the club. Railings lined either side of it, protecting the precious VIPs from falling in with the rabble below.

Kano peeked over the railing. A sea of people danced beneath his feet, thousands of them, bouncing shoulder-to-shoulder to the beat of the music. He was relieved not to be trapped in the middle of that, though that didn't make the VIP section any more welcoming. The VIPs themselves sat at row after row of bars and card tables. None of them were smiling. Some grinned as he passed, but it was an unsettling grin, the kind that made Kano want to sit as far away as possible. That would probably be for the best anyway, at least until he could figure out what was happening to him. The energy was returning to his hands in waves now, each one a little stronger than the last. He would need to see Nobara again – tonight, if possible. Maybe after she closed the tavern…

"Kano, look alive," said Jaden, nudging him with his elbow.

"Huh, what?"

"I brought you both here for a very important reason," whispered Jaden as he led them along. "Tonight, beautiful women from all across the galaxy will be leaving the festival and coming to the humble Sphere for a drink. It is our job – nay, our duty, to meet as many of them as possible."

"I'm honored to be chosen for this task," said Makoto, adding a little swing to his step as he passed a group of ladies lounging on the railing.

"Hi *Jaden*," they cooed in unison.

"Ladies," Jaden answered, quickening his pace.

Makoto waited until they were out of earshot to snap at Jaden. "Why didn't you introduce me?!"

"I'm doing you a favor." Jaden hushed his voice. "Their boyfriends work for the Taipa Kanani."

"Well that's a damn shame," sighed Makoto.

Perfect, thought Kano. Not only were his powers getting steadily out of control, but now he was in the presence of the most dangerous gang in the quadrant, maybe even the galaxy. He had half a mind to slip back through the blue door before any of these Taipa Kanani boyfriends showed up.

"Don't you worry, Makoto," assured Jaden, "I'll find you a good one. I know everyone here…" Jaden trailed off, his eyes fixing on the bar. "Except that one."

Kano knew what was happening. It happened every time Jaden went out. He was stricken. Infatuated. Whoever it was, he would spend the next week talking about her. He scanned over the bar, lowering his expectations to match Jaden's tastes, when his eyes fell upon a figure that made his jaw drop. She had brown hair that fell down around her shoulders and a red gown that blanketed her tall, thin frame. Her eyes were like sapphires; he could have sworn they flicked in his direction. His heart skipped. He tried to think of the right words to describe what he had just seen, what he had just experienced, but all he could choke out was, "Now that's a woman."

"Very observant of you, Kano," said Jaden, smoothing his over-gelled hair. "Now if you'll excuse me, I'm feeling the gravity well pulling me in that direction."

Kano rolled his eyes. This would be over in minutes – though if Jaden did somehow manage to keep the conversation alive, it could be the perfect opportunity to slip away undetected…

He watched as Jaden descended upon the bar like a man with newfound purpose, hopping into the seat right beside the poor girl and lazily signaling the bartender with one finger. "I'll take a Scorcher, hold the Pílu—" Jaden paused, glancing at her for dramatic effect. "In fact, make that two."

"Oh, that won't be necessary," she said as Kano and Makoto claimed the open barstools beside Jaden, neither glancing in her direction, but keeping their ears tuned to every detail.

"Please, it would be my pleasure! I'm Jaden by the way, Jaden Upton."

"Oh, I'm well aware of who *you* are," she laughed.

"Of course you are, I am, uh…" he let out a fake cough, "pretty popular around here."

She turned back to the bartender, raising her eyebrows in a cry for help.

He's sinking. Kano could see the panic setting in on Jaden's face. He was about to step in and say something just to keep the conversation going when Jaden blurted, "I…take it you're new in town."

"What makes you say that?" she asked.

"Your dress. No one wears big-name designers outside of the Central Systems. Not to mention your perfume; they don't sell Divonné anywhere *close* to here. Believe me, I've looked."

"Oh, so you're a traveled idiot," she teased.

"I'm afraid to say I spent more time enjoying the galaxy than actually learning about it." He succeeded in coaxing a giggle out of her and smiled. "Do you have a name?"

"I might."

He was in love now, Kano could see it. "How about a game then? For every drink we order, you give me a letter."

A sly smile crossed her face. She nodded.

Thank goodness, thought Kano. He started to stand, the girl's eyes quickly flicking over to him before returning to Jaden.

"Marky, the Scorchers!" shouted Jaden.

"That's not my name," the bartender mumbled as he slammed two glasses in front of them, each bubbling with a bright orange fizzle.

"So, first letter?" urged Jaden, waving the drink in his hand for effect.

"Nah-ah, you've gotta finish it first," she said with a wave of her finger. Jaden shrugged and began to chug his drink.

She smirked. Just as Kano started creeping away, he caught her passing her drink to another gentleman beside her, who shrugged and began chugging as well.

Jaden slammed his empty glass on the counter. He turned to her, his eyes longing for the first letter, but his mouth shut tight to suppress a burp.

"C," she said as two more drinks landed in front of them.

Looks like he's met his match, thought Kano as he slipped away.

<hr>

Files were scattered across the computer screen, each one more confusing than the last. Junior rocked in his seat, frustrated. Dozens of missing people with nothing in common. Not only were they different species, but from different planets with different occupations. At first, he had thought they were accomplices of Taranis, helping him plant bombs and then disappearing once they went off, but somehow he doubted a Nurrano carpenter or a Braiman mechanic could be behind such sinister plots.

Were they victims? Some of the reports matched up with Taranis's attacks, but many only coincided with sightings of him, and those were shaky at best. Anyone could don a mask and fool people, and in several reports that had been confirmed to be the case. There had to be something else, though. Something that his dad and Novak saw here that he didn't.

There was a knock at the door. *Speak of the devil.* He switched off the screen.

He opened the door and the scar stared right back at him, a deep ravine in his father's cheek. One day he might finally get used to the sight of it, but that would be after his father finally told him where it came from.

They stood silent for a moment. Hendricks cleared his throat. "Novak tells me you were having a…um, off day today."

"I'm fine, I just need some sleep." He tried to shut the door but his father caught it halfway.

"You understand what's happening, don't you?"

"I would if someone gave me a straight answer every once in a while."

There was a long pause. Long enough to make Junior fill it himself. "Taranis is coming here, isn't he Dad?"

"I don't know. My contact on Darraden is still missing after the attack." Junior's eyes widened. "He could be dead in the rubble, but…if not…"

"Dad, what does he know?"

"Enough to get us both killed. It may not come to that, but if anything should happen, I need you close. Taranis knows that his best way to me is you."

"If something happens, I'm not going to sit on the sidelines like a child. I have a duty to protect this city. A duty *you* gave me."

"Your duty is to follow my orders. You're to stay here. Novak is sending men to watch the house. If an attack happens, go to my study."

Junior took a long, hard look at his father. This wasn't the first time he had been told to stay inside. His father had earned his fair share of enemies during the war and had a tendency to switch into panic mode at the tiniest suspicion of their presence, but something was different this time. Something in his eyes told Junior this was no exercise.

"Dad, I need to know what's coming after us."

"I wish I knew." Hendricks turned to leave, but stopped halfway to the stairs. "I'm proud you want to help, but this one can't be your fight. I promised your mother a long time ago I would never let you get wrapped up in this."

Junior froze. He couldn't believe his ears. He *never* talked about her. To even mention her now meant the man in front of him was completely over the edge.

Hendricks descended the steps without another word. Junior waited until the last stair creaked before he raced back to his computer and reactivated it. Now the files had new meaning. These were his father's contacts. As he scrolled through them, though, it still didn't quite add up. There were hardened criminals on this list, certainly not his father's top-choice for trusted allies. Then again, he did have contacts in strange places…

I heard your dad paid them a little visit last night, Jaden's voice echoed in his head.

Most of what happened in the Archives was a blur, but that one comment had stayed with him. Why would his dad visit the Sasakis right after the attack? They were a completely normal family – well, except for the fact that they had adopted a…Human…

What of the boy, Hendricks? echoed the old man's wheezy voice.

Kano. They had been talking about Kano downstairs – but *why*? Did they know his parents? No one else seemed to. In fact, he didn't know much about Kano at all. The only time they had ever crossed paths was today at the Archives when he…broke the viewing glass.

It would take a sledgehammer to leave a crack like that, echoed Novak's voice.

He looked at the missing person's reports on his screen, his eyes widening. He grabbed his coat and raced out the door.

Chapter 7

Hellfire

The quiet of the lounge area was a welcome change. Kano had tried leaving the club, but the red-vested attendant had informed him that he couldn't exit through the blue door (at least not without injuring himself), so he would need to find an exit tunnel instead. After twenty minutes of searching, though, all he had found were more gangsters to keep him on edge. They screamed at each other at the card tables and shouted over each other at the counters as if getting the bartender's attention was a sport. Kano felt his powers swelling in his hands every time one of them strayed too close to him. He knew he needed to get away from it all – the gangsters, the crowds, the music, and the shouting – before something happened.

To his relief, he had stumbled on this little enclosure tucked within the VIP section. He would have passed it by entirely had it not been for an attendant who, probably seeing the frightened look on his face, opened the door and politely directed him inside. All the walls were glass. Every way he looked, he could see people walking, dancing, and drinking along the walls of the Sphere, something he could appreciate much more now that all the noise was blocked out. He could have drawn the curtains, but he figured he would enjoy the view while he had it, considering he had no intention of coming here again.

He sank deeper into the cushy couch he had claimed for himself. There were others spread around the edges of the room, but no one else was here to claim them. For the first time today he could relax without any crowds, schemes, or drama.

He looked down. The floors were glass too, and beyond floated the outside world. The Dockyards stretched on for miles beneath his feet, its spotlights cutting across the starry night sky, beckoning ships toward its many landing pads. Strange: he thought the Dockyards would be much more crowded for the festival. There were hardly any ships left in the sky, either. He checked his communicator.

Past midnight? How long had he been sitting here? The Dockyards were about to close, and that meant Nobara would be closing shop soon as well. The tavern was just a short climb down; he could make it on foot. He just needed to find one of those exit tunnels. He stood up and made for the door when he spotted a red and black face talking to the attendant outside.

Makoto. His brother must have been looking all over for him. The poor guy was probably miserable watching Jaden make a fool of himself.

The attendant pointed to the glass. Makoto caught Kano's gaze and mouthed something Kano couldn't make out, and probably didn't want to. A moment later, the Nurrano was bursting through the door, allowing a thousand voices to enter with him.

"Why the hell did you run off?" he asked, plopping into the nearest couch while the attendant shut the door behind him.

"I wasn't running, I just—"

"Needed some space?" Makoto concluded with a smirk. "How's your um…?" he waved his hand around as if he had powers coming through it.

"It's fine," mumbled Kano. He sank into the couch across from Makoto, his eyes lost in the sea of spotlights beneath his feet.

"You must feel pretty useless here, don't you?"

Kano looked up. "Excuse me?"

Makoto smirked. "You know, the Nurranos at school tell stories from back home on Tikata about heroes like Kenji the Kraken or Wakumi the Wise or, my personal favorite, Shinzo the—"

"They're just stories," interrupted Kano. He already knew where his brother was going with this.

"Maybe to you, but not to my people. You can be one of them Kano. You can do the impossible things that only they could."

"They didn't even exist."

"Yes they did. Mom and Dad believe in them. I believe in them too, no matter what they say in school or on TV. You're living proof that they existed."

"I'm proof that powers existed, not heroes."

Makoto leaned forward. "Do you know why we like telling these stories so much? When the Poterians destroyed our home, these stories were all we had left. Look around you. The suits, the music, the dancing: the people here don't care about these stories because they don't need them. They have everything they could ever want. But spend a day on what's left of Tikata and the people there will treat you like a god."

"I don't want to be a god."

"You don't have to be. You can be Kano – Kano the Kraken, that has a nice ring to it."

"You know what my powers can do. I'd do more harm than good."

"Maybe now, but with the right teacher—"

"Teacher? If I had a teacher, I'd be putting them in danger every time I came in for practice. And there's no place I can practice here without being discovered. Your mom and dad had it right: *'Never use these powers and they will never betray you'*."

"Who said anything about practicing on Famora?" said Makoto. He pointed down at the ships flying out into the blackness of space.

"I can't just *leave*," said Kano. "What about school, and – well, *school*?"

Makoto chuckled. "I'm sure there are other schools on other planets. And maybe they'd be more appreciative of your powers."

Kano stared at the starry sky, wondering. Was there really a teacher somewhere out there? He remembered the man from the dreams. The man on fire. He had powers too. Horrifying powers, but powers nonetheless. Maybe he could find him – if he was even real…

The door swung open and the music blasted back into the room. Kano expected to see Jaden standing there, but what he saw instead made him jump out of his seat.

"Marcus," he said, his legs shaking. The cadet entered with a whole horde of his comrades behind him. They packed in shoulder-to-shoulder before shutting the door and dousing the room in silence once more. Kano counted at least a dozen, and they were all wearing red vests.

"How did you find us?" demanded Makoto.

"We work security here for a little side money," answered Marcus, his fingers drumming against his baton. "Imagine our surprise when Jaden's name came up on the VIP list. I didn't realize he was such an esteemed member of the community."

The cadets maneuvered around the edges of the room, shutting all the curtains. The only light left came from the spotlights flashing by beneath their feet, casting harsh shadows on the cadets' faces. Kano's heart was racing. He had never been in a fistfight before, and this was the worst possible time to break his streak.

"Guys, I promise we didn't mean for things to go—"

"You had us running through half of Downtown like idiots!" shouted Marcus. The cadets inched closer. "Colonel said we were so slow to catch up with you guys that he's gonna have us run ten miles every morning until the next festival!"

He drew the baton from his belt.

"You wouldn't dare," said Makoto, raising his fists.

"What? Does a little sting frighten you?" The tip of Marcus's baton sparked with electricity, illuminating the devilish grin on his face.

"Marcus, we're *sorry*," begged Kano. His hand pulsed. His powers were coming whether he wanted them to or not.

"Hear that, boys? He's *sorry*!" The cadets laughed. "Now let's take them down."

The cadets swarmed. Most went for Makoto, knowing him to be the stronger of the two. Only two cadets attacked Kano, but both were much larger than he was. It took them only seconds to pin both of his arms to his sides.

Marcus marched toward him, the baton crackling with electricity.

"Do something," Kano told himself. He tried wriggling free, but their grips were too strong. He jerked his arm, and the cadet holding it stumbled into the path of the baton. Kano felt the electricity shoot through the cadet and into his own arm. His muscles seized, and he collapsed beside the cadet, who lay there staring at him, unblinking. *He's stunned.* Kano felt a tingle in his own arm. He wiggled his finger; he was fine. *But if they think I'm stunned, maybe they won't fight me.*

Marcus grabbed him by the collar and hoisted him into the air. "Damn you," he seethed, staring into Kano's wide, unmoving eyes. "Are you pretending to be stunned?"

"I…*no*," defended Kano.

Marcus dropped him. Kano tried to scramble back, but the other cadet stood in his way.

"You three are just full of tricks, aren't you?" said Marcus. He swung at Kano's head. Time slowed down for Kano. He ducked, and suddenly the energy surged into his fist. Without thinking, without warning, his fist drove straight into Marcus's gut. He felt the breath forced from the cadet's lungs and saw the shock on the cadet's face as he went hurdling back.

Marcus smashed through the wall. The curtains collapsed in a shower of glass and the light poured back into the room. Everyone stopped: the VIPs, the bartenders, the cadets who had been struggling to get a hold of Makoto. They all stared at Marcus.

The cadet groaned. He lifted his head off the ground and stared at Kano. "You…" he whispered. "You're…you're a…"

Makoto burst from the mob of cadets and swung his foot into Marcus's skull. The cadet was out cold before his head even touched the ground.

Makoto turned to Kano, who stood there horrified. "*Come on!*" he shouted.

Kano snapped back into motion. He raced after Makoto, the whole Sphere spinning around him. *Marcus knows my secret.* Soon everyone would know. He had to get out of here. He had to get out of here *now*.

◁◆▷

"C-E-R…what was that last one you said?" slurred Jaden, tipping forward as the weight of his head suddenly became too much for him to handle.

"A," she answered, trying hard to hold back her laughter.

"Cera! I like that name! That's a good…good game. Let's play another. *Marky!*"

The bartender shot her an annoyed look. "I think we're good on drinks," she replied, pointing to the mass of empty glasses in front of her.

"Nonsense!" exclaimed Jaden. "I have free drinks for life!" He leaned in and whispered, "I'm have a pin."

"Yeah, you mentioned that," she said. "So, what happened to those two friends you came in with?"

"You mean Kano and Makoto? They were just here a minute ago…" He looked back and forth, realizing that everything around him was now one big blur.

"Tell me about them," she said. "How long have you all known each other?"

"Oh, we go back a couple cycles. Now with Makoto, what you see is what you get, but Kano on the other hand, you'll find he's full of surprises."

"Like what?" she pressed, leaning closer.

Jaden smiled. "Well, for starters—" He paused. A large, blurry figure was charging toward him, its familiar scowl coming into focus.

"Junior!" he cheered.

"Where's Kano?!" shouted Junior.

"We were just wondering the same thing!" said Jaden, joyously. "You want a drink? I get them for—"

"Has anyone seen Kano?!" Junior shouted.

"Is that them over there?" asked the bartender.

Junior spun around. Kano and Makoto were racing straight for them with an army of cadets not far behind. He rushed to meet them, his big frame blocking their path.

"Not him again!" cried Makoto.

"Out of the way!" screamed Kano.

"Kano, stop, I'm here to help—" Junior fell forward before he could finish. The floor had turned to jelly beneath his feet. The whole Sphere shook. The cadets tripped over each other. Jaden tumbled out of his barstool. Kano and Makoto flew into the railing, clinging to it while the dancers below screamed and toppled over each other.

"That wasn't you, was it?!" asked Makoto.

Kano shook his head. "I think a hoverpad just went out!" *Or worse.* Whatever it was, it had bought them some time, but not much. He could already hear the batons sparking behind him.

"We have to get to the bottom!" shouted Makoto, pointing to an exit tunnel far beyond the VIP section that the crowd was now clamoring for.

So that's where it was. Kano gulped. They would have to cross a sea of terrified people to reach it. Then again, maybe they didn't need to…

"Makoto, the shoes!" he exclaimed, unlacing his own.

"You're a genius!" shouted Makoto, ripping his off.

Kano felt gravity yank him up into the air, but not in the way he had hoped. He spun and flailed, every spin bringing him closer to the gravity well.

"Makoto, we're going the wrong way!"

"No kidding!" Makoto shouted back as he somersaulted through the air.

Kano felt a rush of wind whoosh past. He looked over his shoulder – *Junior*. The cadet was arcing around the inside of the Sphere like a bullet, his legs pressed together and his arms held tight to his chest.

Damn he's persistent. The cadet rocketed past them again, this time closer. They were running out of time.

Kano saw the tunnel flash by in his spin. He pressed his arms and legs together, feeling his momentum slow. He heard the whoosh of the cadet; he must have been just inches away that time. He would have them on the next pass, Kano was sure of it. There was no time to think. Kano grabbed Makoto by the shirt and pulled him closer, his other hand aimed in the direction away from the tunnel.

"Kano, what are you doing?!"

"I have no idea." The power rushed into his palm. He steadied his hand. *Three…two…* Something hit them hard. He couldn't stop it now. The power burst from his hand with a crack. They hurtled back, Makoto still clutched between his fingers, and two burly hands wrapped around his chest.

"Let go!" he screamed.

"Kano, you need to let me explain!" cried Junior as he sailed with them.

The Sphere disappeared, replaced by narrow metal walls. *The tunnel.* The cool night air hugged him. Their momentum slowed as they passed through to the other side. He could see the stars hanging over his head and—

Stars?

"Kano!" screamed Makoto.

"What?!"

"That wasn't the bottom!"

The gravity shifted. He started falling, Junior and Makoto on either side of him. *Stupid gravity well. We were going up the entire time!*

Makoto struck the Sphere first, lights dancing underneath him as he slid down its curved surface. Kano slammed down next, his shirt caught between Junior's bulky fingers, and together they tumbled. Kano kicked out his legs. His socks skidded along the surface, but without shoes he had no traction to slow him down.

An arm wrapped around his neck, the communicator on its wrist digging into his chin.

"Hold still!" Junior shouted as they slid together. He reached his other hand around and pushed a button on his communicator. "I'm trying to help you!"

"That's a load of—" Kano stopped. Something wasn't right. The night sky, it looked...*orange*. The air felt warmer as they descended. He looked down at the Dockyards and his heart almost stopped.

Fire. Fire all across the Dockyards.

Smoke and ash plumed from each of the hundreds of landing pads. In the distance, docking stations exploded into balls of fire, the flames rising high into the night.

Makoto turned around, still well ahead of them, his eyes wide with fright. "Kano, I think you might be right about—" He didn't get to finish. He passed the widest point of the Sphere and plummeted off its surface toward a thin gap of abyss hanging between the Sphere and the Dockyards.

Kano fell after him with Junior still wrapped around his throat. *Two bubbles in one day*, he thought miserably. Suddenly, he felt Junior's weight swing forward. The abyss disappeared from under them, replaced by fire. The stupid cadet was angling them *toward* the inferno.

"Are you crazy!" screamed Kano, the wind lashing against his face. "We need to follow Makoto to the Trampoline!"

Junior ignored him.

Kano heard a familiar roar. He looked over his shoulder. A jet-black speeder bike was diving after them without a rider, and it was gaining.

The cadet was a quick thinker, Kano could give him that. He jabbed Junior in the stomach and felt the grip on his neck loosen. Kano slipped out of the headlock, but when he tried to angle himself away, he felt Junior's massive paw clench around his leg. With the other hand, Junior grabbed onto the speeder and pulled himself into the seat. He yanked on the throttle, trying to pull the speeder out of its nosedive.

Kano dangled helplessly at Junior's side, feeling the heat of the fires as they closed in on their collision course. "You're insane!" he cried.

Junior gritted his teeth, refusing to ease up on the throttle. He screamed as he pulled it in as far as it would go. Kano closed his eyes, certain this was the end. The speeder arced, the G-force coming down on them like a ton of bricks. Kano felt the speeder slow, and when he opened his eyes again the rubble was just inches beneath his face, whizzing by as Junior steered them through what was left of the Dockyards.

"What are you doing?" demanded Kano, his head heavy from being held upside down.

"Saving your life," said Junior, lifting the speeder back toward the night sky. "Taranis is here and—"

"I can see that he's here, but why are you after *me*?!"

"Because I think he came here for you."

"*What?*" Kano's head felt suddenly heavier.

"I don't know for sure, but it has something to do with your powers."

Kano let that sink in. He knew. Of course he knew, his dad must have told him. "How…how would Taranis know about that?"

"He kidnapped a customs agent on Darraden. That's how he tracked you here. I can take you to my father; he can protect you."

Suddenly everything fell into place. Hendricks's visit, Novak putting a tracker on him: they were all trying to protect him. All this…just because of him? There had to be a mistake; it couldn't be him. He felt sick. He stared into the raging fires, expecting it to wake him up like it always did.

A docking station exploded beneath them. Kano felt the force of it smack him across the back. Molten chunks of metal rocketed overhead in great, fiery streaks. Junior veered out of the way, but it was too late. One of the burning projectiles struck his arm. He screamed and lost his grip. The next thing Kano knew, he was plummeting through the smoke.

"*NO!*" screamed Junior. He dove into the rising plume, the ashes burning his eyes and scalding his lungs, but he couldn't stop himself. He couldn't let Kano die under his watch.

Junior heard a crack, and then a force smashed into him, knocking the breath from his lungs and sending him into a tailspin. It took all his strength to hang on as the speeder spun round and round, turning the flames into a fiery whirl. By the time he had leveled out, he had no clue where he was. He felt sick. Kano couldn't have survived that fall – unless…unless *he* was the source of that force. Junior had felt the same rush when they were floating through the Sphere: it had carried them all the way to the tunnel; surely it could have been strong enough to break his fall? He felt the blood trickling down his arm. He grabbed the molten chunk and ripped it out. His arm screamed in pain, but he would worry about the wound later. Right now he had to find Kano, before someone else did.

He jetted through the smoke-filled sky over the Dockyards – or what was left of them. All the docking stations had been reduced to piles of rubble. Whole ships sat engulfed in flames. The air smelled thick with ash and burning fuel. He spotted flashing lights through the smoke, accompanied by sirens: emergency hovercraft, dozens of them, dumping water and formula over the flames. It wasn't enough.

The smoke grew thicker. The streets and ruins below began to disappear, and still no sign of Kano.

Why would Taranis strike at night when the Dockyards were closed? Didn't he know that no one was here? Then Junior remembered: the bombs were only a distraction, a smokescreen. It was meant to cover Taranis's hunt – and he had just dropped Kano right in the middle of the killing ground.

He swooped down to the street, the ash and smoke choking him. He tore off his sleeve and wrapped it around his mouth and nose to keep from coughing. If only they hadn't ruined his helmet. On and on he drove, the burning corpses of buildings zipping past him, and still there was no sign of anyone. He stopped. The smoke swirled around him, taunting him in devilish wisps, hiding the very person he had just put in danger.

"Stupid, stupid, stupid!" he cried, pounding his fists against the handlebars. He swung over and over again, but it didn't make him feel any better. Only angrier. *Deep breaths*, he reminded himself.

A cry echoed from the distance. Kano? He spun the speeder around. He heard it again – it was coming from across the street. He flew alongside the nearest building, an old five-story warehouse. The windows spat fire at him in greeting. He heard the cry again, this time louder.

It was coming from the rooftop. He jetted up and spotted a worker in a gray uniform waving.

"Thank goodness!" he cried as Junior landed beside him. He was a short, stocky Human, his golden teeth twinkling as he spoke. "My buddy's trapped down there. I tried gettin' him out, but the debris was too thick. I've been tryin' to flag down an emergency craft…"

"I'll take care of it," interrupted Junior. It may not be Kano, but he couldn't turn away now. It was his duty. "You take my speeder down to the ground."

"But you'll be trapped!"

"I can call it back with this," he replied, flashing his communicator. "You get down there in case I don't make it out in time."

"Bless you," he said, climbing on as Junior stepped off. "He's two floors down, on the left."

Junior nodded and raced down the stairs. The air down here was thick with black smoke. Embers singed his face as he ran. He could see the fire eating through the walls and into the support beams like they were all made of paper. The floor groaned beneath his weight, and by the sound of it, he had only minutes to find the person and get out.

⊲◆⊳

"Hold still Nama."

"I am. It's your hand that's shaking, dear."

Li took a deep breath and steadied herself. Her hand glowed again, hovering over the gash in her grandmother's forehead. New skin began to form, but it stopped at the edge of the gash, refusing to heal over. Li pressed harder, the white light growing brighter, but still the skin wouldn't move. She kept pressing, the pressure mounting. She started to see spots. *Breathe. Remember to breathe.*

She gasped and dropped her hand, its light fading away.

Nobara smiled. "In time, child. For today, we can stick to the medical kit."

Li nodded, her chest heaving. She got up and crossed the tavern, her shoes crunching through the splinters and broken glass that littered the floor. The bombing had felt like an earthquake. First it shattered all the bottles, making the place stink even more than usual, then the glasses spilled out of the cupboards and smashed across the floor. Finally, the barstools and chairs began to topple over one another into mounds of broken wood. Looking around, Li hardly recognized the place anymore.

There was a knock at the door. She stopped and spun around, her fists clenched. It could be *him*; she wanted it to be him. She wanted to face the monster who had just destroyed her home.

Nobara shot her a stern look. Despite the wound in her head, she still looked as resilient as ever. "Stick to the plan," she whispered.

Li looked to the door, then back at her grandmother. *"Be careful,"* she mouthed, not daring to make a sound. She retreated to the kitchen and shut the door behind her, keeping her ear pressed against it. *"It's just someone looking for help*," she told herself. That would've been easier to believe if Hendricks hadn't come to warn them this morning. She had been looking over her shoulder all day, expecting to see someone in a mask among the crowd of patrons, but she had never expected *this*.

She listened to her grandmother's slow footsteps tread across the tavern. "*Please, please, please*," she prayed. There was the click of a lock and the creak of a door. Then there was a scream.

Li burst from the kitchen and dove over the counter, but when she saw what was in the doorway, she froze.

Kano. He was coated in a layer of rubble and white dust, his arms and legs stained with dried blood and his body teetering.

She rushed over and caught him as he toppled. He felt limp as a noodle. She led him to one of the few tables that was still standing and laid him across it while her grandmother raced behind the counter for the medical kit.

Li could see the light fading from his eyes. "Stay with me, Kano," she said, patting his face. He started to stir.

"The bombs...I saw them going off...Makoto and I, we...*Makoto*!" Kano shot up and immediately stiffened, pain seizing him.

"Lie down," said Li, soothingly. She eased him onto his back. "You're in no condition to go back out there."

Nobara arrived with the medical kit and a wet rag. She wrapped the rag around Kano's forehead, its icy chill soothing his entire body. Then she went for the halocine and cotton balls in the kit.

"He's still out there," coughed Kano, suddenly aware of all the dust in his lungs.

"I'll call the first responders," said Li, raising her communicator.

"Wait!" He grabbed her wrist and she froze. They stared at each other for a few moments, until Kano remembered what he had wanted to say.

"Tell no one I'm here," he whispered.

"Okay." She punched an alert message into her communicator, her hand trembling.

"Kano, what's happened to you?" asked Nobara, pressing a cotton ball to his knee.

"I fell from a speeder," he began. Li felt his grip tightening on her wrist as the halocine soaked into the cuts. "I broke the fall; it threw me sideways into the debris." He looked at the cuts running up his arm as if seeing them for the first time. "Ah jeez…"

"You're very lucky," said Nobara.

"We need to hide. Taranis…he's here, and he's looking for someone…someone like us."

Li looked to her grandmother; her eyes wide.

"Whoever this terrorist is after," said Nobara, "I doubt it's either of you."

It took Kano a moment before his eyes lit up with realization. He sat up again, swallowing the pain.

"How many others are hiding in Famora?" he blurted.

⊲◆⊳

Junior felt his communicator buzz as he raced through the smoke and flames. He smacked the center button with his palm and brought it to his mouth.

"Where the hell are you?!" his father's voice boomed through it.

"Now's not the best time, Dad," he answered as he ducked under a fallen beam.

"What's that sound? Are you in the *Dockyards*?!"

"Don't worry, I'm fine. I'm checking for survivors."

"No, you need to come home *now*! You're in danger!"

"So are these people!" He stopped. A pile of wooden beams blocked his path. Behind it, he could just make out the shape of a limp body on the floor.

"This isn't up for debate; you're coming home now!"

"Dad, I'll have to call you back!"

Junior smacked the center button again, cutting his father's tirade of obscenities short. He steadied himself and began kicking the beams out of place. It stung without shoes, but he pressed on, sweat pouring from his face as the wood crumbled beneath him. When the opening grew wide enough, he reached down and scooped the man up by his gray uniform. *A dockworker*. He checked the man's neck. Faint, but there was a pulse. He threw him over his shoulder and raced for the stairs. Another creak echoed through the building as he ran, and a pile of burning beams came crashing down in his path.

Dammit. He looked back. The way was blocked by fire. His only option was through these beams.

He raised his communicator and hailed the speeder. It cruised through a broken window, its laser guidance leading it around the flames. When it reached the pile of burning beams, though, it stopped. Junior jammed on the button over and over again, but the speeder refused to push through the obstruction.

The floor groaned. He felt his feet sinking. *It's now or never*. He glanced every direction. No one was here, and he doubted anyone outside could see him through the smoke. He took a deep breath and raised his hand toward the burning beams.

The fire lifted off them. It waved delicately through the air in wisps that settled into the palm of his hand and formed into a ball, a ball which shook harder and harder the more he added to it. Soon he had sucked all the light out of the hallway save for the fiery aura in his palm. His face reddened. His muscles tightened. With a mighty push, he hurled the fireball forward and blasted the beams apart. He jumped onto his speeder and zipped through the open window just in time to watch the building crumble behind him.

Chapter 8

The Zoboros

A cold wind crawled up Kano's spine. He stared up the mountain, its black rocks of volcanic glass dripping with rain and glistening with each flash of lightning. The mountain looked like a field of spikes, climbing all the way to the swirling black clouds that concealed its peak.

Something was climbing up it: one – no, two people, dipping in and out of sight as they weaved between the rocks. A man and a woman, their faces concealed by shadows. When the lightning flashed, Kano saw something glint off the woman's neck.

Kano checked his pocket. *The necklace*. It was gone. He raced up the mountainside, weaving between the spiked rocks. He couldn't explain why he was running after it; he just needed that necklace back.

Rain pelted his face. The rocks kept getting larger, closer together, their pointed edges harder to squeeze between without a sharp prick. Blood streaked down his arms and legs to join the water gushing down the mountainside, but still he pressed on.

Hours went by. The air became colder, harder to breathe. Wind howled through the rocks, stabbing through his soaking clothes and into his flesh. He looked up again. The clouds were close above now, the man and the woman hiding somewhere inside them.

It grew dark within the clouds. Too dark. He had to wait for a flash of lightning just to see where to reach next. Still he kept climbing. His arms ached. His hands were covered in blisters. He gritted his teeth every time he pulled himself higher while the rain washed the blood from his arms in red rushes. *How much farther?* he wondered.

His foot slipped on a rock. *No, no, no!* Before he knew it, he was on his belly and into the rapids. Down he slid, his momentum gaining, until he slammed against the flat face of a rock, pain shooting through his chest as though he had been struck by a hammer.

At least I missed the pointy end, he thought miserably.

How far he had fallen, he had no idea. Clouds still surrounded him, but something was different. No more rain. Lightning flashed and he saw a ceiling of rocks shimmering overhead, stretching on into the unknown.

A cave. He couldn't see how deep it went. He went to activate the light on his communicator, but found his wrist was bare. Rising onto shaking knees, he wondered what else they had taken from him.

He stepped forward. The ground here was smooth. Dry. A welcome change. He kept walking with his hands out in front of him, relying on the quick flashes of lightning to show him the way, though soon he had strayed too far even for that. He knew he should turn back. He didn't know why he kept going. Maybe it was the fear of facing the mountain again. Or maybe something else…

Blue light streaked across the roof of the cave, lighting the path before him until it zipped out of sight. It was a straight shot. No turns, no rocks, just flat ground. He started into a jog. Another blue flash streaked overhead. He ran faster, trying to keep pace with it. The cuts in his legs were screaming, but he couldn't stop now, not until he knew where it was going.

The light stopped. He skidded to a halt, and just in time, too. At his feet was a glowing pool of deep, murky-blue water. It stretched on another thirty feet to an opposite bank, where two figures stared back at him, shadows covering their faces.

"Who are you?!" he called. There was no answer. He searched for a path, but the pool took up the whole breadth of the cave.

The light he had followed dripped from the ceiling, and as it splashed into the pool, something else splashed out.

Please no, not him. Kano stumbled back as the man emerged, glowing water pouring from his blood red cloak.

The room brightened. Kano looked up. The roof of the cave had vanished, replaced by a night sky. Millions upon millions of stars hovered over his head, the blue bands of the galaxy weaving through them. He had never seen a sky like this on Famora.

The man reached a pale, veined hand into the air and the cosmos began to rotate around it, faster and faster, swirling into a vortex that descended gently into his palm. The light of the pool began to fade, until all that was left was a white aura glowing in the man's hand.

Kano heard a whisper. It didn't sound like an ordinary voice, though. It sounded like a thousand echoing as one.

"Find us."

Every instinct told him to run, but he couldn't move. His heart kept beating faster. These voices, he didn't just hear them, he felt them, shaking in rhythm with the power pulsing inside him. The man reached out his glowing hand. It trembled there in the air, waiting to be taken. *"Leave…leave now!"* something screamed in the back of his mind, but the voices were screaming louder.

"Find us! Find us! Find us!"

He had to know who they were…

"Find us! Find us! Find us!"

He had to know where they were…

"FIND US! FIND US! FIND US!"

He reached out and took the man's hand.

Everything went dark. The screaming became silence. He felt a rush of wind, and then everything sped into fast motion. He was flying, out of the mountain and into space, past asteroids and stars, through planets and valleys and oceans and cities the likes of which he had never seen.

And then it was over. He gasped as he glanced around. He was back in the cave, sitting on his knees, the rocks hanging over his head and the pool glowing in front of him, but the two figures on the other side were gone.

The man stood beside him, pointing to the water. Kano stared into it. His reflection stared back at him, but he didn't recognize it. His hair was shorter, his arms bigger, his face…hairier. He reached down and touched the water's surface, so cool it soothed the blisters on his hands. The man's reflection stood beside his own, the cloaked face nodding to him. Kano nodded back. He knew what to do.

The water quivered as his power pressed into it, at first slowly, then faster and faster, churning into waves that splashed out over the edges of the pool. The water tried to slither back, but his power kept pushing it away, farther and farther, and still it was only a fraction of what he could do. He pressed harder, and the water began to part beneath his hand. Before he knew it, he was falling, his hand still pushing, the water clearing away from it. He struck the rocks beneath the pool, but they crumbled at his touch. The whole mountain crumbled. Deeper and deeper he fell through mountain and earth, past fire and magma, straight toward a light that grew brighter and brighter until…

Kano snapped his head up, gasping. Sweat dripped from his face. His heart was pounding. Darkness surrounded him once again, only this time the air wasn't cold. It was stuffy and warm and smelled of old wood.

He found his communicator was back on his wrist. When he touched the screen, he felt fresh cracks running through it. *The fall.* The whole night came rushing back to him. The Sphere, the bombs, and *Taranis*...

The last thing he remembered was lying on one of Nobara's tables, panicking. She had claimed that no one was coming for him, but how could she know? Hendricks had come to warn *him*. Novak had put a tracker on *him*. He checked his wrist, but all he found was a bump in the skin where the tracker had been. It must have broken off when he hit the pavement. He could feel the panic setting in again. He was stranded right at the place of the attack with no one to protect him – unless Nobara had taken him somewhere else.

He switched on his communicator. The broken screen flickered to life, dimmer than usual. New messages ran all the way down it, probably from Yuchi, but the cracks rendered them unreadable. He activated the communicator's flashlight and swept it back and forth. There was nothing but giant barrels of liquor looming over him, one after the other, each a deep, rich brown.

Nobara's storeroom.

He rested on a pile of flour sacks, soft yet firm, the fabric soaked in his sweat. Something grazed his forehead. He reached up and grabbed it: a pull chain. He gave it a tug, his eyes wholly unprepared for the surge of yellow light that swept across the room. He blinked away the spots, the long line of barrels coming into view. There was something else, too: a small glass on the floor, placed perfectly beneath the tap of a barrel. A gift from Nobara, he assumed. Considering the night he had had, it felt like an appropriate time to put it to use.

He rose. His knees screamed. Deep red lines ran across them, each one glistening with halocine. He had to hobble to the tap, every painful step sending flashes through his mind. He saw Jaden drunk at the counter, and Makoto falling into the abyss, and Junior spinning away on the speeder. Where were they now? He saw Li hovering over his wounds with her hands, and Nobara with that terrible gash in her forehead, and the Dockyards blazing with a fury that lit up the night sky. He could still smell the smoke, still taste the ash like sand against his tongue. And that mask, the one he had seen on TV, staring back at him…

By the time he reached the tap, his heart was racing again. He collapsed beside it, his whole body shaking.

It couldn't be true. What could Taranis want with him? Powers or not, he was just a kid. Nobara had said there were others hiding in the city, probably stronger ones too. Ones who actually knew how to use their powers.

Sighing, he stuck the glass beneath the tap and pulled the stopper. Nothing happened. He tugged over and over again, each time harder, until the whole tap snapped sideways with a loud click. He jumped back, expecting booze to come shooting out, but nothing happened. With a cautious hand, he grabbed the tap and pulled ever so gently. It felt weightless against his fingers. The whole face of the barrel creaked open, and not a drop of liquid spilled out.

Alright Nobara, what surprises do you have for me today?

He aimed his communicator's light into the barrel. Crates were stacked on either side, each overflowing with junk. Wood carvings, silver trinkets, tribal masks: treasures from worlds he had never seen and had probably never even heard of. A narrow walkway cut through the center of it all, just wide enough for him to crawl through, and at the end of it sat a wooden chest, his light glinting off the keyhole.

Kano crawled inside. His knees burned with every movement, but he was too fascinated by the chest to let that stop him. Surely it was what Nobara meant for him to find, but there was no key on the floor. *It could be in one of the crates – one of the many, many crates…*

Another idea crossed his mind. He didn't know if it would work, but he figured it was better than digging through mountains of junk. He pressed both hands to the sides of the chest, his power trickling through his fingertips. The chest began to rattle, at first slowly, then faster, louder, clunking against the barrel beneath it. *Come on…*

There was a jolt. The lock unlatched and the chest swung open. Kano reeled, startled at his own success. The smell of old paper rose to greet him. There were hundreds of leaflets at the top, their edges yellowed. He brushed them aside. Beneath them he found a black, leather bound book, wide and thick, with a golden seal embroidered into its cover that twinkled in his communicator's light. His eyes widened. He reached into his pocket and drew the necklace. When he held it next to the seal, it was a perfect match.

"If you see one like it, you are in the presence of a friend."

The light flickered out. He tapped on his communicator, but nothing happened. Dead. He sighed. Yuchi wouldn't be happy about that. In fact, she wouldn't be happy about a lot of things that had happened in the last twenty-four hours. He scooped the book from the chest and cradled it out into the light.

He plopped back down on the flour sacks and flipped it open, its pages thin and fragile. The first page was covered in letters that he had never seen before. They looked like music notes, with curves and dots all around them, only they ran vertically instead of horizontally. A few of them seemed vaguely familiar, though he wasn't quite sure where he had seen them before…

The mask.

He shuddered. Whatever language this was, Taranis knew it. He flipped to the next page, relieved to find pictures this time, each one hand painted in such a way that they all blended together, telling a tale of warriors who could command the seas and winds and fires great and terrible with just a wave of their hands. He kept flipping through. The pictures told everything: a group of warriors on their quest to save the galaxy from mighty foes on far-off worlds…

<hr>

Terror had seized Famora General. The injured poured in by the dozens, so many that the hospital rooms had all been filled. Now beds lined the sides of every hallway, the moans and cries of their occupants joining together in a chorus of pain. Some had been burned at the Dockyards, but most had come from Downtown, having been trampled in the mad rush to flee the festival.

Junior marched between the beds as fast as he could, dodging nurses as they rushed among patients. Like everyone else here, his clothes were charred with black soot, but he hadn't bothered to change. After his search through the Dockyards had failed, he raced straight to the hospital, knowing Kano would have been brought here by whoever found him.

Unless Taranis found him first.

The attack on the Dockyards had made one thing very clear to Junior: Taranis was not alone. Those explosions came from beneath the docking stations, within the very hoverpads that kept them afloat. Not just anyone had access to those; only engineers or city officials with enough clearance…that could be any of at least two hundred people in the city. And whoever they were, they might still be on the hunt. He had to get to Kano first.

He rounded a corner and spotted a blue suit standing by the information booth, cufflinks shimmering on each wrist.

Junior dipped behind the corner. What was he doing here? He peeked around, watching the man lean up against the booth, the curly haired girl behind it laughing at whatever he was saying. She handed him a card, and he pinched her cheek before walking away. As soon as the man was out of sight, Junior raced up to the booth, the girl still beaming.

"Where's he going?!"

The girl turned, finally noticing his existence. "Oh, Dr. Carmichael needed to check on one of his patients."

Doctor Carmichael. That man was many things, but not a doctor. "Which one?"

"Ummmm…" she glanced at her computer screen, "…Marcus Antolini. Say, aren't you the one who saved the man from the Dock—?"

"What room number?" he interrupted.

"1306, but—"

Junior sprinted off before she could finish. He heard her shout, "You can't get into the ER without a pass!" but that didn't stop him. If Carmichael was here for Marcus, then he wasn't far off Kano's scent. Junior had overheard the cadets' radio chatter on the way here; he knew the two of them had had some kind of a fight, one that didn't end well for Marcus.

He dipped left and right through crowded halls and passages. Carmichael may have had a head start, but Junior had delivered enough drunken students here on his night patrols to learn the layout of the hospital inside and out. He could get there faster; he just needed a way inside the ER…

A nurse rushed past him with a bright white coat in her hand, stopping beside a doctor who was attending one of the hallway patients. The doctor rose, a tall man, almost as tall as Junior, his coat covered in soot and blood. Junior's eyes locked onto that coat as the doctor shed it and tossed it to the nurse. The nurse handed him the fresh one and raced off, unaware that Junior was tailing her. She stopped at a large, box-shaped bot that was floating slowly overhead, its hollow inside overflowing with rotten scrubs. The nurse balled up the coat and tossed it up into the pile, then hurried away.

Junior slowed down and casually approached the bot. It may have been out of reach for the nurse, but all Junior needed to do was stand on his tiptoes to snatch the coat out of it. He glanced around. Everyone was either too busy or too hurt to pay him any attention. He unrolled the coat and threw it on, the bloodstains feeling cold and fresh as they soaked into his T-shirt underneath. He marched on, patients groaning as he passed. They thought he was going to help them, he realized. He kept moving, trying his best to ignore their pitiful cries and focus on how he would get inside the emergency room. A coat still wasn't a pass, and if security was as tight as he expected tonight, it wouldn't be enough to get him through.

"*Hey kid!*" boomed a voice from down the hall.

He was caught. He turned around, steadying himself so he could flee at a moment's notice, but it wasn't a doctor coming for him. It was a short, stocky man in a gray uniform stained with soot. Junior recognized him almost instantly from the rooftop.

"Thank goodness I caught ya! I can't thank you enough for what ya did back there!" He gave Junior a firm pat on the shoulder, the grease between his fingers sticking to the white coat. The man's eyes narrowed with sudden realization. "Say, I thought you was a cadet?"

"Well this is more of a…temp job," replied Junior.

The dockworker grinned. "Anyways, they says my buddy's stable now. I'd be with him, but they won't let anyone inside the ER. They says you got him here just in time."

Junior spotted an empty bed over the man's shoulder. An idea began to form. He gave the man a once-over. Beneath the grease and soot, this looked like someone who knew how to exchange favors – and do so discretely.

"Would you like to see your friend?" he asked.

◁◆▷

Kano pored over every page, every drawing, every word that he didn't know, his hands shaking with excitement as they flipped deeper and deeper into the story. Three heroes were sailing from planet to planet on their quest, passing over forests of green and castles of gray and…

Mountains of black. The book fell to the floor with a thud.

"You best pick that up," came a voice from across the cellar. "It's an antique."

Kano leaped off the flour sacks. Nobara stood over him, on a flight of wooden stairs that led up to the cellar door. Even from this distance, he could see the smile on her face. "Where did you find this?" he called up.

"You sound troubled. Would you like some tea?"

"Answer the question," he snapped. He felt a sudden urgency. There were so many more questions he wanted to ask.

She sighed and hobbled down the stairs. "You seemed surprised last night when I told you there were others. I wanted you to know the truth. To *see* the truth."

"These are just stories, Nobara."

She glanced at the book lying at her feet, its pages still open to the pictures of dark mountains of volcanic crystal.

"Are they?" she asked.

He gulped, feeling a sudden energy pulse through his hand. "Who were these people?"

"Did Yuchi never tell you the story of the Three Kings of Mogaddu?"

Kano shook his head.

She held out her palm. "The necklace, child." Kano fished it out of his pocket. She snatched it and held it up so the light gleamed off its golden center where the three arrows met. "Long ago, the planet of Mogaddu was divided into three kingdoms. Between their kingdoms was the Temple of Iramwerta, an ancient place said to hold the power of the gods. For centuries the kingdoms warred over it, but no matter who conquered it, the door to Iramwerta would not open." She knelt and flipped to a new page, which pictured a giant wall of stone, its surface etched with those same strange markings.

"No hammers could crack it; no ram could breach it. Whole armies could not push it open with all their strength. It was not until the three kings came together at

Iramwerta and laid down their swords that the temple door finally opened.

"When they passed through, they entered a new world entirely, where land could float and water turned to fire in the sky. It was here they encountered an old, blind traveler carrying a heavy pack on his back. He asked the kings for their help, but they refused him.

"Seeing how he still had such a long way to go and so much to carry, the old traveler told them they could each take an item so as to lighten his load. It could be any item of their choosing, but he warned that they must choose wisely.

"The first king was a learned man; he chose a book that the traveler said could teach him anything he wanted to know. The second king was a strong man; he chose to take a sword to replace the one he had offered to the temple. The traveler said it could win him any battle so long as he held it up to the heavens. The third king was a clever man; he chose to take the pack. The traveler obliged him gladly.

"What they didn't know was that this traveler was no old man. It was Categaris, the trickster god, in disguise. When the three kings brought their treasures back to Mogaddu, they soon discovered that a terrible curse had been placed upon them. The first king learned truths from his book that no mortal man should know, and the knowledge drove him mad. He set his palace afire whilst he was still inside it. The book survived, but all anyone found within it were blank pages.

"With the first king gone, the second king set out, sword in hand, to claim his kingdom. The sword won him the battlefield, but when his generals saw its power, they poisoned him and stole it. It passed through many hands after that, but not a single one ever won a battle with it.

"The third king never used what was in the pack. He had given its contents away as gifts to his people. When he learned what had befallen the other two kings, he sent his soldiers to every corner of his kingdom to collect the cursed items. It took cycles, but when he finally had them all, he returned to the door with the pack slung across his back. He offered them to Categaris, but the trickster god just laughed. 'Those trinkets are useless now,' he said. 'Their job is done.'

"You see, the curse did not remain with the items. Its power passed to whoever first claimed them. The first king gained knowledge, the second gained power, and the third king, well, he now had a hundred subjects spread across the land with powers great and terrible.

"The king asked how this could be undone. Categaris said there was no way, that the power of the gods was now unleashed on the mortal world, as had been his plan all along. The king pleaded, and so Categaris struck a deal with him. He would grant the king the power to oversee any and all who had been cursed with his gifts. In return, the king would be bound to serve him for all eternity. The king agreed."

"But it was another trick," said Kano.

"Yes. Categaris gave him the power, but in doing so bound the king to his temple in the dark mountains, where he could never leave, cursed to watch his creations whilst being unable to stop them. He watched them tear his kingdom apart, and a thousand kingdoms since then, always trying to speak to them, but unable to reach his Zoboros."

"His who?"

"The Zoboros. It's Ancient Mogaddan; it means 'the cursed people'."

"Oh…" said Kano, staring at his empty palm, opening and closing it.

"That is not to say you have a curse, Kano. Many great Zoboros have come before you. They have used their powers to end wars, prevent catastrophes, free slaves. They have guided the course of history, even if they don't teach you about it in school."

"Why wouldn't they?"

Nobara shook her head. "Because many Zoboros have done terrible things too. Over the centuries, the Republic of Planets came to trust them less and less. Laws were passed to keep control of them, and little by little the Zoboros started becoming second-class citizens. Some could not even leave their homes if they were deemed too powerful. That is why the Zoboros sided with the Poterians when they attacked. The Poterians offered them freedom.

"After their defeat, the Zoboros who survived were banished for their betrayal, and those who remained in the Central Systems were hunted down." She paused for a long time. "They were stricken from the history books, never to be spoken of again."

"Which is why I have to hide," muttered Kano.

Nobara picked up the book, closing it so its seal stared Kano right in the face. "Fear has made the galaxy turn its back on the Zoboros, and not for the first time. Someday soon, they will face something they fear even more, and on that day, they will call upon you again."

"What if I'm not ready? These powers – the galaxy would be better off without me."

"One day they will embrace you. But first you must embrace yourself."

Kano felt the energy pulse in his hand again, softly, almost like a whisper. "Do you…do you think I could stop Taranis?"

"With the right teacher, you could take on a thousand of him."

Kano closed his eyes. He saw the glowing pool and the man in the cloak with the power of the cosmos in his hand. He picked up the book and flipped back to where he left off. "This king in the mountain, could he teach me?"

Nobara sighed. "Many Zoboros have sought him. None return."

"Well someone must have, if they wrote it in a book."

"But not the same," she whispered. She whirled around and started up the stairs while Kano let that sink in. "Besides, there are far safer ways to learn."

"What are you talking about?" he asked.

"Are you going to stand there asking questions, or are you going to learn how to use these damn powers of yours?"

⊲◆⊳

"My leg! It burns, *IT BURNS*!"

"Out of the way!" barked Junior, wheeling the bed through the crowd of people, his stolen white coat flapping at his sides. The dockworker flailed and convulsed in the bed, screaming. Overselling it a bit, but it seemed to be working. The crowd was parting. Now nothing stood between them and the doors to the ER except two burly security guards. They took one look at the bloody rag wrapped around the dockworker's leg and stepped aside. Junior wheeled on through, thankful he had snagged that rag from the laundry bot before they charged in.

The doors swung shut behind them. Junior found the ER decidedly quieter than the rest of the hospital. All the rooms were filled, their doors closed. No beds or loved ones crowded the hallways here, just a handful of nurses and doctors rushing between rooms.

"There it is," said the dockworker, pointing to one of the doors.

1306. Junior looked around. No sign of Carmichael.

The dockworker climbed out of the bed. "It's been fun, Junior. I'm gonna find my buddy, maybe lay low until all the excitement dies down." He reached out a grease-covered hand.

Junior took it. "Thank you."

"It's the least I could do, now go see your friend."

157

As Junior made for the door, he heard the dockworker call after him. "The name's Cassius by the way! If ya eva need anything, ya come to the docks, any docks, and ask for me. Ya got that?"

Junior nodded. He had no idea what else he would need from this Cassius guy, but it felt good to know that there was at least one person in this city he could trust.

When he opened the door, he found Marcus sitting upright in bed, though not by choice. His entire abdomen wrapped in bandages, the back of his bed was raised up so he could look straight at Junior with his injuries on full display. IV tubes ran clear liquid from his arm to a monitor beside the bed. An icepack was taped to the side of his jaw, which had ballooned to about three times its normal size.

"Juyior!" he exclaimed, wincing. His jaw didn't want to move.

Junior shut the door behind him. "Marcus, what happened to you?"

Marcus looked away, his smile vanishing. "Juss a fight, dat's all."

"Marcus, I need to know what happened at the Sphere. It's important." He sat on the edge of the bed while Marcus dodged his stare.

"You wouldn't bewieve me if I toll you."

"I think you'd be surprised what I'd believe." Junior stared at the bandages. A crack echoed in his head, the one he had heard when Kano fell. "Listen Marcus, I don't have much time, but what happened tonight at the Dockyards was an inside job. There's a man coming to see you. I don't trust him. I think he's involved – and I think he wants what you know. Tell me now, did Kano do this?"

Marcus stared at him, wide-eyed. "I didn't know dare were Zobowos in da city."

"As far as this guy is concerned, you still don't." The door began to open. Junior dove under the bed, tucking his long limbs in tight between the wheels. In the corner of his eye, he saw a pair of black loafers clicking toward the bed.

"Cap'n' Carmichael," said Marcus, a little less enthusiastic than before. Junior could hear the ruffle of sheets as Marcus tried to steady himself.

"At ease cadet," said Carmichael warmly, his shoes stopping just inches from Junior's face. "No need to strain yourself. You've had a rough night. I promise I'll be out of your hair in a minute."

"Wha…wha do you need?"

"Just need to fill in a few gaps." Junior heard papers ruffling. "I understand you were with the cadets at the Sphere tonight, yes?"

"Yes sir." The bed creaked as Marcus shifted his weight.

"I spoke with some of the other cadets tonight. A few of them sustained some minor injuries, too, but your case is a bit curious. They say you were hurt *before* the bombs went off."

"Well I…it was dark and…"

Carmichael chuckled. "Don't worry Marcus, I already know about the fight. I'm not here to reprimand you;

that's Novak's job. Nothing you report will be shown to any of your superiors. I just need to know what happened to your chest so I can bring an accurate report back to the IDF."

The IDF! Junior snapped his head up, smacking it against the metal bedframe. He bit down on his lip to hold back a yelp, listening to make sure his injury had gone unnoticed. *They have eyes on Kano. If they can prove he has powers, they'll come for him.*

Marcus gulped. "The fight stawted before da bombs. It was dark, but I fink…" He paused. For a long time there was silence. Junior started to worry: if Marcus sold out Kano, what was to stop him from telling Carmichael that he was under the bed?

"One of dem hit me wit a barstool," Marcus squeaked out. "That's how I went true da glass."

"That's very strong glass to be crashing through," said Carmichael. "So was it Kano or Makoto who hit you with this…barstool?"

There was a long pause. "Makoto, I fink it was Makoto."

"Hmmm." Carmichael's shoes clicked toward the IV machine. "And if any other officers were to come asking what happened, would you tell them the same thing you've told me?"

"Yes sir," yawned Marcus. "Yes I would."

"Good. Thank you for your time, Marcus. You've been a great help. Get some rest now."

Carmichael clicked away. Junior poked his head out as the door opened, just in time to watch Carmichael tuck a syringe into his pocket.

When the door closed, Junior shot up. "You did alright, Marcus, but I don't think he bought..." He found his friend was snoring in the bed. "Marcus?" He patted Marcus's cheek, but that only made him snore louder. Junior turned to the IV machine. The fluid inside had gained a purple tint that was quickly diluting.

Sleeper serum. Junior recognized it from training. Carmichael was after Kano, and he was making sure no one else could follow the trail. But why? He crept through the door. Not a soul was there, not Carmichael or a nurse or even Cassius. All was quiet. He stepped out into the hall and felt an arm wrap around his neck.

"We've been looking for you," a voice hissed in his ear. He felt the needle in his neck, and everything went dark.

Chapter 9

The Ripple

The Sun rose over the clouds. The rays that would once have cast shadows over the Dockyards now ran uninterrupted across fields of rubble and ruin. Smoke rose from the smoldering heaps where docking stations once stood, poisoning the sunrise into a light shade of red. Emergency crafts dotted the skies, their crews digging wherever they heard a cry for help.

There were so many. Kano stared through the hole in the wall that had once been Nobara's window, teetering at the edge of his barstool as he watched a team of medics cart away a body on a stretcher, unsure if the person in it was alive or dead.

A loud thump almost spilled him out of his seat. He turned. A wooden bowl sat on the counter before him, water sloshing along its edges. He licked his lips. He still hadn't gotten that drink.

"What, are all the cups broken?" he asked, raising the bowl to his mouth.

Nobara smacked his hand. "No!" she barked.

He dropped the bowl, water splashing out across the counter. "What the—?!"

"This is your first test. I want you to move the water."

Kano eyed her for a moment. He grabbed the bowl and scooted it across the counter.

She smacked his hand again. "With your *powers*."

He rubbed his reddening hand. "If this is gonna become a regular thing, I'm leaving."

"The door is that way," she replied shortly. "If a slap on the hand is too much, then clearly this training is not for you."

He took a deep breath and sat up straight. He wouldn't be dismissed so easily.

"Very well," she continued. "I want you to use your powers to create a ripple."

"A ripple?" Kano chuckled. "You mean like a wave, right?"

"No. Waves are unstable. They fold and crash over themselves. I want a push so gentle that it guides the water without spilling it."

Kano watched the water settle in the bowl. "No offense Nobara, but I don't think I'm gonna stop Taranis with a ripple."

"Then make one already so we can move on to the next lesson."

He rolled his eyes and aimed his palm at the water. His hand shook as the power trickled through. Soon the bowl started shaking, too. Too much and that bowl would fly across the room, he reminded himself. He dialed it up one notch at a time. The water sloshed harder with every extra ounce he put in, his muscles tightening as water crashed up the sides of the bowl.

"Enough!" said Nobara. He stopped and shook out his hand. It felt stiff. "You can make it shake all day long, but it will never move forward unless you push it."

A push, he thought, refocusing on the bowl. Just one push. He aimed again. Gently. His power rushed to his hand again. But how much was gentle?

The energy fired out with a crack. The bowl sailed into the back wall and fell to the floor, leaving a trail of water in its wake. A few moments later, Li burst into the room in her bathrobe, her eyes wild, a rusty pan in her hand ready to swing.

"What happened?!" she cried. She followed the trail of water from the bowl to Kano, grumbled something to herself, and retreated back into the kitchen.

"Try again," said Nobara, refilling the bowl in the sink. She slammed the bowl back on the counter, the thud echoing in Kano's ears long after the room had quieted. *This is such a waste of time*, he thought. His powers weren't meant to do more than this.

He aimed again. Just a little bit…just a… The crack sent the bowl spinning through the air. Water splashed over him, cold and irritating.

Li entered with the mop just in time to watch the bowl land. She huffed and tossed the mop at Kano.

Nobara picked up the bowl and refilled it.

"Again." Thud.

"*I need a quicker release*," he told himself. He steadied his hand. Just for a second. A half second. He caught the burst as soon as it started and the bowl skidded across the counter. It teetered on the edge for a moment before toppling over.

"We're gonna have an indoor pool at this rate," said Li.

"I'd like to see you try!"

"Not my power, not my problem," she said with a cruel smile.

"Again!" Thud.

This time the bowl flipped upside down, water snaking out across the counter.

"Seriously, someone's gonna have to clean this up," teased Li.

"*Oh would you shove it!*"

"Focus Kano," said Nobara. "And you, *shoo.*"

Li gave a bow and slipped into the kitchen.

Nobara turned back to Kano. "As long as you are unstable, your powers will be, too."

"My powers have *always* been unstable!" he blurted. "They aren't meant to help people. They're meant to be locked up where they can't hurt anyone."

"Did your family tell you that?" Nobara's black eyes stared right through him. He looked away. "Did your teachers tell you that?" Her words kept cutting deeper. "Did you friends tell you that?" She stepped right in front of him, her eyes boring into his.

"Or did you tell yourself that?"

Kano slumped back, letting the words sink in. The truth was he had been afraid of his powers from the moment they first pulsed through his fingers. Yuchi's constant warnings about being discovered hadn't helped, either. He had seen glimpses of what they could do: a chair flipped across the room; a window shattered at his very touch. No one should have that kind of power, he'd always thought.

"Tell me, Kano, what could your powers do right now if you didn't hold them back?"

Kano felt sick at the very thought. "They'd destroy everything."

"And that is why we start from the bottom. Let us discover the smallest your powers can go and build from there. That is how you master them. That is how you learn control."

"How much weaker could a shockwave be?" he asked.

"We will find out." Thud. "Again."

The lights were fiery beams, blurring in and out of focus as they passed. An awful scraping sound filled Junior's ears as he woke – the sound of his own body being dragged across the wooden floor. Whoever was dragging him looked very blurry and short…and very blue…

"The boy awakens," hissed his captor.

"Awake and pissed off you son of a bitch." Junior tried moving his arms, but found them completely limp.

"I am son of Ephos and Dorimas. Remember this or I will tie your limbs together so many times you forget which ones to walk with."

"I doubt your master would want you damaging his prize."

The little captor shrugged. "He would not mind a few bruises."

Junior tried lifting his head to see where they were going, but his neck could barely move. Everything could barely move. *How did they find me?* he wondered, though the more he thought about it, the more he realized that the better question was *How long were they tailing me?*

A door opened. Junior breathed in a whiff of bareno smoke. The wood turned to wooly carpet beneath him, rough and stale from cycles of wear. Even with his vision blurred, he knew exactly where he was.

"I told you to come back," said a voice like grinded chalk.

Junior slowly balled his fingers into a fist, about as much movement as he could manage in the moment. "And do what? Sit here and meditate with you all day? People are dying out there."

Fire flickered in the hearth. His father knelt beside it, prodding it with a metal poker. "And how am I supposed to protect them when I can't even protect my own son?"

The feeling returned to Junior's right arm. He put all his weight on it, pushing until he could sit up straight, his left arm still hanging limp at his side.

The study came into focus. Empty leather chairs surrounded him in a misshapen circle. It was just the two of them — no, three; the creature sat idly on the edge of his father's mahogany desk. Junior had known about his father's secret henchman for some time now, but this was the first time he was seeing it in the flesh. Its long arms swayed over the edge and its stretched face contorted into some kind of sadistic smile. Junior found himself staring at it when he said, "It's my job to protect them, too."

"Taranis isn't after *them*." Hendricks scraped away the ashes from the back of the fireplace. Junior spotted something shiny back there, a silver triangle etched into the stone. "Did you use your powers?"

"No one saw me."

"*You don't know that!*" Hendricks spun around, red in the face, the poker aimed at his son. "I warned you not to play hero. Not here, not now."

Junior felt the blood rushing back into his legs. He put his weight on them, rising up taller than his father. "Why didn't you tell me that he was coming after Zoboros?"

"Because if I had, you would have done something stupid. Turns out you would have done that regardless."

"I saved a man's life!"

"And if Taranis had gotten his hands on you, a thousand more would be in danger." Hendricks turned his back on him, fuming. "Do you understand *why* he's kidnapping Zoboros? He wants to turn them into weapons, just like the Poterians did. I spent cycles making sure this would never happen again – but now he's traced my work here and compromised everything."

"*Work?*" spat Junior, pointing to the empty chairs. "You mean your little teatime with the rest of the retirement home?"

The creature's bulbous eyes locked onto him. "His work saved your puny life."

"Stay out of this, imp!"

"I am Akio, and you are *imp*!" Green spit launched from its mouth and splattered on Junior's face.

"Enough!" shouted Hendricks. "We're going downstairs."

"We are downstairs," said Junior, wiping the spit away.

His father knelt beside the fireplace, pushing the poker into the triangle at the back until there was a click. Suddenly, the mantelpiece snapped out of place. Hendricks pulled it from the wall like it was any other door, revealing a staircase that led into darkness.

Junior realized it led straight to the hoverpad.

He felt rough, moist hands clamor up his back and hook onto his shoulder. "Hurry up, unless you wish to be dragged again," Akio hissed in his ear.

"Get off of me," said Junior through gritted teeth.

"You do not give orders," Akio hissed back. "Only head of house can do that."

Junior watched his father disappear down the stairs. He followed, his legs wobbling with every step, his hands clutching tight to the railings. "Where did you find this creature?" he asked.

"That creature is a Jakari," answered Hendricks, "and when I found him, he was a slave to the Poterians. In return for his freedom, he offered me *Jonjai*."

"The life debt, as you would call it," Akio whispered in his ear.

Life debts, sleeper serum: Junior was liking this creature less and less. Even the way it breathed made him uneasy. It was so soft, almost silent; had the creature not been clinging to his shoulder, he probably wouldn't have known it was even there.

Light flickered through an entrance at the bottom of the stairs. He moved as quick as his wobbly legs could carry him, down the stairs and into a room far wider than he had anticipated, its contents hidden in shadow save for a round table at the center. At least twenty blue holograms glowed in the seats around it, some with faces he recognized from last night's meeting.

The old woman's eyes flicked over to him. She spoke first. "Good. If Taranis had found your boy out, Hendricks, then we'd all be doomed."

"I'm inclined to disagree," replied Hendricks, claiming the only empty chair at the table. Junior stood awkwardly to the side, watching. The Jakari leaped from his shoulder and into the darkness, silent as a ghost. "I don't believe that Taranis knows nearly as much as we think he does. That's why his attack was meant to cripple our evacuation capabilities. He wants to keep the Zoboros stranded here while he hunts down their identities, which is why we need to get them out."

The old man with the breathing problem stirred in his seat. "But if we load them onto transports…we paint a target…on their heads…everyone will know…"

A Taloan, plump with purple scales and dressed in a fine silk robe, turned to him. "My people can send ships to assist with the evacuations." Her voice was light and melodic. "We can mix the Zoboros in with the rest of the evacuees and no one would know."

"No, Taranis knows we plan to move them," said Hendricks. "An evacuation would only prompt an attack on the loading bays. I have a different plan, one that gets *all* of our Zoboros off-world without anyone ever knowing it happened."

Off-world? Junior inched back into the shadows. They couldn't take him away – not now, not when the city actually needed him…

The back of his head struck something metal, the clang echoing through the hollow room. Twenty blue heads snapped in his direction, then slowly returned to their conversation.

He turned, rubbing the bruise as it ballooned, but all he found was darkness. He flicked on his communicator's light; it bounced off a metal surface and back into his eyes with a fiery sting. He staggered back, blinking away the spots until he could make sense of what he was staring at.

An engine. It hung several feet in the air off a razor thin wing. And not just any engine. A Phantom 850. He stepped closer, inspecting the grooves woven into its metal. They had stopped making these cycles ago. And they only ever built them for…stealth fighters.

A blue hand smacked his wrist, knocking the light out.

"*Fool*," Akio hissed. "They will see."

Junior glanced back at the table, at all the faces lost in argument. *He's going to do it himself, but he doesn't trust them enough to tell them.*

"Hendricks, I can't get behind your plan if you won't tell us what it is," said the Taloan.

"Let me worry about it. I need the rest of you focused on the big picture: capturing Taranis."

"Not all of us are soldiers, Hendricks," said the old woman.

"You don't have to be. Novak is the one on the hunt, and what he needs from us is information. Every ship, every transport, every bus in this city needs eyes on it. We need to know who's moving where and why. Keep eyes on your Zoboros as well; have them ready to move at a moment's notice while we narrow our search. It won't be long before Taranis runs out of places to hide."

"I wouldn't be so sure," came a cheery voice that Junior recognized all too well. He clenched his fists, wishing the man himself were here, instead of a hologram of him, so he could punch his stupid smiling face. "Taranis is a master of deception. If at any point you think you're close to catching him, it's because he *wants* you to think that. Whatever he has planned for us, it's far from over."

Before Junior could call him out in front of everyone, a woman leaned over the table, her hair short, her shoulders broad beneath a uniform decorated in medals. "Is that why you failed to catch him on Darraden?" she asked, her cold eyes aimed at Carmichael's hologram.

"Yes," he muttered, "but my team learned a lot from that experience. We've been studying his tactics, identifying patterns, uncovering weaknesses. Believe me, there is no team better equipped to take on Taranis than mine. They're stationed on Darraden now; all I have to do is make the call."

"Thank you, Carmichael, but I would prefer—" Hendricks stopped. The projections started to fizzle with static. Something wasn't right. Junior could feel it too. Confused glances darted around the table, their nervous whispers fading in and out. A new projection materialized between the Taloan and the woman in uniform. Its figure came in staticky and unstable, a cloak wrapped around its slim, flickering body, and its mask angled toward the floor, as if the face behind it was too shy to look anyone in the eye.

"This is a secure channel!" cried the Taloan.

The mask tilted toward her. "Who told you that?" His low voice was hoarse and filled with static.

"Why are you here?!" shouted the old man. He made to get up out of his chair, but the effort proved too much of a struggle for him. He leaned back, his breath slowly settling.

The mask hung there for a moment, allowing silence to chill the room. "I came to make a bargain, though I don't suspect you'll like—"

"Get on with it, snake," said Carmichael, cracking his knuckles against his palm.

"Impatient as usual, Carmichael," said Taranis, "but what I want is simple. Many cycles ago, your Chief Hendricks hid a child here on Famora. One of many, I'm sure, but this one comes from a lineage that is of particular interest to me. The rest of you may not know who I speak of, but he does."

All heads turned to Hendricks, all except Taranis, who just kept staring at the floor.

"And if I refuse?" asked Hendricks.

Taranis looked up for the first time. The static became stronger, more frantic. "Then I will blow up a building every hour, on the hour, until I have that child!"

Junior felt goosebumps crawling up his arms. Even in hologram, he could feel Taranis's presence in the room.

The woman in uniform rose, her voice louder than the static threatening to cut it out. "Your time will run out faster than you think. When I arrive with my troops, there won't be a hole for you to crawl into. Go ahead and throw your threats around all you like, but you will *not* get this child."

Taranis paused for a long time, his mask tilting toward the floor once more. For a moment, it seemed like his mind had wandered out of the room. Finally, he spoke. "Then, *General*, expect to arrive to a much smaller city."

Another flicker of static and he was gone. The room sat in silence. Junior scanned over the crowd, each face looking more worried than the last.

It was Hendricks who spoke first. "I was wrong; Taranis knows. Cancel all prior arrangements, he's not here for any of your Zoboros. Keep your people hidden and stay off this channel. And Carmichael –" He paused to meet the captain's eye. "I'll expect your team here in six hours."

Carmichael smiled. "They can be here in five."

The holograms disappeared, shrouding the room in darkness. White lights flickered on overhead. For the first time, Junior could see the room in all its bleak glory. It was round, and its white walls were covered in weapons of all shapes and sizes. Pistols, rockets, machine guns, knives – there were some he couldn't even put a label on, with odd, curved shapes and lights that glowed within the stocks. They looked more like machines than actual weapons. Still, they were nothing compared to the beauty sitting behind him. Its silver belly shimmered in the lights, its twin phantom engines just waiting to be flown. Judging by the dust, they had been waiting quite some time.

Hendricks pulled on his overcoat. "Akio, if all else fails, you know where to go."

"Aye, the place at the Edge of the Moon."

Hendricks made for the stairs. Junior followed him, his head spinning. He had so many questions swirling around his head. Finally, he blurted, "Why didn't you tell me about Kano?!"

Hendricks stopped. Junior felt Akio crawl up onto his shoulder, so nimble it barely took the creature a second to do it. "Clever like the father," it said in his ear. "Perhaps this one can be of use to us."

"It's that same cleverness that makes me nervous. You stay here, Junior. I'll be back soon to get you and Kano off-world."

"Off-world?!" he spat back. "But you said it yourself: he's not here for me!"

"But he can use you to get to me. We've been over this; you're not safe until he's caught." Hendricks started up the stairs.

"No one's safe with Carmichael in the city!" blurted Junior, rushing after his father while the Jakari clung to his shoulder.

Hendricks stopped and turned. "What are you talking about?"

Junior climbed until he had caught up to his father. "I heard Carmichael digging around for information on Kano, but it seemed like he already knew the truth. Does he?"

"No, none of them know about him, as was the arrangement, but..." Hendricks paused, thinking. "No, Carmichael wouldn't betray us."

"The *father* of Carmichael would not betray us," said Akio, "but the father is dead, and the son is lost in his shadow. Maybe too lost."

Hendricks nodded. "And I just gave him the okay to bring his people into our city. Akio, stick to your mission. I'll deal with Carmichael."

"Dad, let me come with you. I was there, I can speak for what Carmichael did. I can help you stop him."

"You already have," his father said. For a brief moment, Junior thought he saw his father smile.

Something wasn't right. He felt the Jakari's weight shift on his shoulder. He reached up and caught Akio's little blue hand before the syringe could pierce his neck. His adrenaline spiked. Without thinking, he pried the syringe from its fingers and thrust it forward.

Hendricks stumbled back. He pulled the syringe from his chest, looked at his son, and collapsed on the stairs.

"Fool, fool, fool, fool, FOOL!" cried Akio, smacking him on the head again and again. "Without him, the plan is ruined!"

Junior grabbed him by his little throat and pinned him to the wall. He set his other hand ablaze and aimed it at Akio's scaly face. He felt the creature relax in his hand. It knew when it was beaten. "There's a new plan, Akio, and a new head of the household."

He held his breath, having no idea if that's how the Jonjai actually worked. His other option was to melt the creature in his hand, though he didn't quite have the stomach for that. Plus, he would need all the help he could get to go up against Taranis and Carmichael.

The black eyes narrowed and Akio spat a wad of green saliva on the floor. "What are your orders, *sir*?"

Junior smiled. "Find Kano."

Chapter 10

The Police Plaza

Jaden awoke to an earsplitting buzz. He snapped his head up off the table, his cheek smothered in his own drool. He tried looking around but the bright lights stung his eyes, and his head pounded as though someone was hammering a nail into it.

What happened last night? He ran his fingers across his scalp, dredging old clumps of gel through his hair as he did so. He remembered being at the bar with a pretty girl next to him, what was her name –Sierra? Oh, it didn't matter. At some point he saw Junior, and then people started running, and then Kano and Makoto started flying…

What was in those drinks?

The room began to materialize around him. A single, hydraulic door stood across from him. Fluorescent lights beamed overhead, bouncing off the metal table in front of him and aggravating his headache even more. There was a long mirror to his right taking up most of the wall, reflecting his matted blond hair and wrinkled dress shirt.

I need a bath and some hot cocoa. He doubted he would get either here. Judging by the blank walls and the one-way glass, he must have spent the night in the Police Plaza. Whatever he did last night, he was sure some underpaid, under-interested officer would be here soon to explain it to him.

Another buzz rang through the room, piercing his ears like a hot knife. He whimpered, shutting his eyes and rubbing his forehead as the hydraulic door flung open.

"Jaden?"

He opened his eyes. There stood his Nurrano buddy, both feet firmly planted on the ground this time, his red and black hands bound by handcuffs.

"Makoto?!" he blurted. "What the hell's going on? How did we get here?"

"They picked me up at the Trampoline. They didn't tell me anything; they just threw me in a hovercar and brought me here."

"What?!" He started to rise, only to feel a tug at his wrists. Handcuffs. They had him chained to the table. "Makoto…what happened last night?"

Makoto sighed. He told Jaden everything: the cadets' ambush, the bombs, how Junior had disappeared with Kano on his speeder. It was all sounding more and more like a bad dream, like any moment Jaden would wake up in his penthouse and find his friends passed out on the couch.

"But why was Junior so bent on getting Kano?" he asked. "Shouldn't he have been on duty in the Dockyards or something?"

"I don't know," shrugged Makoto. "I heard him say something about trying to help Kano, but I wasn't buying it. You should've seen those cadets, the way they came after us…"

Makoto continued on his tale of woe, but Jaden's mind wandered from the conversation. *Junior's smarter than the other cadets. If he wanted revenge, he would've come after me, so why chase Kano?*

Another earsplitting buzz rang out, breaking his train of thought and making his head scream again.

The hydraulic door flung open. A young man dressed in a blue suit and tie marched through, his black loafers clicking against the concrete floor. One look was all Jaden needed to know that this man reeked of Vasilia: the single loud color encompassing his entire outfit, the false smile beaming across his pudgy face, the excessive amount of cologne that made the whole room unbearably musky. *You're in a police station, for crying out loud.* Whoever this man was, he was an assault on all the senses.

"Jaden and Makoto!" the man exclaimed, extending his hand. Makoto hesitated before he shook it. Jaden just stared at it, unamused, until finally the overdressed man took it back. "I've been looking forward to meeting you both."

"Since when?" asked Jaden, his eyes narrowing.

"Since I arrived yesterday," he replied, dumping a stack of reports on the table. "You two have caused quite the stir – crashing the festival, breaking into the Archives—" he squinted at the page, "taking off your shoes? Apparently, that's a big no-no at the Sphere. Anyway, here I thought nothing interesting happened on Famora."

"If that's what you thought, then why come?" asked Jaden.

"To keep this city afloat," he replied, his smile suddenly gone. "Where are my manners, though? I haven't even introduced myself. I'm Captain Damien Carmichael of the Interplanetary Defense Force."

A bell rang in Jaden's head. "Carmichael? You don't mean like *the* Admiral Carmichael, the one who defeated the Poterian fleet with a force an eighth of its size?"

"A tenth of its size," corrected Carmichael, "but yes, that was my father."

Jaden couldn't help but laugh. *This* was the son of the mighty admiral? He had to be twice the size of the admiral, and in all the wrong places. Jaden could certainly see *some* resemblance to the old pictures of the admiral – the blue-gray eyes, the high cheekbones – but where the admiral had a fierceness that could quiet a room, his son only had a goofiness that could make the whole room stand up and laugh in his face. Or at least, that's what this Carmichael wanted him to think.

"So if you got here yesterday," said Jaden, "then you must have already known Taranis was coming."

"I had my suspicions. Taranis's attacks may appear random, but a pattern is beginning to emerge, and that is where I need your help, Mr. Upton."

"*My* help?" Jaden spat back. *If he expects me to hack something for him, he can take that request right now and shove it up his...*

"Do you need my help too?" asked Makoto eagerly.

"Why yes, young Mr. Sasaki," said Carmichael, his smile returning. "Yes I do."

Makoto beamed at being called 'Mr. Sasaki,' but Jaden wasn't buying into the flattery. "What could we possibly help you with?" he asked. "The IDF should have all the resources it needs to track down Taranis."

"They do, but tracking Taranis isn't my concern at the moment. What I need from you is far simpler, and hopefully less dangerous."

"Ah, so we're in danger now?" Jaden fired back.

"Mr. Upton, everyone in this city is in danger. If there's one thing I've learned during this investigation, it's that Taranis has people everywhere. Fortunately, so do I." Carmichael tapped his hand on the table and the lights went out.

"What the hell is this?!" shouted Jaden. He tried to get up, but the cuffs tugged him back down. It didn't matter, though; it was pitch black and there was nowhere to go.

"Relax Mr. Upton," said Carmichael, activating the light on his communicator so his floating face became the only thing visible in the entire room. "We have about ninety seconds before they can hear us again. I do apologize for the theatrics, but I would prefer that the rest of our conversation takes place off the record."

"Why?" demanded Jaden.

"Because I know what your friend is, I know where he comes from, and I know why Taranis is after him."

"What?!" blurted Makoto.

Jaden felt his whole world flip on itself. "What could Taranis want with Ka—"

"Don't say his name!" blurted Carmichael. "Don't even let it cross your lips. A man disappeared during the embassy attack, a man with a direct connection to your friend's relocation. We believe he was tortured and gave information that led Taranis here, though not enough to confirm your friend's identity. That's why I need your help to find him before Taranis does."

"What would he want with Ka— our friend?" asked Makoto.

"His powers. Taranis is kidnapping Zoboros all across the galaxy for a purpose I have yet to discover, though never has he gone to such lengths to capture any single Zoboros."

Jaden stared him up and down in the dim light of the communicator, sizing the value of his words. He could be a spy for Taranis. That would certainly explain all this off-the-record business. Then again, if he already knew Kano's secret, he could have kidnapped Kano yesterday and no one would have been the wiser. Whatever this game was, Jaden knew he would have to play to learn more. "What would you have us do?"

"Locate your friend," said Carmichael, tossing each of them their communicators. "I have my contact already saved to both your comms."

"Does Hendricks know about this?" asked Jaden.

"No. He has his own plan for escape. It will fail, just like every other plan to beat Taranis has so far. I had my suspicions as to why I couldn't catch him before, but the attack on Famora confirms it: Hendricks's inner circle has been compromised, and it's allowing Taranis to stay one step ahead. That's why, while Taranis tracks Hendricks, I'll be the one to find your friend and get him to safety. *That* is how we beat Taranis."

Jaden scratched at his wrists beneath the cuffs, finding the wristband still attached to him.

"Aren't you already tracking him?" he asked.

"We found Novak's tracker smashed to pieces in the Dockyards, which makes you two my only link. I can't risk anyone else finding you, so hold out your arms." They raised their chained hands. Carmichael drew a metal pin and swabbed it against each of their wristbands. Both pieces released and clattered onto the table. "We need to move quickly; if Hendricks gets to him before we do, then Taranis *will* find him. There will be an agent waiting outside to drive you to him. If your friend doesn't respond to your calls, check the places he's most likely to be.

"Understand that you do not have to accompany this agent. You can walk away, which would be your safest option, though it also means your friend will likely be captured."

Jaden and Makoto glanced at each other. Jaden knew he had a million reasons not to trust this man. For starters, he had openly admitted to betraying their chief of police. But if they didn't play his game, then they'd have little say in Kano's fate. By the look in Makoto's eyes, he seemed to have come to the same conclusion.

"We'll help," said Jaden.

"Good." Carmichael tapped his communicator. He leaned back, seeming to be waiting for something, but they simply sat in silence. He tapped again. "Eines, hit the lights. *Eines!*"

Jaden perked his ears. Something was happening on the other side of the glass. He heard a thump…muffled shouts.

A body covered in plastic armor smashed through the glass and tumbled onto the table. Carmichael leaped to his feet. He pressed a button on his communicator and an energy shield materialized, just long enough to cover his forearm.

"Stay behind me!" he ordered, stepping in front of them. Jaden craned over his shoulder for a look – not at the broken mirror, but the communicator on Carmichael's wrist. Whatever tech had just generated that shield was not something available on the market.

With the mirror gone, Jaden could see the armored troopers on the other side of the opening. They scrambled around, their weapons drawn, the flashlights on them blazing in every direction.

"Did you see it?!" one of them shouted.

"It's gone!" cried another.

Suddenly, one of them fell below the opening and out of sight.

"Over there!" cried another. A moment later, he fell too.

Jaden watched them fall one by one, their armor thumping against the hard ground. He checked on the man sprawled across the table. No blood, just a bruise on his head the size of a melon.

When he looked up again, all the troopers were gone. Everything was silent. Carmichael held his ground, ready for a fight.

A flash of blue dove through the window. Jaden heard the patter of feet. Carmichael swept his light back and forth across the ground, but found nothing.

"*Show yourself!*" he shouted. A blue flash dove from the ceiling and slammed him against the table.

What the hell! Jaden fell out of his chair, his chains rattling with him as he landed on the concrete. He felt something on his chest. Two giant black eyes were staring right at him, just inches from his face.

"Jaden of Upton," it hissed, drawing a thin knife from its gray poncho, "I have been sent for you."

"*No, no, no!*" cried Jaden. He closed his eyes, heard the swish of the blade, and felt the cuffs fall from his wrists.

He opened his eyes. There was no blood, no pain (save for the headache). The creature grabbed him by the hand and pulled him to his feet. "Come, we must hurry!"

Everything was spinning around him. He recognized this creature – he had seen its kind in old war footage – but what was a Jakari doing out here beyond the Rift? And why was it saving him?

"Wait!" he blurted, spotting his Nurrano friend hiding behind a chair. "What about Makoto?!"

"He was not part of arrangement."

"Free him or I'm not a part of your arrangement, either."

The creature mumbled something to itself in another language. It scampered back, knife in hand, and cut through Makoto's handcuffs with a single slash. "Now come Upton boy, you are needed."

"By who?!"

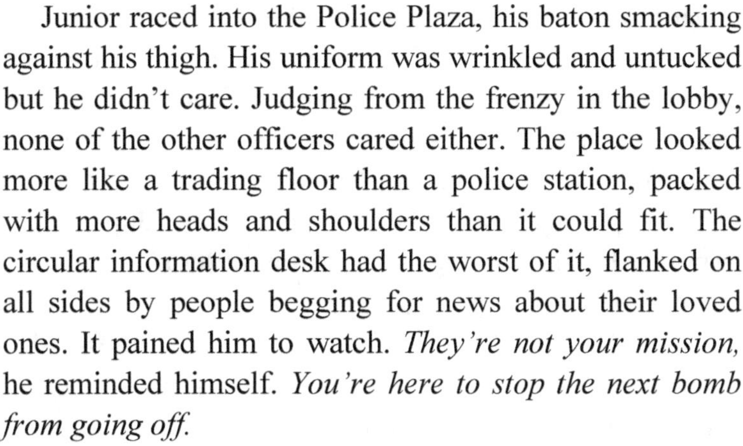

Junior raced into the Police Plaza, his baton smacking against his thigh. His uniform was wrinkled and untucked but he didn't care. Judging from the frenzy in the lobby, none of the other officers cared either. The place looked more like a trading floor than a police station, packed with more heads and shoulders than it could fit. The circular information desk had the worst of it, flanked on all sides by people begging for news about their loved ones. It pained him to watch. *They're not your mission,* he reminded himself. *You're here to stop the next bomb from going off.*

Off to the side, a swarm of cadets were making their way toward a set of stairs that sank beneath the lobby. He raced over and caught one by the arm, her auburn hair hitting him in the face as she turned.

"Where have you been?" she asked.

"That's not important, Sandra. Why's everyone going downstairs?"

"Novak's orders. There's been a breach in the detention level. We have to stay in the barracks until we get the all-clear."

The Jakari. That creature was supposed to wait for his signal. "Where's Novak now?!" he blurted.

"Upstairs, but—"

Junior released her and ran. Some officers yelled at him to rejoin the cadets but he ignored them. He wouldn't let anyone stop him; he had to warn Novak about Carmichael before it was too late.

At the top of the stairs, he found Novak marching toward him with an entourage of other officers at his heels. They each carried machine guns, with the exception of Novak, whose pistol was holstered at his side with a hand hovering over it.

"Colonel!" he shouted. Novak kept marching, his narrowed eyes so focused on the path that he didn't seem to notice Junior standing right in front of him.

"Novak!"

Novak snapped out of his trance. "Junior!" He stopped, his officers stopping behind him. "You're supposed to be with your father."

"I needed to warn you first. I couldn't risk it being intercepted on my comms. I think I know who's behind the attack—"

"This is no time for games." Junior could see Novak's hands were trembling. "There's been a breach, and your father isn't answering his—"

"He's not going to answer you. Now I need to *talk* to you."

Novak eyed him carefully, seeming to take his meaning. "Come with me. The rest of you, to the detention level!"

The officers marched on, but Junior and Novak dipped around the corner and hailed an elevator. Novak began typing away at his communicator while they waited.

"What happened to him?" he muttered under his breath.

"I needed answers," said Junior, "and he didn't give them to me."

"*What did you do?*" Novak hissed. The elevator doors pinged open and they stepped inside.

"What was necessary." He watched Novak press the top button as the doors closed. "Carmichael is working for the enemy. His 'investigation' isn't to find Taranis; it's to catch a Zoboros – *the* Zoboros that Taranis is looking for."

"Did you read my report?" snapped Novak, but Junior didn't respond. "And how are you so sure it's Carmichael? You realize this is the same Carmichael who flunked every physical he ever took?"

"I wouldn't have unleashed a Jakari on the detention level if I wasn't sure."

"Oh great." Novak drew a flask from his jacket pocket. "I knew today was gonna be a long one."

The elevator opened as he took a swig. A runway laid before them, its black asphalt stretching on and on until it met the hazy glow of the morning sky. Normally, police hovercars lined the runway by the hundreds. Today,

Junior counted no more than thirty. The rest would be on patrol for any sign of the masked man.

"How did my father get mixed up in all this?"

"Your father tended to attract other…forward-thinking minds," said Novak as he led him down the runway, their footsteps echoing through the emptiness. "Kind of strange, considering he's the least social person I've ever met, but they admired him because he was a great soldier. Do you know what makes a great soldier, Junior?"

Junior glanced at him, puzzled by the sudden question. "Courage…I guess? Strength?"

"Those are just words people like to throw around. Any man who steps on the battlefield is courageous, and many of them die. Too many."

What was wrong with him? Novak was supposed to be the optimistic one. Junior watched the colonel take another swig. And he never drank either.

"Great soldiers are the ones who can keep their wits in a fight. Your dad could; he did it so well that he saved more lives than I could count. But he's old now. *I'm* old now. Even our methods are old, and they won't protect us the next time the Poterians attack."

The colonel paused. He offered Junior the flask with a shaking hand.

He's losing it, thought Junior. Cadets were forbidden to drink until they came of age. He had been one of the few who had actually stuck to that rule, but this didn't seem like a test. By the look on Novak's face, it seemed more like a command.

He took a quick sip, which was all he needed to set his taste buds ablaze. He passed the flask back to Novak, using all his strength to swallow the bubbling booze.

"What was it like, fighting Poterians?" he asked through tight lips, the fiery liquid still clinging to his taste buds.

Novak shook his head. "If you had seen them in the field, how they could tear a man in two with their bare hands…you wouldn't be able to sleep at night knowing that they're out there just beyond the Rift, probably regrouping as we speak. We need to be ready for them."

They had reached the hangar's edge. A sea of buildings bobbed beneath them. Junior could imagine the people cowering inside each one, hoping theirs wasn't the next to explode. If they couldn't stop one masked man, how could they stop an army of Poterians?

Suddenly, a gunship rose in front of them, black as night, with four grand machine guns poised on each of its short, angled wings. Its engines whipped at their faces as it spun around so its rear liftgate faced them.

Junior jumped back. Novak caught him before he could run, holding him steady. "I'm sorry Junior, but I needed to get you home!" he called over the engines. "I do apologize; I know it's not as graceful as your speeder!"

"Don't send me back!" he pleaded. "I have a plan! I can help you stop Taranis!"

"You can't. Taranis—"

The earth rocked beneath them. Junior fell forward onto the asphalt, his face looking down over the edge of the hangar, watching as fire blasted out the windows and smoke billowed up into his face. *Not here. How could Taranis strike here?*

He pulled himself away from the edge, coughing, his face black with ash. He saw Novak sprawled out on the floor beside him.

"*NOVAK!*" he cried, the engines and the explosions combining to overwhelm his ears. He pulled Novak upright. The colonel didn't seem injured, only shaken. "Novak, there's still time, you can stop Carmichael." He felt his communicator buzz and punched the center button. "Akio, is that you? Can you hear me?"

"Yeah, I can hear you!" came an annoyingly familiar voice. "Just making sure you weren't burned toast."

"Jaden?"

"No, the Jakari. Of course it's me!" Even over the communicator, Junior could picture the smug look on Jaden's face. "We're at your speeder, where are you?"

Junior looked back. The gunship was landing at the edge of the hangar, its engines blasting the smoke away.

"Jaden, I'm not gonna make it to the speeder," he said. "You have to finish the mission. Akio has everything you need. And be careful of Carmichael; he can't find out about Kano."

"But Carmichael already knows about Kano!"

"*Kano?*" repeated Novak, rising to his feet.

"Jaden, what are you talking about?"

"Everything's compromised," said Jaden. "It's all part of Taranis's plan. Carmichael wants to get Kano off-world before…can…" Static spat from his communicator.

"Jaden, Jaden what was that? I'm losing you!"

Jaden's voice became jumbled with static. One final word leaked through.

"*…traitor…*"

Everything went silent: the gunship, the fires. Junior's ears homed in on the one thing that mattered, the cock of a gun behind him.

"NO!" he cried. He shot a tiny fireball that knocked the pistol away. Novak screamed, his hand seared red. His pistol hit the floor and a blue stun bolt fired off into the distance.

"It can't be you!" cried Junior. "*It can't be!*" He tried to spark another flame in his hand, but it puffed away in a cloud of smoke. "What the hell?!"

Novak drew the flask from his jacket and smashed it on the ground. Green liquid oozed out between the broken glass, vile and foul-smelling.

"*What have you done to me?!*" screamed Junior, falling to his knees. Without his powers, what good was he in the face of an attack? In the face of…an *enemy*?

"You might survive this yet!" shouted Novak, his eyes reddening with tears. "But he can't know what you are. *He can't know.*"

"WHO?!" he cried. He heard a blast of compressed air. It tingled up his back and pushed away the smoke. He turned, slowly. *Please, no…*

The liftgate lowered. Through the smoke and mist emerged a metal mask, scarred with markings of another time. The long, thin body was shrouded in a black cloak, and sheathed in its belt was a sword.

"Stay back!" cried Junior, drawing his baton.

Taranis kept marching toward him.

"I said, stay back!" He let the tip of the baton pulse with electricity, but it did nothing to slow the monster down.

"Don't be a fool," said Taranis, his voice like ice. "I won't hurt you if you come quietly."

"Over my dead body!"

"I promise you that's the last thing I want." Taranis unsheathed his sword. The metal was thick and dulled, but the edge was bright and razor sharp, engraved with markings that matched the mask.

Junior swung first. Taranis blocked the baton with his blade and Junior stuttered back. "You killed all those officers – even the *cadets*!"

He swung again and Taranis knocked the baton from his hand with a lazy flick of his wrist. "No cadets died today; your *colonel* saw to that."

"We didn't put any bombs...in the barracks..." Novak's eyes had gone wide. He sat there on his knees, shaking, as if he could feel the souls burning beneath his feet.

"*We?*" Junior saw the metal gauntlet coming for his neck. He dove back, rolling across the floor until he was back at his baton. He rose, twirling it anxiously in his hand, staring into the eye slits of the horrid mask. "Why did you kidnap all those Zoboros?!"

"Kidnap? I *freed* them. Freed them from the shackles that your father bound them in." He took a deep breath, smoke exhaling through his mask. "Freedom comes at a price."

"You just want to use them as weapons!" Junior cried.

"Is that what your father told you?" Taranis thrust his sword back into its sheath. He opened his arms, inviting an attack.

Junior charged. He drew the baton back, the force of every muscle in his massive body coming down on Taranis.

"Junior, *don't*!" cried Novak.

Junior smashed the baton across Taranis's mask in a burst of electricity. He stumbled past the monster and staggered to a stop. It was a good hit. He looked back, but Taranis still stood in place, his head tilted slightly to the right, as if the impact had been no more than a slap on the cheek. *He should be stunned.*

Taranis turned to face him. "Are we done here?"

Junior charged again. This time, he drove the baton into Taranis's chest and held it there, letting the electricity crackle against the cloak. It zapped at his fingers, but he held firm. He had to bring Taranis down. But the monster just stood there, its mask staring off lazily into the distance.

"Hmmm," Taranis sighed. He wrapped his gauntlet around the electric end of the baton, allowing the bolts to leap between his fingers.

Junior felt his grip slip away. The baton crashed to the floor. None of this made any sense. "You can't be…" he mumbled. "You're…"

Taranis raised his gauntlet, electricity swelling between his fingers. "*Free.*"

Junior felt the electricity pump through his chest. He sailed back and landed on the asphalt, his muscles convulsing. He had to fight, he had to run, but all he could do was watch the gauntlet wrap around his uniform and drag him onto the gunship.

Chapter 11

The Broadcast

The bowl was overturned. Water dripped onto Kano's lap as he leaned against the counter, his head in his hands, his chest heaving. He had never used his powers so much in such a short amount of time. It took more out of him than he realized. His arms were sore, his knuckles cracked and bloody, his head a little light. *"I need to stop,"* he told himself. He was still battered and bruised from the night before; any more pushing and he might just pass out on the counter.

The Sun was high in the sky now, cooking the fields of rubble below. Rescue teams still dotted the horizon, but at this point they had been outnumbered by the troop transports flying in from all corners of the quadrant. IDF troopers poured out of them by the dozens, each clad in blue armor built of thick plastic plates that made them look twice their actual size. As Kano watched them march, he knew it was decided now. Famora was no longer a city; it was a warzone.

He threw the bowl across the room. How many more people were going to die? He was a Zobos...or Zoboros, whatever Nobara called him; he was supposed to protect people from Taranis. Instead, he couldn't even make a ripple.

The kitchen door opened. He didn't bother looking to see who it was.

"Well, at least you've gotten pretty good with the mop."

Kano drew a long breath. "Look, I…" He spun around and froze. Li had swapped her bathrobe for a blouse, bright gold to match the diamonds of her skin. Her eyes shined like emeralds, staring up at the ceiling as she leaned her back against the counter. "I guess I'm just getting used to it, that's all."

"I wouldn't sweat it too much. You'll get it eventually. Why not take a break?" She grabbed a remote off the counter and switched on a TV that hung over the bar, the volume too low to hear.

"Was it this hard for you?" he asked.

"What, the training, or dealing with Nama?"

"Both I guess."

She laughed and drew a fireflower from her front pocket. At least, Kano thought it was a fireflower; it was so gray and wilted that it was hard to tell. It looked like a single touch could make it crumble.

"It gets easier," she said, playing with the flower in her palm. "The toughest part is figuring out how to channel it. But once you do…" Her hand began to glow beneath the flower. The stem changed to a royal blue and the petals erupted in a flurry of reds and oranges. By the time her hand stopped glowing, the flower had tripled in size. She placed it in his hand. It felt warm.

An idea sparked. Kano pointed at the scabs running up his arms. "Do you think you can get rid of these, too?"

She frowned. "Someday. Nama says the best healers could have things like that cleaned up in minutes. For right now, though, I think I'll stick to plants."

"Well isn't that convenient?" he said.

"Here." She got up and grabbed the bowl from where he had tossed it. "Let's try this one more time."

"What happened to relaxing?" he asked, though in truth he couldn't relax, not with the wreckage outside constantly on his mind.

Li started filling the bowl. The mere sound of the water made Kano sick.

"You've tried the same approach a thousand times," she said. "If I've learned anything from Nama's lessons, it's that you need to think outside the box." She slammed the bowl in front of him, the impact like a gunshot in his ears.

Li peeled a petal off the flower and placed it into the center of the bowl. It floated delicately there, its red and orange reflection glowing in the ripples it made. "It'll be easier to visualize now that you have something to push across the water – just don't let it spill out."

"I don't see how this makes it any easier."

"Because you're not changing your perspective. You're just gonna shoot a shockwave and spill it again."

"Exactly!" he said. "It's a shockwave. That's what shockwaves do. They roll over things: the water, the bowl, the flower, the…counter." His eyes widened.

Li leaned forward. "Go on – think back to science class when we were kids."

"The vibrations travel through everything…but when they move through solids…" He pressed his hand to the counter, a cautious excitement welling up inside him.

Li smirked. "Like Nama said, one clean strike."

He nodded. His fingers sank into the cracks in the counter, feeling the wear that twenty cycles of patrons had inflicted on it. If it could hold against them, it could hold against him too. He looked to Li.

"Do it," she whispered.

The energy swarmed into his palm and burst against the counter in one pulse. He kept his hand pressed there, feeling the energy roll through the wood. His eyes were glued to the bowl as it shuddered on impact. The water wobbled. For a moment it seemed like nothing happened, and then the petal swam gently to the other side.

"*You did it!*" shouted Li. She rushed up and hugged him while he stood there, starstruck. It was the smallest thing, yet watching the petal move might have been the most beautiful moment of his young life. That, or he was just really thankful to be finished with this lesson.

"Not bad," said Nobara, her frail body leaned against the frame of the kitchen door. "A slow learner, but you can be taught."

How long had she been watching? It didn't matter. "Hopefully I get a real compliment after the next lesson," he said, collapsing happily into a barstool. He could only imagine what her next exercise would have in store for him.

Li screamed. Kano almost fell out of his seat. He saw the gold had flushed from her face until there was only gray. She pointed to the TV screen. A huge body hung there, its arms suspended from chains and its head sagging beneath its shoulders, which were covered in a wrinkled green uniform.

Junior. But how?

A figure entered the frame beside Junior, cloaked in black, its mask shimmering beneath a single lightbulb that hung over the nightmarish scene.

"Now that I have your attention," said Taranis, his voice crackling with static, his face never once turning toward the camera, "I'd like to tell you all a story – the story of a child abandoned by treasonous parents and left under the protection of a man who you call your chief of police. For nearly twenty cycles this child has hidden among you, pretending to be one of you, but this is a lie. This child is a Zoboros, one of many that your police chief has hidden in your city."

Kano glanced at Li. Her hands were shaking.

"People of Famora, some of you know whom I speak of. I ask you, for the sake of your families and your city, that you come forward and give us the child's identity. Once I find the Zoboros, I will leave Famora and bring no further harm to any of you. Wait too long, and more will die.

"Hendricks…" he paused, wrapping his metal gauntlet around Junior's chin, "if you do not hand over the child soon, there won't be much left of yours to collect."

Electricity burst from the gauntlet. Junior screamed. Bolts wrapped around his face and smoke rose from his burned skin as he thrashed, the chains clanking in a wicked chorus.

"NOOO!" cried Kano.

The screen turned to static. Kano stared into it, the lightning still flashing in his mind's eye. *He was talking about me.* It had to be. Nobara could deny it all she wanted, but he knew it was true.

But he still doesn't know who I am.

Only a handful of people knew his secret, and they would never give him away. But Junior – he knew too, and how much more electricity could he take before he finally gave in? Or worse. What if Junior died in that chamber? Suddenly, the whole tavern was shrinking around him. He couldn't just sit here and watch people suffer, not when he could end it all right now. He stood up and marched for the door.

"Where are you going?" asked Li, almost in a whisper.

"Don't be a fool!" shouted Nobara. "If you go, there is *no* coming back."

I know that. Kano spun around, the room shaking as the power rushed into his fists. "You saw what he did!" he cried. "What he's about to do! People will die because of me."

"People will die," said Nobara, "but *not* because of you."

Kano reached for the doorknob. It felt cold against his trembling hand. He wanted to turn it, but he couldn't.

"Kano," said Nobara, her voice firm but calm, "whatever this Taranis has in store for you, I fear it will cause even more death to follow. There was a time when the Zoboros could have stopped all this. But the galaxy rejected them, outlawed them, took them away…" She trailed off, taking a long, deep breath. "We failed you, Kano. That is why you suffer."

Kano let his hand slip from the doorknob, his powers shrinking away. He saw tears welling in Nobara's eyes – not for him, though, for something deeper, something he was just now realizing.

"Li isn't the only Zoboros in your family, is she?" he asked.

"She is now."

Kano looked to Li, but she turned away. He sat down on one of the few remaining chairs, the weight of it all bearing down on him.

"I owe Hendricks a debt," continued Nobara, "and I repay it today by keeping you safe until he can get you on his ship."

"*His ship?*" Kano leaped back onto his feet. "I can't just abandon everybody!"

"A moment ago you were fully prepared to," she fired back.

"I wasn't leaving Famora, I was just making sure that Taranis didn't come after anyone else."

"And then what?" she snapped. "What would you do when you confronted him? *Fight?* There is a reason no one has caught him yet."

"He'll kill you," whispered Li, still turned the other way.

Kano threw out his arms. "But I can't sit here and do nothing."

"Then Taranis wins," replied Nobara, quietly. "If you go, he will either take you or kill you, and the galaxy will lose all the wonders you could have brought it."

Kano sunk lower in his seat, his head feeling heavy. Every direction he turned, it seemed like he would lose. He could hear Nobara hobbling toward him. He looked up, his voice choked. "What do I do?"

"Train, like I told you. When you are ready, you come back and show everyone why we need you."

Kano sat there for a long time, trying to process all of this. "But why me?"

Nobara looked away. Kano rose. He took her wrinkled hands in his. "There are other Zoboros in this city, you said so yourself. What makes me different? Why is he willing to blow up half the city just to find me?"

"Something to do with your parents," she whispered. "Hendricks never told me what."

"My parents..." He looked from her to Li and back again. Pieces suddenly started snapping into place. "Nobara, do powers pass through bloodlines?"

She nodded. "But not always the same power, and sadly not to every family member." She waved her wrinkled hands. "You must come from a powerful family, Kano, and power attracts. Taranis may frighten you, but he is only the errand boy. Others have sent him; others who go by many names and wear many faces; others who wish to turn you into something that you are not."

How many others are there? he wanted to ask, but he knew she didn't have the answer. As far as he could tell, everyone in Famora could be his enemy right now, hunting him just like Taranis, wearing masks all of their own design.

Not everyone, though. "What about the other Zoboros in the city?!" he blurted. "They must have people close to them. If someone outs the wrong person, they could be compromised too!"

"Hendricks tasked other protectors to each Zoboros," said Nobara. "I guarantee you they are safe. Only he knows the identities of all the Zoboros and their guardians. That way they couldn't all be compromised at once, not unless he was compromised first."

"But he is!" said Li, the color finally restored to her face. "Taranis is torturing his son. It's only a matter of time before this all falls apart."

"It's already falling apart," said Kano. "He's wiped out the Dockyards, the police, and now Hendricks."

"Hendricks will come," said Nobara flatly.

"Nama, he was supposed to be here hours ago! Has he even contacted you?"

Nobara hobbled to a nearby table, leaning on it for support. "He will come," she repeated. "He always does."

She looked like she was about to fall. Li walked over and hugged her tight.

"He saved us," her granddaughter whispered, "but he might not be able to save Kano."

"There must be another way to beat Taranis," he said. "There has to be someone who can." He paused. He heard something outside. It was getting louder, a roar, strong enough to make the floor rattle. Not a bomb, though, something else…something familiar…

Junior! Kano raced out the door. The speeder thundered over him, its phantom engines spraying him with rubble as it skidded across the walkway and into an awkward stop. The rider stumbled out of the seat and fell to his knees, his blond hair falling over his face.

"Jaden?" He saw Makoto leap off the back of the speeder, a strange blue creature perched on his shoulder – the same creature from the Archives. "Who's that?!" he blurted.

"We'll explain inside!" shouted Makoto as he rushed into the tavern. Jaden trailed behind, leading the speeder toward the door, his eyes wild with excitement.

Kano grabbed him by the shoulders. "Jaden, *what's going on*?"

A grin stretched across Jaden's face. "We know how to find Taranis!"

Chapter 12

The Hideout

The rattle of chains filled his ears. Junior fell to the floor, landing before a pair of bare feet, gray in color and each one larger than his face. He looked up into a pair of red eyes, Gorv eyes. The beast unhooked his chains from the ceiling and wrapped them around its brawny arm.

"Be gentle Dimitri," echoed a cold voice from across the empty chamber. The Gorv grunted in acknowledgement.

Gentle's a strong word for you, Taranis. Junior reached a shackled hand up to his cheek. It flared at the touch. He swallowed the pain, the strange pain he had never known. His own flames had never hurt him, nor any other flames, but it seemed lightning was too hot even for him.

"I apologize," said Taranis, "but I needed something to motivate your father."

"Don't bullshit me," said Junior, wincing. It hurt to talk. "You enjoyed every minute of it."

He squinted across the room at the monster seated quietly on the floor. *Is he meditating?* Three candles burned around his frozen figure, their flames dancing across his mask.

Junior rubbed his palm, hoping it would warm. Still nothing. Whatever poison Novak had given him would need to clear soon; he suspected Taranis didn't intend to keep him alive much longer.

"Get him out of here," ordered the masked man.

The Gorv tugged lazily on the chains. It was enough to drag Junior across the floor. He stumbled to his feet and followed the beast to the door, all the while staring at Taranis. He could hide behind that mask all he wanted, but he couldn't hide what he was. "Why do you keep your powers a secret?" Junior called over the rattle of his chains.

There was silence. The Gorv waited a moment, but when no answer came, it opened the door and tugged Junior along.

"And sour my people's reputation even more?" came Taranis's low voice. Junior stopped again, and fortunately so did the Gorv. "Bad publicity was our downfall."

Ours? Or yours? Junior could see right through the mask now. "You were discovered, weren't you?" he said.

Taranis rose suddenly. "Change of plans, Dimitri. Prep the gunship. I will take him from here."

Dimitri dropped the chains and skulked through the door, the patter of his bare feet echoing long after he had disappeared.

Taranis lifted the chains slowly. They clinked inside his metal gauntlet.

Junior gulped. All Taranis had to do was pump one lazy zap of electricity into those chains to send him into another convulsion. He followed Taranis down a dark corridor, not daring to speak another word, his eyes on the sword sheathed in his captor's belt.

"Contrary to what you might think," began Taranis, "I don't hate your father." The words came out so smoothly, so quietly, yet still they felt like venom. "He did a noble thing, protecting the Zoboros from the galaxy's wrath, but that was in the past. Now he only pacifies them."

"And your solution is to turn them into weapons?"

Taranis tutted. "It was *your* government who turned them into weapons." He led Junior into a hallway along which orange lights glowed out of deep cuts in the walls. The cuts curved and looped into patterns that Junior recognized. *Ancient Mogaddan.* His father had taught him its alphabet, every one of its sixty-two letters, but he still couldn't decipher the messages written all around him.

"What do you do with the Zoboros, then?" he asked.

"I give each one a choice," answered Taranis. "To join me, or choose their own path."

My ass you do. "And if I were Zoboros, what would you tell me?"

"That I don't extend the same courtesy to my prisoners."

Taranis opened a hatch in the wall. The stench of sewage and decay filled Junior's nostrils. In the dark, dank room sat a pale and shriveled man, his white officer's uniform torn and stained with blood, his face inflated by bruises. Junior squinted. Even beneath the bruises, he knew that face. He had seen it all over the news.

"Dominic?" he asked.

The man looked up with sad, broken eyes – eyes that widened at the sight of him.

He knows who I am.

Junior felt the gauntlet wrap around his arm, as cold and hard as the shackles on his wrists. One push and he was on his knees beside the other prisoner.

Taranis knelt in front of them, pressing his mask right into Dominic's beaten face. "If the boy doesn't spur your friend into action soon, then I'm afraid you won't be making it out of here alive."

Dominic flashed a giddy smile that flaunted a few broken teeth. "We both know I was a dead man the moment you found me."

"True," said Taranis, "but I thought I'd give you the comfort of a false hope."

"You're too kind."

"I'll show you kindness." Taranis drew his sword, its old metal ringing long and deep as he pointed the tip at Junior's neck. "Pain may not break you, Dominic, but how long can you stand to listen to it?"

Electricity shot up and down the blade with a wild bluish glow. It cracked and swirled, the bolts leaping off the tip to zap Junior's face. He scrambled back, his cheeks screaming with every zap.

Taranis followed him slowly, steadily. "Tell me who it is," he said to Dominic, though his mask was focused on Junior.

"Leave him out of this!" cried Dominic. He crawled after them, his own chains scraping against the metal floor.

Junior hit a wall. There was nowhere to go in this tight little chamber. *I need to get out. I need my...*

A spark flared in his palm, just for a moment. *Yes.* He clenched his fist, feeling it warming. *Not fast enough.* His muscles tightened as he tried to summon it back into his hand.

The gauntlet clenched around his chin and tilted his head up, the blade glowing just inches from his eye. "Shall I give him a scar to match his father's?"

"*Enough!*" pleaded Dominic. "If you hurt him, Hendricks will come after you with everything in his power!"

"I'm well aware of what power he possesses," said Taranis, "just as he is aware of mine." The blade was no longer the only thing glowing. Electricity shot through the mask, filling the grooves and markings with blue light. Even the eye slits began to glow.

Come on, come on... Junior held his hands behind his back, the sweat on them steaming away. *Just a little more.* He clenched them around the shackles, feeling them sizzle. *Come on – melt already...*

"You can't gain anything from this!" cried Dominic. He threw his frail body at Taranis, but Taranis needed only throw an elbow back to knock the man into submission.

"This can all end," hissed Taranis. "The torture, the bombs. All I need is the name you conjured when you helped Hendricks bring the child here."

Junior felt his fingers sinking into the metal as it dripped into a pool at his feet. He smelled smoke.

He caught Dominic staring at him from behind Taranis, a smile creeping across his battered face. He smelled it too.

Dominic started to laugh, a loud laugh, a mad laugh that consumed every ounce of his shriveled body. "You're so close to figuring it all out, Taranis!" Dominic rolled across the floor in his chains. "But you're too *stupid* to see it."

"See what?!" shouted Taranis. The glowing mask twisted in Dominic's direction, and just in time. The shackles fell away in a puddle of warped metal. Junior felt his power surge back into his fists. He threw them forward and they exploded against Taranis's chest in a flash of flame and smoke.

Junior screamed. His fingers throbbed. *More metal.* When he looked, Taranis was gone, blasted back into a cloud of smoke. He'd be back, though: Junior knew his fire hadn't been enough to penetrate that armor.

"The sword!" shouted Dominic, pointing.

Junior found it laying at his feet. He took it up in his aching fingers, expecting the thick metal to carry some weight to it, but it felt light as a feather, and perfectly balanced.

Dominic offered up his chains. Junior swung at them, surprised when the blade sliced through them like butter.

"Come on!" urged Dominic, pulling Junior up by the arm and leading him into the smoke-filled hallway. A bolt of lightning exploded over their heads, sparks raining down on their shoulders.

"*YOU!*" screamed Taranis. He emerged from the smoke, a gaping hole in his cloak where it had been singed away. In its place was a plate of silvery armor, still reddened from where Junior's fists had struck it.

Now I'm dead. Taranis raised his gauntlet, and Junior watched the jets of lightning shoot from the monster's fingertips and charge straight for him.

Dominic shoved Junior out of the way, taking the sword in his hand and aiming the tip at Taranis. The lightning bolts rallied to the blade. They swirled up it as Dominic pivoted, and when he swung, the lightning shot back at Taranis and sent the maniac hurtling back once again.

"*What kind of weapon is that?*" Junior wanted to ask, but Dominic pulled him into a sprint before he could even form the words.

Kano and Li stood in the middle of the tavern, reeling at the news Jaden had just unloaded on them. Of all the crazy details, though, one thing clearly stood out.

"*Junior* broke you out?!" they blurted in unison.

"I know, crazy right?" said Jaden. He had spent the past twenty minutes tinkering with Junior's speeder, his mouth moving a mile a minute while he worked. "Well technically the blue guy broke us out, but Junior sent him so we could save you. And, in an ironic twist of fate, we now have to save him."

"And how exactly do we do that?" asked Kano.

Jaden unscrewed an antenna from the back of the speeder and began digging his fingers through the opening it left behind. "The speeder is linked to his communicator. If Taranis was stupid enough to steal the communicator, then we can track him."

"The signal on those barely covers a block," said Li. Kano nodded sagely in agreement, knowing absolutely nothing about speeders or their tracking devices.

"True," said Jaden, "but I can boost the signal to cover a wider range."

"How wide?" asked Li. "Enough to cover the city?"

Jaden smiled. "And then some."

This all seemed too good to be true. With Jaden, it usually was. "What's the catch?" asked Kano.

Jaden paused his work for the first time since he had started. "Before any of you get hysterical, I want you all to know that I've kept your best interests at heart—"

"Oh just spit it out!" shouted Li.

Jaden rolled his eyes. "I'm very proud to announce that I've negotiated a deal with a very prominent member of the IDF who's going to help us."

"Negotiated?" blurted Makoto. "All you did was say yes!"

"What can I say? The man spoke my language."

"The IDF?" repeated Nobara. "Jaden, do they know where we are?"

"Nah, he's waiting on us to call him. We were supposed to meet some agent, but we bailed on that. Figured we'd do a better job searching on our own, right Makoto?"

"Sure, but should we even call him?" asked Makoto, rubbing his bald head. "I mean, I don't know that I trust this guy taking my brother off-world."

"Off-world?" said Kano. "But that's Hendricks's plan!"

"Hendricks sleeps," said the strange blue creature. It was perched on all fours on a barstool, its eyes constantly scanning the room. "His spawn filled him with serum. We will not hear from him for a few more hours."

"I'm sorry, who *are* you?" asked Li.

"I am Akio, son of Ephos and—"

"Yeah, we got it," interrupted Jaden. "The point is, Taranis is following Hendricks's every move. If Hendricks comes for Kano, which he can't presently do, Kano will be captured. That's why this IDF guy wants to sneak Kano out undetected. *However*, in light of the discovery of this speeder, I think we can negotiate a new deal – one where we give Carmichael the location of Taranis, *he* captures Taranis, and Kano gets to stay. It's a win for everybody!"

"You've entrusted the safety of Kano to a *Carmichael*!" screamed Nobara. She hobbled over to Jaden, swinging at him with her purse.

"Ow! Would you just—" Jaden caught the purse in mid-swing and wrenched it from her wrinkled hand. "He's the son of the admiral, the one everybody likes!"

"Everybody *except* Zoboros," she said. "He killed them."

"Yeah, when we were at war. Everyone fought the Zoboros."

"He was pushing for anti-Zoboros legislation BEFORE. WAR. EVEN. STARTED!" shouted Nobara, pounding her hand on the table with every word.

"Well, I mean, it was a different time…" mumbled Jaden.

"She is right," hissed the Jakari.

"You stay out of this!" shouted Jaden. "I brought you here to help, not to take sides!"

"I am here to rescue son of Hendricks. Now give me location and stop wasting time with stupid ideas!"

"You hear that?" said Li. "The new guy called you stupid."

"Yeah well, I got a few names for you too, honey!" Jaden returned to digging through the speeder's insides, drawing out a yellow wire and connecting it to a port in his datapad. "But first, let's find the bastard responsible for all this."

"And then what?" asked Kano. "What if we can't trust this Carmichael guy?" Kano was anxious enough with Taranis in the city; he didn't need some anti-Zoboros agent coming after him too.

"Despite the family issues, I've got a good feeling about him," said Jaden. "I mean, he's Vasilian after all."

"That's not a good thing," mumbled Makoto.

"Listen to me, Kano," urged Nobara. "The Carmichael family is powerful, and none of them acts without an agenda. Whatever his plans are for you, they are no better than Taranis's."

Kano felt the walls closing in. It seemed everywhere he turned there were more people looking to hurt him. The only ones he trusted were assembled in this very room, and none of them had the power to stop Taranis. In fact, they were in danger just by being near him.

"Nobara, is there another way to get me out of the city?" he asked. "We can still give Carmichael the coordinates; he'll just have to settle for those and not me."

"Hendricks mentioned a backup transport," she answered, "but I don't know where he's hidden it."

"I do," said Akio, pointing at Kano. "You, boy who hides in kitchen. I can take you there."

Kitchen? Kano looked around. Is this what his species called a kitchen? Unless he meant… "Were you spying on us?!" he blurted. "Two nights ago, when Hendricks was in our house—"

"You were spies," rejoined the Jakari with a hooked finger. "I was protector to you, as is my charge. When I get you to destination, my charge will be complete, and then I may go rescue angry Hendricks child. We must move quickly though; he does not have much time in hands of maniac."

"No he does not," agreed Jaden, returning to his datapad.

"Does this mean Kano's leaving?" asked Makoto, looking down at his shoes.

Akio nodded.

A beep echoed from the speeder. Everyone looked. Jaden grinned. "You guys, I think I got it!" he exclaimed. His eyes followed a stream of coordinates as they scribbled along his datapad, his grin fading away. "That's impossible…"

"What's impossible?" asked Kano. He began to walk over when he felt something bump his foot. He looked down. A little ball was rolling away from him, its surface blinking with white lights.

The Jakari was on it before he had time to blink. "*Everybody down!*" cried Akio, scooping the ball in his long arm and tossing it out the broken window.

He wasn't fast enough. The ball burst with a flash of white light. Kano fell to his knees, his ears ringing, his eyes stinging. He felt a hand wrap around his own and pull him up to his feet. All he could see was white. He stumbled along, trusting wherever the mysterious arm was leading him.

He began to see shapes. The kitchen door. The arm leading him forward, gold diamonds on gray. The ringing died down. He heard crashes from the other room, shouts, thunder pounding on the walls.

Ahead he could just make out the kitchen counter, gray with green spots that he assumed were chopped vegetables. There was something at the edge of it, tall and thin, bright orange at the top with a wide base at the bottom. The fireflower. Li had decided to plant it.

Suddenly, a red and black blur dove across the counter, throwing lettuce into their path as it slid right into the flowerpot.

"NO!" cried Li, catching it just inches from the ground.

"Sorry, sorry, sorry!" said Makoto as he hopped back to his feet.

"Makoto, what's going on?" asked Kano, his own voice sounding foreign in his ringing ears.

"They followed us!" gasped Makoto."The IDF! They sent the blues in!"

"Everybody into the cellar!" ordered Li. "There's a backdoor we can use to—"

A blue blur dove into their path. It was tall, far too tall to be their new acquaintance with the poncho. Kano's vision was coming back to him; he could see the rivets holding the blue plates of armor together. A helmet topped it all off, blue with a white stripe running down the middle.

"Hands up," said the trooper, his eyes watching them through a thin visor in his helmet.

Kano raised his hands, as did Makoto beside him, but Li kept hers on the flowerpot.

"What are you waiting for? Raise them up," Kano whispered in her ear.

"What's your rush?" she snapped back. Her eyes flicked down. He followed her gaze to her hands. They were glowing.

"Drop the flower," ordered the trooper.

Li nodded. She bent down, lowering the pot gently to the floor. Suddenly, she tossed it up into the trooper's plated chest with a crash. Dirt and shards of clay rained down, but the plant stuck to the trooper, its blue stem wrapping round and round his armor. He tried aiming his weapon, but the stem kept tightening around his sides, growing thicker with every pass. Li's arms started to tremble, but she kept pushing until the trooper's abdomen was completely cocooned. She gasped, her arms falling to her sides. Her hands lost their glow and she stumbled forward.

Kano caught her, completely at a loss for words. All that came to mind was what Nobara had said to him this morning. "Not bad."

She smirked. "You flatter me."

Jaden barreled past them, his shirt torn, his blond hair mussed and tangled. He knocked the trooper over in his mad rush. "I hope you have more of those plants!" he shouted, swinging the cellar door open, "because there's a whole army outside your door!"

He froze. Standing on the other side of the door was another officer in blue, much shorter and rounder than the last one. Everyone leaped back, ready to strike, but the officer drew no weapon. Instead, he tugged off his helmet to reveal a pudgy and smiling face.

"Carmichael?" said Jaden. "How did you get in there?"

"There's a backdoor," he shrugged, "though the other officers don't know that. I can help you escape, but we have to hurry. Do you trust me?"

The moment of truth. Kano looked from Jaden to Li, the first nodding and the second shaking her head. "*They never act without an agenda*," echoed Nobara's words in his mind. Whatever agenda this Carmichael had, though, surely it was better than falling into the hands of the army rushing at their heels.

"For now," said Kano.

"Good enough. Do exactly as I say – and someone please untangle Eines."

Chapter 13

The Prisoner

They ran and ran through halls of orange. At times the path forked into hallways that glowed green or purple, each carved with the same ancient letters as before, but Dominic kept them on the orange path. Junior had no idea how long they had been running, only that Taranis couldn't be far behind. He didn't dare look over his shoulder, though; he just kept going.

They rounded a corner and into a dead end. Junior stopped, panting. "I thought you knew where you were going!"

Dominic ignored him, running his pale hand along the wall, his fingers gliding over the glowing grooves until his thumb caught something. He pushed it in and part of the wall gave way. A door opened, outlined by the glowing markings.

"You were saying?" said Dominic.

Junior was getting pretty sick of these doors. It had his father written all over it. Junior followed Dominic inside. There were no markings on the bare, white walls here, just a line of suspended lightbulbs leading on to an unknown destination.

"How did you know that was there?" he asked as Dominic sealed the door behind them.

"I helped your dad set this up back in the day. It's a safehouse – or at least it was."

"A safehouse for who?" The lights flickered out, shrouding them in darkness. Junior sparked a flame in his palm that revealed a smile on Dominic's face, one that told him everything. "How many were there?" he asked.

"Hundreds," answered Dominic, "refugees, fugitives, you name it. Almost every species I know of, and most were children. We couldn't send them all out into the world at once, or we would risk them being discovered, so we siphoned them out slowly to people we could trust, took our time to cover our tracks."

"You built this whole place to do that?" asked Junior.

Dominic chuckled. "No, this place was built long before we arrived. For what purpose, I don't know. It's a maze of passageways and dead ends. Purple is the main path, likely the one our host has mapped out. Green leads you in circles – he probably has that one figured out by now too. Orange, though, that one has all the best tricks, and I doubt Taranis has figured them out yet."

"How did you find this…facility?" he asked.

Dominic shook his head. "That's a question better put to your father."

"And how did you find my father?"

"He found me, is more like it. I was about your age, living on Kakono." He paused. "Have you ever heard of Kakono?"

Junior shook his head.

"No surprise. It's buried deep in the Outer Territories. A small planet, but the trees there grew as tall as mountains. My village was carved into those treetops, up where we could farm the fresh fruit and catch the rain in baskets. Imagine living your whole life high in the sky on rickety bridges. Well, I guess it's not so hard for *you* to imagine, but believe me, there were no tractor beams up there. Needless to say we got pretty good at climbing.

"We were hidden from everyone but the occasional traders that flew in for fruit and lumber. They never even had to chop down a tree, a branch was all they needed to fill their cargo hold. In return we would get medicines, exotic foods, all that good stuff. They taught us your language, and my family spoke it every day so I could learn to speak with the men that came down from the sky." He stared at the sword in his hands, its blade glowing red in the firelight. He shuddered.

"One night, I heard screaming. When I looked out my window, I saw my village burning. Entire homes ablaze. Ropes snapped and bridges fell into oblivion. Everywhere I looked, people were scrambling up the branches and into the cover of darkness. Everyone except one: a shadow, coming straight for my home.

"My parents burst into my room and opened the window. They told me to run as far and as fast as possible and never look back. I started to climb, but…I couldn't get myself to go very far. Not without them. When I turned back, they were still standing in my room, waiting, while the shadow entered.

"What I saw that night was a monster unlike any I had ever seen. His face was green and scaly, his eyes a wicked yellow, his dark hair pulled back in a ponytail that was almost as thin as he was. In his hand was a sword with markings just like this one.

"I don't know what they said in that room. There was shouting from my parents, but the shadow never raised his voice. He only laughed – a sick, twisted laugh. I watched him cut my parents down. I should have looked away, but I couldn't. I remember…wanting to scream, but I couldn't do that either…I couldn't make a sound. Then, I remember those yellow eyes locking onto me, watching my tears fall…and the shadow smiled.

"For three days I hid in that tree, watching the last embers of the fire disappear, but still I couldn't move. I barely ate or drank anything. I could have died right there in that spot had it not been for your father. He came down in his shiny ship with his team. They tried talking to me, but I ran away as fast as I could. Eventually Novak caught up with me. He talked to me – about slifeball, I think. I didn't even know what that sport was at the time, but whatever he said must have calmed me down."

"Novak is a traitor," said Junior, touching his burned cheek.

Dominic stopped. "Are you sure?"

"I wouldn't be here if he wasn't."

Dominic drew a long, deep breath, staring at his own reflection in the blade. "We knew it had to be someone close to Hendricks. Everything Novak ever did, he did to protect people. If what you say is true, then perhaps he's lost his way."

"He'll lose a lot more when I'm through with him." Junior marched faster down the passageway, the light going with him. Dominic followed.

"Your dad had a similar vendetta with the shadow creature," continued Dominic. "He called it the Jaculus, said they had been tracking it for weeks. An assassin from the Poterian Empire. Their best assassin. No fingerprints, no DNA matches, and no connection to any person or species in the known galaxy."

"Did they catch him?" asked Junior.

"They caught up with him, but when they did, he was ready for them." Dominic ran his finger down his cheek. "Your father was never the same after that fight."

Junior nodded. It felt strange, learning the truth from a complete stranger. "Why was my father after him? You said the Jaculus was an assassin; who was he hunting?"

"From what I heard, it wasn't a *who* so much as a *what*, though whatever it was, it must have been incredibly valuable for the Poterians to send their snake after it. I begged your dad to let me help him in his search. I was angry: I wanted my parents' killer dead and I wanted to be the hand that did it, but your dad said there were better ways that I could help. He sent me to Vasilia, said he needed people he could trust for something he had planned. He suggested I learn about immigration. I took him up on it, and now everything you see here is a result of our work."

Junior stopped. "Including Taranis?"

"From a certain point of view."

"*A certain point of view?*" The flames flared in his palm. "He burned my face because of this. He's trying to bring the Zoboros out of the holes you've hidden them in, and he's willing to kill me to do it."

"And he's not alone," replied Dominic. "The Zoboros have been in danger for a lot longer than I've been around. Their exile after the war was the culmination of centuries of abuse. We searched far and wide for a place where they would be safe, but there were none. Even in the places where they weren't banned, gangs would hunt them down and sell them into fight rings. As horrible as it is, hiding has been the best thing for them."

"And what happens if Taranis reveals them?" asked Junior. "What happens if he gives my secret away?"

"You can try Poteria," shrugged Dominic, "if you can get there. The Poterians are the only ones who ever truly embraced the Zoboros, in a twisted sort of way. Still, don't expect much affection from them."

"But there are others like you, right?" asked Junior. "Others who will help us."

Dominic shrugged. "Yes, but…when your life is on the line, how many people can you really trust?"

Something creaked beneath their feet. Dominic signaled him to stop. They were standing on a rusted metal grate, a bit of light leaking through its edges. Dominic pulled a latch on the floor and the grate folded away, leaving an opening just wide enough to squeeze through.

Junior knelt to get a better view of what laid below: switchboards, row after row of them, each about four feet high with wires snaking between them. A control room. A hundred screens climbed up the back wall, each flashing with security footage. Two guards sat in front of it, switching rapidly from screen to screen.

"They might be tunneling through the waste lines," suggested one.

"Checking," said the other.

Junior perked his ears. He recognized those voices…from the Police Plaza. He had heard them plenty of times in passing. Novak's men. The ones who had been marching down to the detention level with him. The ones who were marching away from the bombs they had planted.

The guards chattered back and forth, every syllable making Junior's palms grow warmer. They'd pay for what they did. He steadied himself for the drop when he felt Dominic's hand tug him back. The skeleton of a man shook his head and took Junior's place at the edge of the opening, placing a hand on either side for support while his legs dangled lower and lower into the control room. When his arms began to shake from the weight, he dropped the rest of the way, his feet making the slightest tap. His head snapped toward the guards, but they didn't budge.

Junior passed the sword down to Dominic. As Dominic took it, a little wheeled bot squeaked to a stop right at his feet, its single red eye craning up toward his bruised face. Dominic raised a finger to his mouth and shushed it. For a moment, the bot just sat there. Then it was scurrying toward the guards, its red eye flashing and its speakers wailing.

The guards jumped to their feet, each drawing pistols that zeroed in on Dominic before he had time to move.

"Hands up, Mr. Leone," said one of them, inching forward.

Dominic raised his hands while Junior clenched his. He wasn't about to sit around and watch them drag Dominic back into that chamber.

"Where's the Zoboros?" one of them asked.

That was his cue. Junior dropped down, jets of fire spewing from his hands at either guard. They dove behind a switchboard, letting the fire roar over their heads and into the security monitors with a crash.

The pistols popped up over the switchboard, firing wildly in all directions. Dominic grabbed Junior and tugged him behind cover.

"Stay here!" he ordered, and then he was gone, snaking his way around the room.

Screw that. Junior leaped to his feet, hurling fireballs anywhere he heard a gunshot. The guards had split up, each shielding himself behind a switchboard. His fireballs did nothing to break their cover; if anything, it was making it harder to spot them through all the smoke.

Dominic used it to his advantage, weaving out of sight, sword in hand. When he reached the first guard's position, he vaulted over the switchboard and drove the blade down with him. There was silence in that corner. Junior kept his fists aimed at the other guard's position. As soon as the pistol popped up again, his fireball sent it skating away.

The guard ran. Junior tried catching him with another fireball, but the guard was too quick. He rushed to a table in the back and scooped up a stun baton, sparking the tip.

My baton, Junior realized. He spotted his communicator on the table, too.

The guard drew closer. Junior raised his fists, letting the flames swirl around them.

"JUNIOR!" cried Dominic.

Junior turned around in time to catch the sword in his burning hand. Fire swirled up the blade, roaring out of each of the markings in a great aura.

Now this was his kind of weapon.

The guard circled around him, baton raised, searching for an opening. Junior kept the sword aimed at him, holding it in tight to his chest, ready to drive it forward at a moment's notice. His heart was racing, but he kept his breath even, just like his father had taught him, watching as the guard started left, then dipped right, the baton swinging for his chest. Junior swung the blade into it and fire exploded out. The baton spun through the air, as did the guard, flames smoldering on his shirt as he struck the back wall with a clang.

"You did well, kid," said Dominic, marching past him.

Junior just stood there, sweet adrenaline coursing through his veins. He had always wondered what a fight like that would be like, would *feel* like, to face down an enemy outside the safety of the training room. It was exhilarating.

The beaten guard struggled onto his knees, the tatters in his shirt revealing pinkish burns in his skin. Burns he deserved.

"Why did you do it?!" shouted Junior as he marched forward, the thrill of the fight still on him. "We trusted you! We trusted *Novak*! And all of you sold us out! How many more are there?!"

"I don't know," groaned the guard, inspecting his burns. "They didn't tell me who else was an operative. Until today I thought that guy over there was just another officer." He pointed to the body lying beside a smashed switchboard, blood pooling around it.

"He's lying," said Junior, a new fireball readying in his palm.

"Probably." Dominic raised a pistol and fired. The guard fell flat on his face, dead before he hit the ground.

Junior felt what little food he had left in his belly lurch up. "Why did you do that?!" he cried, bile retching out onto the nearest switchboard.

"We don't have time for interrogations. Taranis will be here any minute."

"You didn't have to kill him!" He wiped the dribble from his mouth. It was as green and bitter as the drug Novak had fed him.

"He knows your secret, Junior. That's reason enough for me. Besides, we don't need another one of them tailing us while we make our escape." He opened a hatch in the wall. Inside was a line of woolen coats. He tossed one to Junior. "We'll have to hike to the next comms station. We could've called for help here, but your little entrance snuffed that idea." He pointed to the smoldering remains of the control board on the wall, sparks bursting out of its loose wires.

Hike? There was no hiking in Famora, unless the plan was to climb every walkway from the Dockyards to City Hall. But if so, he would just hail his speeder bike – if he could even reach it from here. He grabbed his communicator off the table and checked for a signal. Nothing.

As he fumbled with it, his foot splashed in a puddle of blood. He jumped back, the color draining from his face. All his life he had been training for combat, but nothing could have prepared him for the real thing.

"How many others have you killed for my father?" he asked.

"I'd rather not answer that, Junior."

He felt sicker. "If we go around executing people, what's to separate us from them?"

Dominic stopped in front of a hydraulic door. He glanced back at Junior, buttoning his new coat over his bloodstained clothing. "Survival."

He pressed a red button on the wall and the door whooshed open. Icy wind rushed in, cutting through Junior's clothes and biting into his skin. He threw the coat over himself as quickly as he could. He had never felt cold like this before. Famora's artificial atmosphere didn't allow it.

Where the hell were they? Sunlight poured through the open door, making it impossible to tell. He stepped through it blind and felt his feet sink into something soft – snow. It climbed up past his ankles. He bent down and scooped some up, letting the cold fluff melt between his fingers. It was so much crunchier than he thought it would be.

His eyes began to adjust. Silhouettes in the distance began to take shape: mountaintops, hundreds of them, rising like giant skewers through a layer of pink clouds that floated between them. There were so many. He had heard the stories of the planet's treacherous mountains. They didn't seem so bad up here, but beneath the clouds, where the light stopped and the darkness began, one misstep could mean death.

"You'll need this," said Dominic, stuffing a flashlight in his hand.

Oh joy. Junior tucked it away. He glanced back at the door they had come through. It was part of a wide, rounded face of metal painted white and concealed in snow. He had no idea where the mountain ended and the bunker began. And neither would a passing ship.

"It's a three-mile hike," said Dominic, "so I suggest you—"

Junior looked up, expecting Dominic to finish. Instead, blood trickled out Dominic's mouth and down his bruised chin. He collapsed in the snow, leaving nothing between Junior and the Gorv except the silenced pistol in its hand.

"*DOMINIC!*" he screamed, but there was no answer.

"Lower your voice." Taranis slid down the face of the bunker, snow plowing beneath his metal boots. He landed in a puff of white, his burned cloak flapping behind him. "Or you'll bring the mountain down on us."

"Don't move!" shouted Junior, aiming the sword at the masked man. He tried setting it ablaze again, but the wind swept the flames away.

Taranis snapped his fingers, allowing a spark to leap between them. Junior felt the sword pull, so fast and so hard that it slipped right through his grip and sailed back into Taranis's hand.

"Who are you?!" he screamed. The mountain seemed to groan at him, the snow trembling beneath his feet.

"Do you want to get out of here alive or not?" asked Taranis, his voice colder than the snow.

"If I come with you, I'm a dead man anyway," said Junior, inching back.

"But you're not a man. At least, not an ordinary one. Tell me, Aaron, why didn't you use your powers at the Police Plaza when you tried to stop me?"

"I couldn't. Novak gave me some kind of…drug."

"He took away your powers. How did that make you feel?"

Empty. Junior stepped back. The snow fell beneath his feet and he stumbled forward. The edge. He could see it just over his shoulder: the drop to oblivion.

"I'm not here for therapy, Taranis." He raised his fists, hoping he could spark a flame. The cold had him shivering, the wind gnawing at his exposed hands.

"With the proper training, not even this cold could stop your powers," said Taranis. "It is a part of you, a part that your city, your government, even your father wishes for you to deny. But you can't hide from yourself forever. I can show you how to unlock your true potential, if you'll let me."

Every word brought the masked man closer. He sheathed his sword and reached out a gauntlet-covered hand.

Junior stared at it, its metal grooves clicking together, waiting to be clasped. *My potential.* No one had ever asked to see what he could truly do. No one had the slightest idea what he could do, least of all himself. But Taranis knew, or at least he claimed to. Junior felt something pulling him forward. His hand was reaching out, almost of its own will, but just as his fingers touched the cold metal, he saw the body lying in the snow. The one person who had tried to help him.

He drew his hand back. "You're nothing like me," he whispered. "You're a murderer."

Taranis took a step back, a flash of blue flickering through his eye slits. "Then perhaps I'm more like your father."

The wind died away, for just a moment – *his* moment. Junior summoned up a fireball with all his strength and hurled it forward, but Taranis was ready with a bolt of lightning. The two forces collided with a crack, and suddenly Junior was flying, falling through icy wind down the side of the mountain while snow rained down from above, and two glowing eyes watched him disappear into the clouds.

Chapter 14

The Cellar

Boots rumbled down the wooden steps. Kano heard them filing between the barrels, dozens of them, the plates of their plastic armor clinking together. He could feel everyone around him holding their breaths. They squatted on hands and knees, piles of old junk looming over their heads, the air so stuffy it was practically choking them. No one dared to make a sound, or else one of the troopers might decide to inspect their seemingly ordinary barrel.

"About time!" shouted Carmichael, sounding exasperated. Kano saw his shadow limp past them, his armor plates hanging off his sides at odd angles, making him look more like a pinecone than a person.

"What happened to you?!" asked a trooper.

"They were stronger than we anticipated…better trained." Carmichael pretended to catch his breath. Kano was surprised how convincing Carmichael sounded; he only hoped the captain's story would have a similar effect on the troopers. "They used the backdoor. Tell the general she's gonna need—"

"Tell me what?" boomed a voice from across the cellar. Kano heard more footsteps coming down the stairs, though these weren't loud and clunky like the others. They were slow, methodical, each one chilling the room into a deeper silence.

Another silhouette arrived in front of Carmichael's, taller and, unsurprisingly, thinner.

"General Mezo!" the pinecone shook as it snapped to attention, one of its plates falling and clattering on the ground.

There was a dreadfully long pause before she finally spoke. "I gave you a second chance, Captain, but if a group of children can elude you just as easily as Taranis did, then clearly you're not cut out for the job."

"I still am," he replied, "and so is my team."

Two silhouettes formed up on either side of him. Kano assumed one was Eines; the other a mystery.

"Thanks to you our only lead is gone. Do you have any idea what will happen if Taranis finds him?"

"We'll find him first. I can promise you that."

"I've had enough promises from you." Mezo spun around, her shadow marching back toward the stairs. "Have the captain returned to my ship at once, along with his *team*."

"But don't you want to know where he's going?" asked Carmichael.

Mezo stopped. "Don't play games with me, Captain."

"You must already know where he's going," continued Carmichael. "It's obvious. Now that you've ordered a whole battalion to storm their hideout, there's only one person left in the city that they can trust to protect them."

Silence filled the room. The general placed a hand on the barrel, just inches from Kano's face. He held his breath. He could practically feel hers as she hissed out the name: "*Hendricks.*"

"The man's been off the grid for hours," said Carmichael. "He's up to something."

"He's going to take the boy off-world," she muttered, pacing away from the barrel. Kano and the four others around him all suppressed gasps of relief. Makoto leaned back, his elbow bumping an overstuffed crate. A silver dish fell out the top and clanged on the ground.

Kano's heart skipped. Outside, all the shadows snapped to attention, all except for Carmichael's, who began patting at his broken armor. "These damn plates," he grumbled. "Clearly not designed for single combat."

The captain wasn't entirely lying. When the Jakari had seen him leading their group into the cellar, it had leaped onto his chest and began hacking at the seams between the plates with its knife. It took both Jaden and Makoto to pry the creature away. When they explained their plan, Akio didn't seem all too pleased. Even now Kano could sense the Jakari brooding in the back of the barrel.

"You and I both know we can't let him leave with the asset," said Carmichael. "If he does, this whole mess starts over again."

Mezo thought for a moment. "I'll take care of Hendricks. You get whatever information you can out of the old woman. When you're finished here, return to the ship." Her shadow marched away.

"But General!"

"You and your team are out," she said. "Everyone else with me." Her shadow stopped while her troopers charged past her in a stampede. "And Captain, fix your damn armor."

Dozens of boots clopped high over their heads as they stormed out of the tavern. It wasn't until the last echoes had faded away that one of Carmichael's team opened the barrel, letting a wave of cool, sweet air rush in to embrace them.

"Oh thank goodness!" cheered Makoto, crawling out and collapsing into the flour sacks.

Kano stepped out after him. Carmichael stood before them, but something seemed different about him. It was hard to say for sure; Kano had only known the man for about ten minutes, yet he could sense the captain's warm energy had turned cold, the smile on his face a shadow of the one he had greeted them with earlier.

"Well, I hope you weren't all planning on visiting the Hendricks Mansion today," muttered the captain.

Everyone turned to the Jakari.

"*Is* that where we're going?" asked Li.

"No," muttered Akio.

"Then you'd be leading them to the Edge of the Moon, I take it?" said Carmichael.

"Where I take them is no business of yours!" it hissed, pointing a long finger at him.

A trooper stepped up beside Carmichael, his helmet off, his hand hovering over a holstered pistol.

"Easy Eines," said Carmichael. "Surely we can talk this one out."

Something about Eines seemed familiar now that the helmet was off. Kano stared him up and down. He was tall, with a thin face and an equally thin black beard that came to a fine point on his chin.

"You're the attendant!" blurted Kano, recalling how eager the man had been to launch them into the heart of the Sphere.

The man bowed until his whole torso was at a ninety-degree angle to his legs. "The very same," he said, his voice melodic, every syllable carefully enunciated. His eyes peeked up from the floor. "I see you never did get your shoes back. Sorry."

Kano felt a hand wrap gently around his shoulder. He looked up. The other trooper stood over him. Her helmet was off too, her golden hair tied in a ponytail that ran down past her plated shoulders. A pair of bright blue eyes stared over his head at the Jakari, her hand on her pistol as well.

"Wait a second!" blurted Makoto. He pointed over Kano's shoulder at the trooper. "We met you at the Sphere too, didn't we?"

She smiled, her teeth white as pearls. She did seem familiar, Kano realized. That face, that smile…

Jaden's jaw dropped, all his drunken memories seeming to line up in that instant. "Sierra," he stammered.

Cera rolled her eyes. When she looked to Kano, her smile returned, sweet and sincere. "We've been searching a long time for you," she said.

"How long have you been following us?" asked Jaden.

"How long would you believe?" replied Eines with a coy smile.

Carmichael stepped in. "When we discovered that Taranis was hunting Zoboros, I decided it was time to call up a few of my father's old contacts. You'd be surprised what information you can get with just a few drinks and some carefully placed questions. Little things start to slip out, about mysterious cargoes and missing refugees. When I pressed further, it seemed the same name kept coming up."

"Kano?" guessed Makoto.

"No, *Famora*." Carmichael leaned up against a barrel, shedding his broken armor. "My father would never have approved of a Zoboros relocation program – at least, not one where they got to stay in Republic-controlled space. But Hendricks was a different sort. When he took over, he made this city the centerpiece of his entire operation. When Taranis struck Darraden, I knew where he would set his sights next.

"Hendricks believes Cera and Eines arrived last night. In truth, they were already here, following his every move, gathering information on who Taranis's next target might be. I knew whoever it was would be under his careful watch."

"Lies," hissed Akio. "If you had been following Hendricks, I would have caught you."

"That's why we tailed you instead, little guy," said Eines, rubbing the Jakari's head.

Akio's bulbous eyes locked onto Eines. "You wouldn't *dare*."

"My father made mention many times of a Jakari who had indebted itself to Hendricks," said Carmichael. "He wasn't a fan, but I saw the value in an ally with such keen eyes and ears. I knew he would be the one Hendricks trusted to protect his Zoboros. I sent my agents to the festival for any leads. I knew finding the Jakari would be like finding a needle in a haystack, but after you three pulled your little fireworks stunt, we caught him following you into the Archives. We knew then that the Zoboros had to be one of the three of you, and since one of you is adopted, the answer seemed plainly obvious."

"We were worried when we lost you at the Sphere," said Cera, "so I made sure to bring Jaden back to the Plaza to help us find you."

Jaden winked at her. She ignored him.

"When we tailed Jaden here, we didn't realize Mezo was tailing us too," said Eines. "So, um…sorry about the troopers, I guess."

Jaden sat himself down on the flour sacks, thinking. "When you had us in the interrogation room," he began, "you said you knew why Taranis was coming after Kano. So what is it that makes him so special?"

"Nobara said it had something to do with my family," said Kano.

"Azral and Jeslow," came Nobara's voice. Everyone turned. She was hobbling down the stairs, cane in hand. "Care to tell him the rest, Captain?"

Carmichael drew a long breath. "They served my father during the war. They were two of his most valuable assets."

"I thought you said your dad hated Zoboros?" said Kano.

Carmichael laughed. "If they were Zoboros, they kept that well hidden from him. They were scientists, not soldiers, working on a top-secret project. To this day, I don't know the details of their work, only that it was critical to ending the war."

Ending the war? Kano's head was starting to spin. "But if they helped us beat the Poterians, then why are they in hiding?"

Carmichael glanced at Nobara. It wasn't until she nodded that he gave the answer. "After the war, they were moved to a facility on Vasilia for more classified work. The kind the government was pumping money by the shipload into. Thousands of scientists, tons of security. Whatever was going on there, it must have…snapped something inside them. That or they were planning it from the beginning. Whatever it was, all I know is that they—" he paused, his eyes shifting from Kano to his shoes, "blew up the facility, along with everyone inside it."

Kano felt a weight sink inside his chest. *My parents…terrorists.* "It…it can't be…"

"It was all over the news for months," said Nobara. "The IDF was willing to pay any price for information on their whereabouts."

"They became public enemy number one," added Carmichael. "But as far as I know, no one has ever found them."

The explosions in the Dockyards flashed before Kano's eyes. He stumbled back, catching himself on one of the barrels. *"They would never do something like that,"* one side of his brain was telling him. *"But you didn't know them,"* said the other.

"But…Hendricks stayed close to them," said Kano. "He must have. He brought me here. Why would he help known fugitives?"

"Now that's the million-dollar question," said Carmichael. "What is this secret game they all play? What connects them all? And most importantly, why do all paths seem to lead directly to you, Kano?"

Kano just stared at him. He had no answer. Only a million more questions.

Carmichael sighed. "Someday we may figure it out. For right now, we need to get you far away from Taranis. I'd take you in my ship, but then Mezo would know and we'd all be fugitives."

"He comes with me," said Akio. "To the Edge of the Moon."

"And we'll come with you," said Li. "To see you off."

"The road is dangerous," warned Akio. "Taranis will have eyes searching for boy."

"We can take the truck," said Li. "They'll never see him in the back."

"Sweetheart," whispered Nobara, grabbing Li by the arm, "I—"

"No Nama, I'm going to help."

"That's not—"

"Nama, I have to go."

"*Li*," said Nobara, loud enough to make everyone pause. "I know you do. That is why when they take Kano, they must take you as well."

"Nama, what are you talking about?"

Nobara smiled. "I raised you here because Hendricks could protect you in this city. Now I see all that protection is gone. Today they come for Kano, tomorrow they may come for you. Leave with him. You can start a new life. You will be safer together."

Li stood there, her eyes welling up, unable to look at anyone save for her grandmother. "Nama, I can't just…this is…we have training. I'm…I'm not ready."

Nobara pressed her hand to Li's cheek, catching a tear as it rolled down. "No one ever is. At least, we never think we are. You just have to do it."

Li hugged her grandmother tight.

"You didn't think you could stay in this ugly dive forever, did you?" asked Nobara.

Li giggled. "No Nama, I…I just thought one day we would be leaving together."

Nobara clasped Li's shoulders in her wrinkled hands. "This is the time when you must find your own path. Ours will cross again, someday – and do not worry: you will not be alone." She nodded over at Kano, who made an awkward wave from the sideline.

"This is all very touching," said Jaden, drawing his datapad, "but let's not forget we have a terrorist to catch." He handed it to Carmichael.

"What's this?" asked the captain, squinting.

"Coordinates," said Jaden. "I tracked Junior through his speeder to this location."

"Using the comms link?" said Carmichael. "But the signal on that barely covers…"

"A block, I know. The manufacturers encode a limiter on it so riderless speeders don't go zooming through the city, so I bypassed it."

Carmichael looked up from the datapad, beaming. "Mr. Upton, you've done us a tremendous favor here."

"And don't think I just give away favors for free, now."

"If a string ever needs pulling, just say the word," said Carmichael with a wink. "Well, it's been a treat everyone, truly, but it's time we went and put a stop to all this." He and his team started up the stairs. "And Kano," he called back. Kano looked up. "Even if we succeed in stopping Taranis, remember that you are still compromised. No matter what happens today, you must still leave Famora."

"I understand," said Kano. He watched them go, the weight of everything they had said bearing down on him – yet he wanted to know more.

"Wait!" he shouted.

Carmichael stopped. "Yes?"

"What did your dad tell you about my parents?"

Carmichael smiled. "That they were good people."

Kano nodded. He watched them walk through the door one by one. Cera glanced back and gave him a smile before leaving; Eines gave him a short bow. And just like that, they were gone.

Chapter 15

After the Fall

"Find us."

The voice echoed through the cave. One voice, or many? Junior wasn't sure. He looked back and forth, but he couldn't see more than a few feet past the fire blazing in his open palm. The blackened rocks around him gleamed in its light, so shiny that they looked wet to the touch, yet it did little to hold back the encroaching darkness. The cave seemed to just keep going, deeper and deeper. And colder, so much colder… He pressed on, wondering how he had gotten here in the first place.

A rush of icy wind whipped at his back, so powerful that it extinguished his flames. He tried to spark it again, but the fire wouldn't come to him in the cold.

What was this place?

The floor disappeared from under him. He splashed down into violently rushing water. Waves crashed over his head. He gasped for air, fighting to stay afloat as the current dragged him deeper into the darkness. He reached his hands out, hoping to discover solid ground, but there was nothing.

He spotted a light glowing in the distance. It grew brighter and brighter as the current pulled him toward it, and suddenly he splashed up onto a steep shore, coughing up water. He propped himself up on shaking arms, his hands sinking into the yellow sand.

This was just a dream; it had to be…

He felt the Sun warming his back. Waves splashed up beneath him, cleansing the sand from his skin.

"*Find us.*"

It echoed with a hundred voices. He looked up, but only one figure stood over him, its back toward him, and its blood red cloak flapping in the breeze.

"Find *who*?!" he shouted. He tried to climb up the shore, but the sand gave way beneath him and pulled him closer to the water.

"*Find us.*" It was one voice this time, high-pitched, almost taunting.

"Who are you?!" He scrambled for a solid hold, but the sand kept falling away beneath his fingertips, dragging him lower and lower no matter how hard he tried.

The figure turned, its cloak rolling back behind its shoulders. Its skin was a scaly green, its eyes as yellow as the blistering Sun, and its thin smile like venom.

"Find us, find us, find us!" it cheered. It stuck out a bare, sand-covered foot and shoved Junior's face with it. He slid back, feeling the sand carrying him down the shore. He waited for the splash, but instead he felt something soft come up beneath him.

His bed. He glanced around the familiar room. It was filled with toys – toys he hadn't seen in cycles. He felt something warm pressed against him. It couldn't be…

"Is something wrong, sweetheart?" cooed his mother's voice. He looked up. She was just as he remembered her, with coal-black hair and bright orange eyes that glowed every time she saw him. And her necklace, a golden triangle shimmering in the lamplight.

"We're almost at your favorite part," she whispered. He realized there was something on his lap, something heavy. The book. He riffled the long, weathered pages under his thumb, the pictures flashing by in a whirl of color. He remembered all of them. They had read through each story half a hundred times.

"This doesn't make any sense," he whispered.

"They're just stories," she said teasingly.

More than that. They were the only thing that had made him feel normal growing up; the only thing he had to remember her by, but his father had taken it away, too.

"Where did you go?" he asked.

"What are you talking about?"

The window flung open. A cold wind howled in. It carried with it a long, black overcoat.

"I'll always be right here, Aaron," she said, pressing her hand to his heart. The overcoat wrapped around her. He felt her hand pull away, and then she was gone.

The overcoat flew out the window, fluttering through the open air like a flag without a pole. Junior leaped out of bed. He was prepared to run out into the cold night and chase it, chase it to the end of the world and onto the next one, whatever it took to find her again, but when he opened his bedroom door, he found a pair of glowing eyes staring down at him.

"No, please—"

"You're coming with me," said the man through his mask.

The gauntlet clenched around his little arm. He felt the heat rise into his palm. *"Bring her back!"* he screamed. He launched a fireball right into the monster's face. It staggered back, its mask skating away.

His face. The monster was turned the other way, recovering from the blow, but Junior couldn't wait any longer. He had to know.

"Who are you?!" he cried.

The monster turned, slowly, and their orange eyes met.

Junior leaped up, gasping. Sweat ran down his face. He was in a bed again, but not his own. Tubes ran under the sleeves of his gown and into machines that beeped to fill the otherwise silent room. Pain ached up his arms and down his legs. He drew back one of his sleeves and found his arm coated in gashes and bruises. He fell back into his pillow, shutting his eyes as tight as they would go.

How did this happen? He remembered the mountain, and *Taranis*. Their powers had collided; there was an explosion, and then he was falling…falling through the clouds and into darkness. Total darkness. He remembered the fire burning in his hands, brighter and brighter, more than he had ever felt before. It blasted out in long jets, roaring, slowing him down, draining every ounce of his strength along the way. The last thing he remembered was the rocky floor coming up beneath him.

I did it, he realized. *I broke the fall.* Still, that didn't explain how he had gotten here – wherever *here* was. He rolled up his sleeves and tugged the tubes out two at a time. Some were dug in deep, he realized, but he pulled them out all the same. When he sat up, all the blood rushed to his head. It took a minute for the room to stop spinning, but once it did he set his bare feet down on the cold tiles. His legs felt like jelly, his knees nearly buckling with every step he took. How long had he been out? He kept waddling forward an inch at a time, out the door and into a hallway where a young woman was upon him immediately. She wore a black flight suit, all nylon, her blond hair tied back in a ponytail.

"We thought it'd be days before you'd be walking again," she said, wrapping her arm under his, her weight relieving some of the pressure from his stumbling feet.

"*We?*" he repeated. The ground shook. He staggered, the woman's grip the only thing keeping him from falling forward. It was in that moment that he realized where they were.

The atmosphere. They were taking him away. He wrenched from her grip and started down the hallway toward a door at the very end of it.

"Aaron, wait!" she called. "You need rest!"

"No one calls me Aaron!" he shouted back, stumbling forward on bare feet, one hand on the wall to keep him steady. The woman caught up to him. She was saying something in his ear, but he didn't hear it. All he could hear was that strange, awful voice screaming *"Find us!"* over and over again.

The door whooshed open automatically. The screaming died, replaced by the beeps and blips of a hundred control monitors. The room was a wide oval shape, its circumference filled with displays feeding data from all parts of the ship. An empty command chair sat at the center of it all while giant holographic maps of Famora orbited around it. Three windshields towered over the front of the bridge, arching up the walls and across part of the ceiling, the pink-blue sunset rushing by as the ship sped on. One man sat before it all, his hands at the controls, his brown eyes staring back at Junior through a mirror taped to the side of his console.

"You're up early," said the pilot, scratching at his pointy black beard.

"Who's in charge, here?" demanded Junior, grabbing hold of a nearby railing to keep himself steady.

The flush of a toilet answered his question. A familiar man in a familiar blue suit stepped in through a side door, shaking a bit of toilet paper off his shiny shoes.

"Junior!" exclaimed Carmichael. "I was wondering when you'd wake up. Cera and Eines were betting at least another twelve hours, but I knew a Hendricks like you couldn't be kept down for long."

"Who's…where…I…" a thousand questions swirled through his mind at once, enough to make his head hurt. He settled for the simple, "What's going on?"

"Well, we found Taranis's location," Carmichael began.

"*Former* location," corrected the pilot.

"The base was unfortunately buried in snow, *but* we managed to find you."

"But…I fell."

"Correct, but you had your trusty communicator. The signal was a bit weak beneath the clouds, but my lieutenant here had the brilliant idea to run a scan for heat signatures. Sure enough, we found a pretty damn colossal one."

"It was incredible," gushed the pilot. "I've never heard of a pyro generating that amount of power."

"He's lucky to still be alive," said the blond lieutenant. "The effort alone could have killed him."

Junior ignored them both. "Is Taranis dead? Did the avalanche bury him, too?"

"Not likely," answered Carmichael. "We detected signatures of a gunship that had departed not long before we arrived. Based on its trajectory, it must have been heading back to the city."

"No," said Junior, clenching the railing tight within his fists. "We can't let him back into Famora."

"Which is why we're heading there now," said Carmichael. "Should only be another twenty minutes out, right Eines?"

"Fifteen," answered Eines.

"Oh, lucky day."

Junior stumbled past the captain, his bare feet plodding to the nav computers. He had seen enough of these in training to know his way around. He pulled up the comms beacon and searched for an available connection to the city.

"We need to get a message to Famora immediately. They've been betrayed."

"We know," said the lieutenant.

"You do?"

"There's only one man Hendricks would turn a blind eye on," said Carmichael. "We don't know who else in the city is working with Novak. If we send a message, we risk Taranis discovering that we're on his tail. Eines, try getting a signal to Hendricks's direct line. It's likely been tapped, so we'll need to be discrete.

Eines began typing. Junior watched him, confused. "What are you people doing?" he blurted. "We need to be blasting this information to the whole city before Taranis makes his next move. We have to—" Junior paused. His heart was pounding. His legs gave out from under him and he collapsed.

Cera was on him in an instant, sitting him up and checking his vitals. The blurry-blue figure of Carmichael stood over him, watching.

"And he's going to continue his merry killing so long as he thinks he has the upper hand," said Carmichael. "If Novak or any of the other traitors get the slightest inkling that we're onto them, they and Taranis will vanish like dust in the wind. We can't afford to let that happen again."

"So you're going to use innocent people as bait?" said Junior, leaning up against a chair, his blood pressure rising again. "The city needs to be evacuated. There could be bombs anywhere. In twenty minutes hundreds more could be dead."

Carmichael knelt down beside him. "And how many more will die if Taranis escapes?"

"No signal from Hendricks," called Eines.

Carmichael eyed Junior. "Cera, escort the good son back to his room. He's not to leave until our mission is complete."

"What are you talking about?!" blurted Junior, trying to wriggle out of Cera's grip. "You can't take Taranis on alone; he's a Zoboros. I can help you!"

"If you're seen alive, Novak will know that he's been made," said Carmichael. "Maybe even set off the bombs early in his haste. You've done an incredible job today, Junior, and you've given us what we need to win. It's time to rest and let us take over."

Cera had him up on his feet and hobbling back down the hallway. "But I can help you!" he called back, his legs feeling limp again. He felt like he was being dragged through the hangar again, when Novak had tricked him into thinking he was being returned home, when he thought Novak already knew the truth about Kano and…

He froze.

"Come on, Junior," said Cera warmly. "We're almost there."

"No," he said. "Where's Kano?"

Carmichael exchanged glances with his team. "Never heard of him. Why do you ask?"

"Because he's compromised."

Chapter 16

At the Edge of the Moon

Kano felt the hovertruck rumbling its way toward their unknown destination. Even inside its steel walls, he could hear the exhaust coughing out the back. He ignored it as best he could; he had enough stressing him already without the thought of a midair plunge.

Jaden and Makoto stood in the back compartment with him. There were no seats, so they each clung to hooks hanging from the ceiling, most of which were covered in black spots that Kano assumed had once been meat; he wouldn't have touched the hooks at all had the truck not been twisting and turning so much. He made a mental note to scrub his hands clean as soon as they reached this "Edge of the Moon" place.

"How much longer?" grumbled Makoto, hopping from one leg to the other to keep himself amused.

"Good question," said Jaden. He slid open a slit in the back wall just wide enough to stick his big mouth in. Li was on the other side of it, steering the truck wherever the little Jakari pointed its long fingers.

"Hey! Are we there yet?"

"Did I say we are there yet?" hissed the Jakari.

"Nope."

"Then *stop asking*!" Akio slammed the slit shut.

"Such a way with words," mumbled Makoto.

Kano wished he could have joined them in the front instead of hiding within this steel cage. Whatever animal carcasses Nobara once stored here in the back still lingered on in spirit. The stench was enough to make his eyes water.

Jaden seemed to have the right idea; he had sprayed cologne onto his hand and cupped it around his nose. Makoto, on the other hand, didn't seem to notice the smell at all; he was too busy swinging from hook to hook, going up and back down the cabin as quickly as he could.

"Want me to time you?" asked Jaden nasally.

"Nah, I've been timing myself," said Makoto. He flashed his communicator at them, and for a split-second the stopwatch on his screen disappeared, replaced by a new message – from Yuchi.

"Wait a second!" Kano rushed over, braving the sticky meat juice as he switched from hook to hook. "Have you been in touch with Mom this whole time?"

"Well, I mean…she's been in touch with me, yeah."

Kano glowered. "When was the last time you got back to her?"

"This morning, maybe?"

Kano ripped the communicator off his brother's wrist. The poor woman must have been worried sick about them. Nobara had assured them when they left the tavern that Yuchi would get an update, but that didn't sit well with Kano. Yuchi was the closest thing he had to a mother; the least she deserved was a proper goodbye. He redialed. As the communicator rang, he racked his brain for the words to say, only to realize he had absolutely no idea how he was going to break the news to her that he was leaving. She would be devastated; there would be tears. He was almost relieved when it asked him to leave a voice message.

"Hi Yuchi, it's me," he said, still eying Makoto. "We're in Nobara's truck heading for some place at the edge of the moon. I don't know what that means, but hopefully you do. I may not get to see you for a while…but I think Hendricks can help you find me. Bye."

He hung up, immediately wishing that he had said more. There was no telling when he could return home again, *if* he could even return home at all.

His mind kept flashing back to the tavern, to his last conversation with Nobara. He had offered her back her necklace. "Until we see each other again," he had said.

Nobara had shaken her head. "Hendricks gave me that necklace a long time ago. He said it could compromise the *child* it was given to." She had pressed it back into his hand, and that was that.

Kano held it in his palm, flipping the triangle over and over again. It felt heavier, deeper, as if twenty cycles worth of questions had suddenly been packed inside its golden edges. *They left it for me. They wanted me to find them.*

The truck shuddered. Kano froze. The coughing had stopped. Either they had landed, or they were about to. Kano braced for the plunge.

It wasn't until the backdoor rolled open that Kano could breathe again. The setting Sun blazed in around Li's silhouette. She beckoned them forward and one by one they stepped blindly into the unknown.

"Careful," said Li, snatching Kano's arm. He stopped right at the edge of the platform – but not just any platform. A *golden* platform. The only golden platform in all of Famora.

He gazed over the edge. The whole city laid at his feet, bobbing and weaving in two long arms that reached down and hugged the clouds between them. Little hovercars drifted between them, like specks of dust against the great floating city.

"It all looks so much smaller from up here," said Li, lost in the view.

"It does," was all Kano managed to say. From up here, even the great towers of Downtown were beneath his feet. They had reached Providence Circle, home to the biggest of the big: politicians, oligarchs, foreign dignitaries looking to skip the winters on their home planets. And here he was in a beat-up T-shirt…

"Is that it?" asked Makoto, pointing. Everyone looked. Farther along the edge stood City Hall, its marble pillars tall and thick, its banners waving down at the city.

"Is it?" asked Kano, turning to Akio. "The Edge of the Moon?"

"No," hissed the Jakari as he climbed down from the passenger's seat.

"But that is," said Jaden, pointing behind them.

Everyone turned. In front of the hovertruck stood a pair of barred metal gates. Leafy vines looped from bar to bar, wrapping around an insignia stamped right in the center: a white circle with a spear running across it.

Makoto was the first to speak up. "Hey Jaden, that's the—"

"I know what it is," said Jaden, his face turning red.

A family crest, Kano realized. Could it be his? He didn't know much about the Upton family, but he had always assumed that Jaden was the only member in the city.

"Well come on," said Makoto, nudging Jaden from behind, "It's time to find out what this Montiki thing is."

"It's a *Montiquo*, and I'd really rather stay with the truck."

"Come boy, we may have need of your brains," said Akio. He waved his long blue arm at a security camera positioned over the gates. There was a grinding sound. The insignia parted down the middle and the two gates opened.

Kano's jaw dropped. Beyond the metal bars was something he had never seen before.

"Is it…real?" asked Makoto.

Kano wasn't sure. He had nothing to compare it to. He stared up the thick base to the long arms hanging high over their heads.

Li reached out a glowing hand to a low-hanging branch and the leaves began to sway.

"It's real," she whispered.

Jaden rolled his eyes. "Ah hell, it's just a tree, guys."

It stood at the center of the yard, the wings of a pearly white mansion flanking it on either side. Its bark was a rich mahogany, its leaves a bright green, though their edges glowed a tinge of orange against the setting Sun, and its branches climbed high enough to scratch the shingles three stories up.

"They know only stone and metal," muttered Akio as he climbed onto Jaden's shoulder. "Nature is mystery to the city that never rains."

Jaden and Akio led them around the tree and up a cobblestone walkway. Kano kept staring up at the branches, wondering how anything could grow to be so massive.

Jaden stopped. A great round fountain roared in their path, the cobblestones arcing around it on either side. Stone figures stood at its center, Humans, each one looking fiercer than the last, with long spears in hand that were aimed and ready, water pouring from their tips like blood.

"Well that's welcoming," said Makoto.

Jaden ignored him, examining the water as it drenched the warriors' feet and spilled into a wide pool at the base. "They must have their own irrigation system built into the platform," he said. "They'd have to get water specially imported just to keep this thing running."

Kano wandered on along the path, uninterested in the splashing water. He was far more fascinated by the leaves crunching beneath his feet, all different shades of red and yellow and brown. He wondered what other life he would discover on his journey, what creatures he would meet beyond the hoverpads, where there were forests and swamps and…

Mountains.

He felt a chill. *Is that where they're taking me?* He shook the thought away. Nobara would never allow that. Then again, Nobara probably had very little say with these Montiquo people…

Up ahead was the white pillared face of the mansion. Two stone sentinels stood on either side of a red door, each with a spear in hand and a Montiquo engraved on their armored chests.

"I'd feel a lot safer if they had real guards," said Jaden. "Preferably ones with guns."

"More guards means more traitors," said Akio. "They cleared the grounds for our arrival."

When they reached the red door, Akio rang the bell. Kano glanced back at the grounds. The yard suddenly seemed longer, tighter, as if the wings of the mansion were angling inward to swallow him.

The door unlocked. Kano turned, holding his breath. Everyone around him seemed to be doing the same. This could be a trap, he realized. Akio had mentioned traitors; who was to say Taranis hadn't taken up residence here?

The door opened a crack. Two green eyes stared through it, widening. "YOU?!" came a young woman's voice. She opened the door the rest of the way, her auburn hair catching the sunlight, her freckled face scrunched as she squinted at them in disbelief.

"Oh, oh!" exclaimed Jaden, snapping his fingers. "It's on the tip of my tongue!"

"It's Sandra, now get inside," she said quickly, glancing nervously in every direction.

They rushed into a wide foyer. Walls of marble climbed high over their heads and a chandelier hung from the ceiling, a thousand bulbs twinkling between its golden framework, yet the foyer somehow seemed dim and shadowy. No windows, observed Kano. He felt a weird sensation. Something was nagging at him…the smell; like vanilla and…cherry, with a hint of tobacco. Why did he know that smell?

"Why are *you* at the Edge of the Moon?" asked Jaden.

"Because I happen to live in it," replied Sandra. "And I was about to ask you the same thing. Your friend was supposed to come alone."

"Where he goes, we go," said Makoto, stepping between her and Kano.

"You don't want to…go where he's going," rasped a voice from another room.

Everyone turned. Through an arching gap in the marble wall sat an old man in a great black reclining chair, its old leather aglow from the grand fireplace blazing behind it. Liver spots dotted his frowning face, and only a few wisps of gray hair still clung to his head. He was squinting, but not at them. He was watching a TV that took up most of the opposite wall where a window would otherwise be. Its screen was divided into eighths, each section featuring news reports from different channels. Kano couldn't help but notice that each section was larger than his TV at home.

"Well if it's gonna be that dangerous, maybe we shouldn't let him go with you at all," said Jaden coolly.

"That's not for you…to decide," the man wheezed.

"Who decides then?" demanded Jaden. "The seniors' bingo club?"

The man grabbed a cane and pressed it against the tiled floor, his face reddening as he rose on shaking knees.

"Grandpa, careful!" Sandra rushed over and wedged herself beneath his shoulder to help him up.

"When Zoboros leave here…they go beyond…Republic borders." The man's face had turned so red that Kano started to wonder if he would pass out. "We cannot guarantee…anyone safe passage."

"If this path puts the boy in danger, then I must go with him," said Akio. "That is my charge."

The old man rolled his eyes. "Jakari and their blood oaths…" he grumbled, spitting a wad of tobacco into a basin beside him.

"Do not insult our guests," came a stern voice. Everyone turned again. A woman had entered behind them, white-haired as well, though her olive skin had fared much better than her counterpart's. She stood about Kano's height in a blue blouse, golden bracelets clamped around each of her arms. She scanned over them curiously, stopping when her gaze found Akio. "We should show our respects to Hendricks's…er…associate."

"A Jakari in our own home…" the old man wheezed as he hobbled around them, "…what has our order come to?"

"Sit down dear, you're not doing yourself any good at that altitude."

The old man mumbled something to himself and settled back in his recliner. The woman's gray eyes flicked back to them. "Who wants tea?"

Tea? Kano had a thousand more important things to worry about than tea. Who were these people? How did they plan to get him off-world? And why were they giving Akio such a hard time? He opened his mouth, but Li cut him off.

"Tea sounds lovely," she said quickly. She gave Kano a sharp look that warned him not to speak.

The old woman smiled and retreated to another room, leaving them with the old grump and their confused classmate.

Kano felt Li's hand cup his shoulder. "Tread lightly here," she whispered. Her attention snapped to a line of fine china arranged on a mantle behind the old man, where Makoto was instinctively prodding the glassware. "What are you doing?" she muttered, marching off to contain the situation.

Tread lightly? As far as Kano was concerned, he had been treading lightly all day. Now he wanted answers. He slinked toward the back of the foyer, his friends too distracted exploring the enormous house to notice him, and found a spiral staircase running up the back wall. There was something strange about it – that familiar smell was growing stronger.

"I had no idea it was you," came a voice from behind. He turned. Sandra stood there; her eyes focused on the cracks in his knuckles. "So many came through here, but I didn't know there were any left in the city."

I've been here before. "How long did they keep me?" he asked.

She shrugged. "You were gone before I got here. Some of the others were still here, though. My grandparents presented this place as an orphanage, which was technically true, but these were special children, adopted by people from very *special* circles."

'Special' wasn't the word that came to Kano's mind. The whole place seemed well-intended, sure, but he couldn't shake the feeling that something was off about it, or at least the family that owned it.

"Are they really your grandparents?" he asked.

Sandra shook her head. "Follow me." She started up the spiral steps. Kano followed, his friends shrinking away as they climbed. These people were going to take him away from them, he reminded himself. That was their job: to take the Zoboros away.

At the top of the stairs was a hall lined with red doors. Sandra led him all the way to the end, where stood a single black door constructed of unusual material. Kano poked it, his finger sinking in. Rubber. He suspected he knew what it was for. He pressed his hand into it and released a quick pulse of energy, but nothing happened. No shake, no reverb. The door absorbed it all.

My door.

Sandra opened it a crack. The curtains were drawn and the room was dark, made darker by the black, rubbery walls surrounding it. A large bed sat in the middle, stuffed animals lining its headboard. Beneath its pink and white striped sheets, Kano found a freckled face. The same face that was standing next to him, only this one was fast asleep, its auburn hair in tangles against the pillows.

"When our grandparents adopted us, your room became the perfect place to keep her," said Sandra, running her hand along the black door. "I was the lucky one. I got to go to school and make friends. She got a tutor and was allowed to spend one hour in the yard every day, but only *after* I got back from school. I couldn't play outside with her either, or else someone might discover there were two of us."

"I'm sorry," said Kano. It was all he could come up with. He watched the girl lying there; she looked so peaceful, locked in her rubbery prison. "They're taking Li and me to a place where we can start fresh. Maybe she could—"

"She can't leave," said Sandra quickly. "Never."

They heard footsteps at the bottom of the stairs. "Sandra, dear, could you give me a hand?" called her grandmother.

"You can join us for tea when you're ready," said Sandra, her eyes locked on the floor. She retreated down the stairs and out of sight.

Kano stood in the doorway, alone. *Once I go down there, everything changes.* He could still hear his friends laughing and arguing with each other in the foyer. He closed his eyes, listening, wanting to stretch this moment on forever. Wanting to stay here, forever.

He heard something…a groan. He opened his eyes. The girl still laid there, her eyes shut, but her face was scrunched and gleaming with sweat. She rolled onto her side, pulling her sheets in tighter like a cocoon.

The noise must be bothering her. He started to shut the door when he heard her whisper something.

"You."

He froze. *Me?* He stood there awkwardly, half-in and half-out of the room. *No, she's probably just having a bad…dream.*

It couldn't be. They were his dreams, his…visions. She could be dreaming about anything – but he had to be sure. He stepped inside and shut the door behind him.

The girl kept tossing and turning, her face reddening. Every fiber of Kano's being was telling him to leave, but for some reason he kept drawing closer. The girl reached her hand up into the air. *For me?* he wondered. *Or for him?*

He didn't know what else to do. He reached out. He was just inches away. If he took her hand, maybe that would pull her out of the nightmare. He stepped closer and a red spark leaped from her hand to his.

The jolt rang through his entire body. Suddenly, the room was on fire. He stumbled back into a wooden dresser and collapsed onto his knees, his scabs and bruises screaming. He blinked and the room was dark again. Safe.

And a pair of green eyes were staring back at him.

"You're the one who used to live here." Her voice was so soft he hardly heard it.

"Apparently a lot of people used to live here," he said, rising. "Do you know where they went?"

"Everywhere," she shrugged. She grabbed the nearest pink pillow and hugged it tight to her chest. "So what can you do?"

"I…what do you mean?"

"Well they wouldn't give you rubber walls if all you could do was turn into a fish or something." She scurried up to the edge of the bed, her eyes searching for the answer.

Kano didn't know what to say. No one had ever asked him what powers he had, much less been excited by what the answer would be.

"Would…you like to see?" he asked.

She shook her head vigorously.

He approached the bed, lifting his hand slowly, letting it shake as his powers swam to it.

"Oooh," her eyes widened. "Do it, do it, do it, do it!"

He felt it getting stronger, his hand shaking faster. It was practically screaming at him, begging to be unleashed. He closed his eyes, and there he saw the man on fire again.

"No," he pulled his hand back, letting the power die with it. "Are you crazy? Do you want this whole house to come down on top of us?"

She shrank away. "I was just asking."

Kano felt hot behind the ears. He hadn't meant to snap like that. The poor girl was probably just excited to finally meet someone else. Someone like her.

"It's shockwaves," he said. "I...I can create shockwaves with my hands. But I have to keep them under control, which used to be easy, but now suddenly it's like, well..."

"Like they're getting stronger?" she whispered.

Kano froze. Her hand was wrapping around his own. "You saw him too, didn't you?" he asked. "Just now, in your dream."

She looked around the room as if someone was watching her before nodding in reply. He felt her grip tighten. "They say he's one of us, but also...not."

"Well then what is he?" asked Kano.

"*A god*," she whispered.

The door flung open. Both of them jumped, their hands separating. Li stood in the doorway with her arms folded. "They're waiting for you downstairs."

"Right," Kano stumbled past her and back into the hallway, turning back at the last second. "It...it was nice to meet you."

"You too," the girl said with a smile as Li shut the door between them.

"Come on lover boy," she said, grabbing his arm and tugging him down the hall.

"We were just talking," he said, blushing. "They're hiding her here; she seemed lonely."

Li stopped at the entrance to the stairs, her voice hushed. "You need to be careful, Kano. These people are dangerous. If they find out you were snooping around, they might decide to lock *you* up in a room so no one can find out what you saw."

"I wasn't snooping. Sandra brought me up here."

"To *warn* you," she interrupted, pointing at the rubber door. "That's what they'll do to you if you can't control it. Nama warned me about this, about these people and their twisted little organization, but for right now they're the only chance we've got."

"Who are they?" he asked, a creeping feeling rising up the back of his neck.

Li shrugged. "All I know is that this teatime needs to go exceptionally well." She adjusted the collar of his T-shirt. It wasn't much of an improvement, but at least his shirt looked symmetrical now. "Are you ready?"

"I thought I was, but now I'm not so sure."

She rolled her eyes and started down the stairs. He followed, feeling as if he was moving in slow motion. Until now, he had imagined his mysterious destination to be somewhere pleasant; probably quiet and secluded, but pleasant. Now he wondered if his new home would be filled with rubber rooms like the one upstairs. It could be a rubber planet for all he knew, locked away in some uncharted system where no one would ever find him.

Not even his friends.

He found them assembled along a table that could seat twelve. The woman sat at the head of it, her gray eyes watching him through a plume of steam as she poured her tea.

"Now Mr. Kano, whatever will we do with you?"

Kano could feel his friends' gazes converge on him, but he kept his eyes locked on the woman's piercing stare. "I was about to ask you the same thing," he said, claiming the seat at the opposite end of the table.

She made a thin smile. "The thing is, we find your situation a bit…complicated. You see, Hendricks was the only one in the city with knowledge of your intended destination. Without him, we are forced to choose between the alternatives that we know of. I'm sorry to say none of them are—"

"Habitable," muttered Sandra. She sat an extra seat away from the others, with her arms crossed.

"*Ideal* is the word I was going for," said her grandmother. "Nonetheless, with Taranis siphoning information from within our own organization, I fear these locations will not be safe for much longer."

"Then what was the point of coming here?" asked Li. She had claimed the seat beside Kano, but it was taking everything she had to stay seated.

"To present you with an alternative," said the woman, leaning forward. "Tell me, have you ever heard of Iramwerta?"

That word stirred something around the table. Beside him, Li had turned stiff as a board. Jaden scratched his head while Akio stood up on his chair. Makoto just looked around, confused.

"It's a temple on Mogaddu," answered Kano. "Nobara told me about it; that's where the Zoboros came from."

"It's also a myth," said Jaden. "Millions have searched for it. *Warred* for it. Not a single one ever found it."

"That is because…they didn't know…where to look," rasped the old man.

Kano blinked. He was just realizing that the old grump wasn't among them. He glanced over his shoulder to find the man still stretched in his recliner across the way, his eyes still glued to the giant TV.

"Our family knows the way," said the woman.

Goosebumps prickled up Kano's arms. "Who are you?" he whispered.

"Why don't you ask your friend?" she replied, her eyes falling on Jaden. "Considering he's been pretending to be one of us for quite some time now."

Jaden flushed red. "They…they're the Orlovs," he managed to get out. "Old blood…Mogaddan blood."

"Much like yours, Mr. Upton," said the woman, spreading her arms as if to welcome the whole table in on their little secret. "His father, and his father's father before him have been the most exceptional of rivals to our family. Tell me, Jaden, when was the last time you saw them?"

Jaden shrank in his seat, offering no reply.

"Anyway, where are my manners?" she continued. "My name is Nina, you already know dear Sandra from school, and the sack in the chair is Konstantin."

Konstantin grunted.

"And you can really get us to Iramwerta?" asked Kano.

"I can get you to Mogaddu," answered Nina. "We have family there who can guide you the rest of the way."

"How?" demanded Akio, watching her every move with his big black eyes.

"Our spears have guarded Iramwerta for millennia. They watch the surrounding lands and ensure that only the worthy may reach its gate."

"What makes me worthy?" asked Kano.

Nina shrugged. "The fact that Taranis is so intent on finding you. When it comes to the Zoboros, he's a bit of a fanatic."

"A psychopath," added Konstantin.

"You may not be the first Zoboros he's sought out," continued Nina, "but you're certainly his favorite, and quite possibly Hendricks's favorite too. We believe you may have a larger part to play here."

"And if you're wrong?" said Li. "If the gate doesn't open for him? You're a Protector; you know what's supposed to happen then."

Kano's heart quickened. He looked to Jaden, who looked away. "What happens at the gate?" he asked.

"Not everyone who searches for Iramwerta comes back, mate," muttered Jaden. Nina said nothing.

"What happens at the gate?!" demanded Kano, pounding his fist on the table. A rumble pulsed through it.

Nina watched her teacup rattle. "That is for you to find out," she said. "Of course, if you don't want to go, we can always take you to one of our hideouts."

"And let the merry chase continue," wheezed Konstantin.

Kano glanced around the table. All eyes were on him, sad eyes, angry eyes, except for Nina's, which he could only describe as curious. Did all this amuse her? How many other Zoboros had she sent to their deaths at the temple's gate?

"Mogaddu is far enough from here," said Kano. "I'll go, but not to Iramwerta. And Li comes with me."

"She is not part of the arrangement," said Nina flatly.

"You must have enough room on your ship for her," he said. "Don't you?" He turned to Li. Her mouth was open, but for the first time she couldn't seem to find any fighting words. "I promised Nobara that she would come with me, away from the danger here."

"Promises can be broken," replied Nina, "as you will learn sooner or later on this journey."

Sandra sank in her seat, her face so red Kano thought she would storm off any second. These people *were* twisted. Shadowy arrangements, rubber rooms, and a destination that would likely get him killed. He had heard enough. He pushed back his seat and rose.

"I'll take my chances with Taranis," he said.

He marched for the red door. No one stopped him. No one even stood up. They all just watched, even Konstantin out of the corner of his wary eye. Kano felt the energy bubbling in his fists. Was he really going to do this? It had all come to him so suddenly, the urge to leave, yet it felt right. It was what he should have done from the beginning.

As he reached for the knob, a knock came from the other side. He froze. The grounds were supposed to be empty. He peeked through the peephole and saw a familiar diamond face.

Yuchi.

He swung the door open. "What are you doing—" was all he managed to get out before his whole world stopped. Through the peephole, he hadn't noticed the gag in her mouth, nor the binds on her hands or the pistol resting against the back of her head.

"Hello Kano," said Novak.

Chapter 17

A Family Affair

Li felt the cold, gloved hand clench around her chin.

"Stay still," cautioned the man behind her.

Six had entered with Novak, each clad from head to toe in black combat gear. Machine guns were strapped over their chests, but not a bullet had been fired. Hardly a word was spoken. They had corralled everyone into the middle of the living room. Everyone but Konstantin sat on the floor. He had silently refused to leave his recliner. No one took issue with it – Novak's goons probably figured standing him up would be more trouble than it was worth. They turned off his TV though, leaving only the crackling of the final embers in the fireplace to fill the void.

The man brought Li to her feet. She could feel the grooves of his gun rubbing against her back. Goosebumps crawled up her arms.

Novak stood before her in a long, gray overcoat, the collar folded up almost to his nose. Yuchi sat in front of him, her eyes wide and filled with tears. Novak rested the barrel of his pistol on the back of her head, his cold eyes peering over his collar at Li.

Traitor's eyes.

Novak's goon nudged her forward. She stumbled but caught herself, straightening her back as she faced him down. *Control*, she reminded herself. *He doesn't know what you can do. Not yet.*

Novak turned to his officers, who had positioned themselves around the room. "She's next," he announced, waving his pistol at Li before returning it to the back of Yuchi's head. "Now I will ask again: where is the transport?"

"We don't have one," answered Nina firmly. She sat on her knees between Sandra and Makoto. "Now let them go. They have no part in this."

"No part?" repeated Novak. "Everyone in this room has played a part in hiding the boy. Hendricks was smart to use Nobara. Someone outside the circle. Someone off my radar."

"Leave them out of this!" shouted Kano. He started to stand. An officer stepped forward and struck him in the back with the butt of his gun.

"KANO!" cried Li. He fell to his knees, groaning. *They're going to provoke him.* She wanted to run over to him, to calm him down before he did something stupid, but she could feel all the eyes of Novak's officers on her. One sudden move and they would start shooting.

Kano laid his hands on the floor. It began to rumble.

"Kano, *don't*," Li pleaded.

"Listen to her, Kano," said Novak. He wrapped his gloved fingers around Yuchi's forehead and began tugging it back against the barrel of his pistol. Li saw tears streaming down Yuchi's face, her sobs muffled by the gag.

Kano looked up at them, his face red and his eyes wide, his breath hissing between his teeth while he seethed. The other officers began training their guns on him. Li held her breath as the ground shook beneath her.

"You used to come to our school," said Kano. "You trained students. *Helped them*."

Novak gave Yuchi's head another tug. "And I'm the only reason they're still alive," he said.

The rumbling slowed. By the look on Kano's face, it seemed like he didn't know how to process that information. Neither could Li.

Novak nodded. He seemed relieved that the conversation was over. "Cuff him," he muttered.

Li couldn't believe it. Did he think *handcuffs* would stop Kano from using his powers? She watched the officer who stepped forward, only he wasn't carrying handcuffs. The thing in his hands looked like a giant metal egg with the top cracked off, its shell covered in blinking red lights, its inside dark and hollow.

"Hands together," said the officer. Kano obeyed, his eyes never leaving Novak while his hands were pushed inside the device. There was a crunching noise. Kano gasped.

What's happening? Li leaned forward. The lights on the cuffs started blinking faster; they were moving closer together. It was shrinking, she realized. Kano fell onto his side and writhed on the floor.

"What are you doing to him?!" shouted Jaden.

"It'll be over soon," said Novak.

Li started forward. "*Stop!* You're hurting him!"

Novak's pistol was on her in a second. "Not another step!" he barked.

She froze, watching the lights turn from red to green. Kano stopped his thrashing. Slowly, he got back onto his knees, his breath heavy. "What is this thing?" he asked, his voice weak.

"Power dampener. A leftover invention from the war."

"Designed to imprison Zoboros," added Nina, the words like poison on her lips.

"No, *your organization* is designed to imprison Zoboros," said Novak. "When this is over, he'll be free – as long as he cooperates."

Kano just stared blankly at the floor, his face pale, his arms as limp as noodles. Li shivered.

"Now take me to the transport," ordered Novak.

"I told you, there *is* no transport," said Nina.

"I wasn't asking you." Novak turned to Sandra, and Li saw the color instantly leave the poor girl's freckled face.

"I...I don't know about a—"

"Save it!" barked Novak, smacking the back of Yuchi's head with the butt of his gun. Yuchi squealed beneath the gag and fell flat on her chest. "Now tell me where it is before I spill this Nurrano's blood all over your pretty floors."

"No please!" cried Sandra.

"That's my *mother*!" screamed Makoto. He started to rise, but Jaden pulled him back down.

Novak scanned over all the frightened faces, his stare blank, while the poor girl trembled in front of him. "Or how about we try your dear old grandfather's blood?" he asked. His gun turned toward Konstantin. The old man didn't even stir.

Sandra shook her head, speechless.

"I'll give you to the count of three. One."

"Sandra dear," said Konstantin calmly, "it's okay."

"Two."

Li stepped forward, ignoring the guns she knew were aiming at her. "Stop…*please!*" she begged.

"Three."

"Okay I'll show you!" cried Sandra. Everyone froze. Novak raised an eyebrow, his gun still aimed at Konstantin. "It's…" Sandra looked around at all the others, shaking. "The passageway is upstairs. I can take you to it."

No, don't do that. Li could already picture the plan Sandra was forming. *You'll get yourself killed if you lead him there, and your sister too.*

"You think I don't know how you people work?" snapped Novak. "The entrance is in this room. I just need someone to show me how to open it. Now Sandra, if you would be so kind." He extended his hand toward the fireplace.

Sandra nodded sheepishly. She crossed the room. There was no fire left, but she grabbed a metal poker anyway and began prodding through the cold logs until there was a click. She tugged at the mantelpiece and the whole thing opened up, revealing a staircase that dipped into darkness.

Novak smiled. "Thank you, dear. That will be all." Sandra rushed back to her grandmother's side and hugged her tight. Nina held her while her gray eyes zeroed in on Novak, filled with disgust.

"Everyone else stays here," continued Novak. He turned to his men. "I'll give you the signal once we're airborne."

And then they'll kill us all, thought Li.

Novak grabbed Kano by the arm and hoisted him to his feet. Kano looked to each of his friends and family, as frightened as he was pale. His blue eyes found Li last, and they stayed there. She felt a knot forming in her stomach.

"I will find you again," he said. "I promise."

She tried to speak, but before she could, Makoto was up on his feet.

"Don't you take my brother away!" he screamed. Two machine guns aimed at him. Jaden tackled him to the floor, pinning him there while he kicked and screamed.

Yuchi wailed beneath the gag, her bound hands reaching out for her adopted son as Novak rushed him toward the stairs.

"Please," Li heard herself say, "don't."

Kano looked back at her one last time. Then Novak nudged him forward and he was swallowed up in the darkness.

Li fell to her knees. Tears rolled down her face, but…she didn't feel sad. She felt *angry*. So angry. She felt the palms of her hands beginning to warm.

The officer behind her jumped back. "No one said she was one of them too!" he cried.

Li looked down. *Oh no*. Her hands were glowing bright white. She looked up, her heart beating out of her chest, and met Nina's gaze.

"*Do it*," Nina mouthed to her.

In that moment, while they stared at each other, Li somehow knew exactly what she meant. *She knows what I can do – but I don't know if I can manage it*. She had never moved something that large before. She felt it, its energy connecting to her palms, but still…

"What do we do?" asked one of the officers, panicked.

"Shoot her!" barked another. He stepped forward, raising his gun.

Konstantin grabbed up his cane. For the first time, Li noticed a metal point protruding from the bottom of it. He aimed it at the officer and a long, thin spear shot out. It slammed into the officer's chest and he sailed into the nearest chair, screaming.

"What the hell?!" cried one of the other officers.

"*Just do it already!*" wheezed Konstantin.

Li felt the energy rush into her palms. She threw her hands out. The TV came crashing down on top of one of the officers as the branches smashed through the walls. They slithered through the air like tentacles, their leaves flaking off as they converged on the nearest officer.

The other officers scrambled away, but this one was paralyzed with fear, a perfect target. She spun her arms, just like Nobara had taught her, wrapping them round and round the man's torso until his arms were pinned to his sides.

Three down, three to go. She saw one in the corner of her eye, his weapon turning toward her. No time, she realized. She ran as the bullets peppered the floor behind her. She could hear them whistling, closer and closer, then suddenly stop.

"We got ya, girl!" she heard Jaden shout. When she looked over, he and Makoto were sprawled on top of the shooter. Jaden had the officer's arms pinned while Makoto pounded on the man's face.

Another officer stumbled past her, struggling. Akio was perched on the man's back, stabbing at it with his little knife, screaming in a language she didn't understand.

That was five. That only left…one. She froze. He was standing right in front of her, his gun aimed at her chest. Her hand connected with the branches, but they were too far away. His finger was already squeezing on the trigger.

"NO!" she heard someone scream. She felt a hand slam into her side as the gun fired and suddenly she was on the ground. She clutched her chest, but there was no blood. No bullet. No pain. She looked up to find Nina standing there, blood trickling through a hole in her blouse.

"NOOO!" she screamed.

"Better me than my children," she whispered, a thin smile on her face. She collapsed beside Li, her gray eyes staring blankly.

"NINA!" cried Konstantin. He started to stand. Two bullets struck his chest and threw him back into his recliner.

"GRANDPA!" screamed Sandra.

The red door burst open. Four more officers in black charged in, all shouting at once. One fired his gun in the air and everyone stopped.

Li was on the ground, shaking. She could hear the boots stomping around her, but she didn't look. She just kept staring at Nina, at the wound that should have been hers.

Someone yanked her to her feet. She found the officers were corralling her friends once more.

"They're more trouble than they're worth," said the one who had murdered their two hosts. "Screw Novak's orders. Line them up and shoot them."

Li felt a gloved hand clench around her arm. She offered no resistance as the man led her into the foyer. She just kept looking over at Nina.

They lined her up along the wall next to Sandra. Makoto, Jaden, Akio, and Yuchi were all assembled on either side of her, their faces against the wall, their bodies shaking. Li kept trying to think of ways to escape, ways to take out all the officers with her branches, but she couldn't even see where they were standing with her face against the wall. Even if she could, she knew she wasn't fast enough to outpace a bullet.

"On my signal!" barked one of the officers.

Li heard the guns snap up. There was silence, and then, a creak. She kept waiting, trembling, but no one fired. The seconds stretched on and on, but still nothing happened. What were they waiting for? When she finally mustered the courage to peep over her shoulder, she found all the officers were staring up the spiral staircase.

She followed their gaze. Up at the top, between the bars that supported the railing, a freckled face was peering down at them.

"Jacelyn, no!" cried Sandra. "Jacelyn, run away! *Now!*"

"Where's Grandma and Grandpa?" she asked softly.

"Jacelyn, listen to me, you need to run!" Sandra tried to step away from the wall, but one of the officers stepped forward and shoved her back into it.

"Why are you hurting my sister?!" cried Jacelyn, rising up.

"Get down here, now!" barked one of the officers.

Jacelyn didn't move. She just shut her eyes and stood there, as if she had just wished them all away. She clenched her fists, her face turning as red as her hair.

"No one…hurts…my…*sister*!"

The lights flickered out.

"What the hell?!" shouted one of the officers.

"Sandra, what's happening?" Li whispered into the darkness.

"*Run,*" hissed Sandra.

There was a flash of red and a scream. The lights snapped back on. Suddenly, the officer in front of Sandra was on the ground, motionless, smoke rising from his vest.

Li looked up to Jacelyn, but she hardly recognized the sweet girl from before. Her face had gone pale, the veins within it suddenly a bright red, and they were glowing.

Bolts of red electricity leaped between the girl's fingers, crackling and hissing.

"RUN!" screamed Sandra.

A web of red bolts exploded from Jacelyn's fingertips. They slammed into walls, furniture, floorboards, singeing everything they touched. The officers ran. A bolt struck one of them in the back and hurled him into the red door.

Li grabbed Makoto and Jaden each by the hand and pulled them around the corner and into the living room. The Jakari bounded past her on all fours. She saw Sandra was right behind her, leading Yuchi by the hand. Red lightning cracked over their heads, arcing along the ceiling and leaving a black trail in its wake.

Faster, faster, faster. She smelled smoke. The Jakari was already at the stairs, waving them on. The lights went out again. Only red flashes lit the way now, sudden, quick, constant. She heard more screams and gunfire echoing through the house, but she didn't dare look back. She kept charging forward, all the way into the stairwell.

Akio bounded down into the darkness, but Li slowed. She couldn't even see the next step. Suddenly, the ground shook beneath her feet and the stairs lit up with a fiery glow.

It's starting. The ship's engines echoed up the stairwell and roared in her ears. She charged down the stairs as fast as she could.

Not fast enough. The light was disappearing. They were getting away. She jumped the last few stairs and charged into the launch tunnel. The walls were round and metal, at least thirty feet high, and the thing seemed to stretch on forever. *It must cover the whole length of Providence Circle.* She saw Akio up ahead, still bounding down the tunnel, but the ship wasn't even inside it anymore. Li could just make it out against the twilit sky before the golden doors sealed the tunnel once more.

She fell to her knees. They were too late.

◁◆▷

"We have a launch!" shouted Cera.

The bridge had been in a frenzy since they got the report of gunfire at Providence Circle. Cera had the comms link pressed to her ear, shouting out the news as it came in. Eines had pushed the ship into full throttle. The whole bridge shook as the engines surged toward Famora. Junior could see it through the arcing windows now, a speck against the pink clouds, growing larger by the second.

Home, he thought. He had never been so relieved to see it.

"What type of transport is it?" called Carmichael as he laced up his combat gear.

"Viron Class VII!" called Cera. "Older model, came out about twenty cycles ago."

"Sounds about right," grumbled the captain. "Eines, can you intercept?"

"Not at this vector!" he called back. "They're too lightweight to…hold on…" He leaned his face into one of the many scanners on his console.

"What is it?!" called Carmichael, loading a pistol and holstering it at his waist.

"We have a second launch."

"One of Mezo's?"

"No, it's…" Eines squinted at the screen, "…gone."

"Gone? It can't be gone." Carmichael scrambled over to the radar.

The realization hit Junior like a train. "Yes it can!" he blurted. Everyone turned to him. "I need my communicator. Who took it?"

Cera pulled it from her belt and tossed it to him. He caught it and dialed his father. No answer. He racked his brain. The Jakari didn't have a communicator, claimed someone could track him with it. That left only one person he knew of who might know what was going on. Desperate times. He redialed the last number that had called him, bracing for whatever stupid wisecrack he was about to endure.

"Aren't you supposed to be dead?" came the nasally voice.

"Jaden, do you know who's on that transport?"

"It's Novak. He turned on us and took Kano! Say, where the hell are you anyway?"

Junior hung up. "Eines, stay on the intercept course. Something tells me Novak's not gonna make it much farther."

Eines turned to Carmichael, waiting.

"Well you heard him," said Carmichael. "Stay on course. Cera, man the guns."

"Aye!" She claimed the seat behind Eines, slightly elevated above him. Two grips rose from the floor into each of her hands. A targeting monitor lowered from the ceiling, positioning itself right in front of her face.

"Use pulse rounds. We don't want to incinerate the poor kid." Carmichael marched for the door at the back of the bridge. "Junior, with me."

Junior rushed after him, fighting to keep his balance while the floor shook.

"Where are we going?" he asked, catching Carmichael at the door. "The fight's here in the bridge. I can help you."

"I'm not about to put you in the middle of a dogfight," said Carmichael. "Make sure your communicator is secure to your wrist."

Junior clamped it on. "Why?"

"I have your speeder in tow. You're no good to me here on the ship, but you might be some use in the city."

Chapter 18

Old Friends

The transport rattled as it pressed into the upper atmosphere. Kano shook beneath his seat restraint, and not just because of the turbulence.

I could have saved them.

He shut his eyes. All he could see were their frightened faces watching as Novak dragged him away. *Why didn't I use my powers?* He would have buried his face in his hands if the stupid cocoon wasn't holding them hostage. Every time he tried to pry it off the thing got tighter, crushing his fingers and digging into his wrists. He was starting to lose feeling in his hands.

He stared down the aisle, down two rows of empty seats that all faced each other. Seats that should have been for his friends. He kept wondering what would have happened if he had put up a fight – if he had at least *tried* to stop Novak's men before they locked him in these cuffs. But he didn't, and now his friends were trapped inside the mansion, waiting to die.

His eyes locked onto his captor at the end of the aisle. The colonel was sunk deep into the pilot's chair, screens blinking all around him as he pulled back on the throttle. Out the windscreen, the tallest clouds were clearing away, leaving only stars above them now.

This wasn't how I was supposed to leave.

"What happens to my friends?!" he called down the aisle.

There was no answer.

Dead. It was like a knife had stabbed through his heart. He wanted to rip off the seat restraint and smash his cuffs over the traitor's head. *I was too afraid. I thought my powers would get them all hurt.*

I held back.

Kano shook the thought away. *They could still be alive...maybe...* His head felt so cloudy. The higher they climbed, the more the pressure bore down on him, as if a weight had been wrapped around his forehead and was slowly pulling him toward the floor.

The cuffs weren't much help, either. They hadn't just taken away his powers; they had sapped his energy too. Even walking down the stairs with Novak had felt like an exercise. Now his eyes kept wanting to close. "*Rest,*" cooed a voice in his head. "*Just for a minute. Everything will be okay...*"

The instant he nodded off, a flaming figure appeared in front of him.

He jolted. His eyes snapped open. The cabin was empty save for his captor.

"Where are you taking me?!" he shouted, his heart pounding.

"It wouldn't matter if I told you," answered Novak, his cold eyes watching Kano through an overhead mirror. "You've probably never heard of it, anyway."

"So then why not tell me? And how about these cuffs? Are they coming off or should I start getting used to them?"

"Patience. Everything will be explained once we arrive."

That answer only made Kano angrier. "And what about your master, Taranis? I'm surprised you didn't pick him up in your rush to leave."

"Taranis is no master of mine."

Kano paused. Those words sat with him for a moment. "He…he doesn't know you took me, does he?"

"He'll know soon enough. By then we'll be far away from Famora."

"But then…why let him into the city? Why let him kill all those people when you could have taken me away from the start?"

"Because I didn't know it was you when this started. When I learned the truth, I took it upon myself to track you down and put a stop to this before anyone else got hurt."

Anyone else? "You held a gun to my mother," he said through gritted teeth.

"She's not your mother. And this city isn't your home, so stop worrying about it so much."

"But it was yours!" screamed Kano. Something snapped inside him. "Your home, that *you* swore to protect. *People* that you swore to protect. How could you just let Taranis murder them?!"

"Because he's our only chance," said Novak. Silence filled the cabin. "Things may seem peaceful now, but that's only the illusion that your perfect little floating rock has created for you. Out there, people are suffering, waiting for a relief effort that was promised but will never come. The Republic failed, is failing, and soon it will collapse as more and more planets turn away. They need something to unite them again."

"The Zoboros," Kano whispered.

Novak drew a long breath. "For too long I sat by and watched Hendricks toss them away. By the time I realized the damage he was causing, it was too late. But now we can change that. Now we can bring them back."

But not like this. "How can you give people hope when you've unleashed a maniac on them?" asked Kano.

"Fear will lead them into action. Fear will give them a common enemy that only the Zoboros can defeat."

Kano felt a chill. "And how many more people need to die before that happens?" he asked.

"Hopefully not many. With you here we can finally put Taranis back on the leash and—"

The transport rocked, like a ship struck by a wave in the open sea. Kano slammed against his restraint.

"What was that?!" he cried.

"Hold on!" Novak called back.

"With what?!" Kano shook his cuffs in the air.

Novak tilted the throttle and the whole ship flipped onto its side. The pressure shoved Kano's head almost between his knees. He couldn't breathe.

The ship leveled out and he gasped. When he looked out the windscreen, he spotted the other ship in the distance, its wings razor thin, its silvery belly reflecting the starlight as it arced around for another pass. If not for the blue glow of its phantom engines, Kano wasn't sure he would have been able to spot it at all.

Blue bolts fired from each of its wings. Novak hit the throttle again and Kano felt the blood rush to his head as they flipped upside down and back around. By the time they leveled out, the ship was gone.

"He's gone back into stealth," said Novak. "But he'll be back."

The ship began to rock back and forth at a gallop.

"What's going on?!" called Kano.

"He took out one of our engines." Novak started flipping switches across the control board. A pulse drummed through the ship. One by one, the lights snapped off, replaced by the soft glow of red, flashing lights.

"Dammit, dammit, dammit." Novak got up and raced down the aisle to Kano.

There was a bang outside of the ship. Kano felt it reverberate through his seat. Then there was another, and another.

"What is that?" he asked as Novak unlatched his safety restraint, but he got no answer.

"Get back there and stay down," commanded Novak, leading him all the way to the cockpit and shoving him behind the pilot's seat.

Kano peeked at the control board. The lights on all the switches had gone out. They were dead in the water, afloat in the atmosphere. But how were they not falling?

Something pattered across the ceiling. Kano perked his ears: *footsteps.* Novak heard them too. Kano's eyes fixed on the pistol as Novak drew it from the pocket of his gray overcoat.

A crackling noise echoed down the shaft. A red flame sizzled through the ceiling at the far end of the ship. It spun into a wide circle. Kano felt his breath get sucked out of his lungs. The paneling within the circle came crashing down and the hull pressurized, slamming Kano into the ceiling and pinning him there. Up ahead, Novak was pinned to the ceiling too, the pistol still clenched in his hand.

A man lowered through the hole on a wire latched to his belt. There was a parachute pack strapped to his back and a pistol in his hand, too. The rest of him was wrapped in a black overcoat.

"Hendricks!" cried Kano. "Get me out of here!"

Novak slowly began to rise, fighting the pressure with all his might as he stood upside down. "Hendricks," he began, "it's too late. You need to let me finish my mission. It's the only way to stop what's coming."

"You took my son," said Hendricks flatly. He aimed at Novak and fired.

Novak tumbled across the ceiling, clutching his shoulder as he screamed. Hendricks marched straight to Kano, the wire trailing behind him, and pulled the boy to his feet. His grip was firm, safe. Even against the pressure, Kano felt like nothing could hurt him now.

They marched their way to the hole in the ceiling. The silvery ship hovered above it, grappling cables stretching from its belly into a web over the transport, keeping their ships locked together.

"Get ready to jump!" shouted Hendricks over the wind as it rushed into the ship. He positioned his feet for the final push-off. Kano did the same. "In 3…2…"

The lights sparked to life. Kano heard the engines engage, and suddenly he was tumbling back down the aisle, back toward the cockpit where Novak had the throttle pulled all the way up.

Snap, snap, snap went the cables. Kano kept sliding down. Hendricks was right behind him, unlatching the cable from his belt and letting it sail back toward his stealth ship that was now shrinking in the distance.

Hendricks took aim with his pistol as they slid. Kano caught Novak's cold eyes watching them through the mirror. The colonel tilted the throttle and Kano felt the ship toss him sideways. His shoulder slammed into the wall. The pain shot all the way up his arm, stopping at his wrist where the cuffs had cut off all feeling. Hendricks crashed in front of him, the pistol flying out of his hand and skidding away.

Novak began to rise from his seat, one hand clutching his bleeding shoulder, the other drawing his pistol once more. Hendricks flung himself into gravity's pull, sailing down the aisle and straight onto Novak. The pistol sailed away, its bullet firing off at an odd angle, while the two men collapsed onto the windscreen.

Kano clung to the nearest seat by his elbows, watching the two men whale at each other in a flurry of punches and kicks. Hendricks kept reaching for the throttle, but Novak pulled him away every time, leaving them locked in their nosedive. Beneath their fighting, Kano could see the sea of pink clouds growing beneath them.

"*Gahhh!*" Hendricks clutched at his neck where Novak had struck him. The colonel clambered back to his feet and stretched out his arms, steadying himself against the walls as he aimed his boot over Hendricks's face.

He's going to kill him. Hendricks had one hand clutched around his aching throat, the other hand laying uselessly at his side.

Wait. Kano saw something shiny beneath the sleeve of Hendricks's overcoat. A knife. He just needed the opening.

"I did this to *save* the galaxy!" cried Novak, readying for the final strike.

"I'm sure you did," rasped Hendricks.

Kano let go of the seat. He slid down and swung his metal cuffs against the back of Novak's head. Hendricks thrust the knife as the boot came down. Novak screamed, one hand clutching the back of his head, the other his bleeding foot. Kano slammed onto the windscreen, watching as Hendricks scrambled for the gun. It was over, he realized, they had beaten Novak…

An arm wrapped around him. He felt the cold, wet tip of a knife poking at his neck, fresh blood dripping onto his shirt. When Hendricks finally spun around with the gun in hand, Kano was no more than a living shield.

"This wasn't the plan, Hendricks," gasped Novak, blood pooling around his boot on the windscreen, "but I swear I'll kill him if you don't put that gun down."

Hendricks held it on him, his eyes searching for the opening. *"Oh please be a good shot,"* prayed Kano silently.

The moments ticked by so slowly, Kano was sure any moment the knife would come driving into his neck, but then Hendricks finally nodded. "Take a deep breath, Kano. This'll be quick."

Kano did as he was told, bracing for either the bullet that would hit him or the knife that would stab him. Instead, Hendricks aimed the gun down at the windscreen and fired over and over again. The glass burst into a shower of beads and Kano felt the pressure suck him into the atmosphere. He was spinning, spinning so fast that the whole world had turned into one mad blur. He could still feel Novak clinging to him, shifting his weight, slowing their fall.

The spinning stopped. The wind smacked against Kano's face as the clouds drew nearer. He noticed Novak sliding the knife back into his pocket, using both hands now to keep a hold on him.

Something slammed into his back. He looked over his shoulder. Hendricks had snagged onto them. The two men were grappling once again, this time without anything to grab onto besides each other. Hendricks landed a punch across Novak's face and grabbed the man by the collar.

Novak appeared to be out for the count, blood dripping out his broken nose as he hung there in Hendricks's grip.

"Why did you do it?!" screamed Hendricks over the roar of the wind. "Why did you tear it all apart?!"

Novak managed a thin smile. "So we could build something greater." He grabbed Hendricks's chest…*no*, not his chest – the pull cord on the pack. Hendricks gave one last, surprised look before his parachute came bursting out. His grip was severed, and Kano watched as the parachute pulled his savior away, leaving him and the colonel to continue their fall.

"YOU IDIOT!" screamed Kano. "You've killed us both!"

Novak didn't respond. He just pulled Kano in tighter as he adjusted their angle. *What does it matter?* thought Kano, imagining the mountains hidden beneath the clouds that were just waiting to smash him into jelly.

Novak pressed his arms and legs together, turning himself into a human torpedo. *Just like Junior had done in the Sphere.* The pink clouds were coming up faster…but there was something else. A speck among them. It was growing larger.

Kano's eyes widened. He knew what the plan was now. They kept rocketing toward it. The buildings were starting to come into view. So were the walkways crisscrossing between them. So many walkways. One miscalculation and they would be bugs on a windshield.

He felt Novak tense. They were back in Downtown, plummeting face-first between two of its mighty towers. The wind lashed. His heart raced. Kano could see their reflections flashing by in the windows, feel the whoosh of each walkway as they passed.

Kano blinked, and they were inside the Crossing, its many loops whirring by. He could see the Launchpad at the bottom, and their target: a sliver of open space between it and the ramp. Kano held his breath. *Get this right Novak. Get this right.* He closed his eyes and felt the swish.

When he opened them again, they were falling through the clouds, a blue bubble wrapping around them, slowing them ever so gently out of terminal velocity.

For the first time since he had left the mansion, Kano could breathe again.

Chapter 19

A Daring Rescue

He hung there in zero-gravity, his heart finally settling as the clouds filtered past and Famora returned to him. Home. It looked so different from underneath. No towers, no architecture, just flat metal discs floating in two long staircases. Glowing spots of green dotted each one, humming with a hazy energy. Kano had no idea what that strange energy was, only that it was the source of Famora's magic.

Novak floated beside him, silent. It was excruciating. It had taken the bubble at least an hour to reel them back in from their high-speed plunge. All Kano had to keep himself occupied was dodging the drops of blood as they floated up from Novak's boot, which proved difficult in the confined space.

The Trampoline was coming up now. Kano could sense the colonel tensing. Whatever officers were left would be waiting there. Waiting for the man who'd betrayed them.

But it wasn't police officers there to receive them. As the bubble crept over the edge of the platform, Kano's heart almost stopped. An army of troopers covered the entire length of the Trampoline, their blue armor shining under the streetlights. Kano counted at least a hundred.

And each one had a rifle aimed at their bubble.

A woman stood at the front of the formation, a few troopers keeping close behind her. She was tall and thin, almost gaunt, with broad shoulders and gray hair cut in a bob. Instead of blue armor, she wore gray combat nylons from neck to toe, with gold streaks running down the shoulders and sides to signify her rank. It was the kind of outfit officers only wore on a spaceship. Kano knew that could mean just one thing.

They were ready to take him away.

He didn't need to look far to find their transportation to the command ship. A blue gunship hovered overhead, its long, thick wings casting a shadow over the troopers, its rectangular belly loaded with two rotary cannons that were aimed right at him.

Kano gulped. There was nowhere to run. The closest place was Lower Downtown, but too many rifles stood between him and it. He found himself staring at that giant glass dome of the Archives as it caught the starry sky in its reflection. He remembered being so afraid of being caught by the cadets the last time he had gone there. He would have traded them for this any day.

There was something odd in its reflection, though. He saw faces – faint silhouettes, lots of them. *The Crossing.* Above the gunship, where the spiraling walkway looped toward the sky, thousands had assembled along the railings, all craning for a look.

Waiting to see who the Zoboros was.

The bubble burst just a few feet from the platform's edge. Kano and Novak stumbled toward the woman, stopping themselves just inches from her. Her troopers flinched, but she didn't. She just stared Kano up and down. There was something chilling in her gaze, like she could see right through to his insides. Even more chilling was the silence. The bubble had blocked any outside noise, so he was shocked to discover that there wasn't any noise to begin with. All of Famora gathered here, and no one had anything to say.

"Are you hurt?" asked the woman.

Kano blinked. Truth be told, he ached from head to toe. Scabs from his fall, bruises from being thrown around the transport; at this point he felt whittled to the bone. Not that he would tell *her* that; he doubted she nor any of her troopers cared.

"I'm fine," he said quickly.

The woman's eyes snapped to Novak. "You *will* answer for what you've done."

"So will you," he replied.

A trooper stepped forward, handcuffs ready, when a voice boomed from across the way.

"GENERAL MEZO!"

Kano turned. Half the rifles turned with him; the other half stayed locked on Novak. A tall figure stood at the opposite end of the platform. It wore black combat nylons with blue streaks marking the shoulders and sides. Only IDF wore those colors. Kano was beginning to wonder how many more officers this platform could hold. As the figure approached, though, Kano realized it wasn't an officer at all.

"Everyone hold your fire!" ordered Mezo. The rifles lowered slightly, their barrels still following Junior as he neared. "You better have a good explanation for this, Aaron."

Junior stopped between Mezo and Kano, the burns on his cheeks gleaming bright red. *So Carmichael saved him, after all.* Kano scanned the platform, but all he saw were blue helmets and visors. If Carmichael was here too, he had no way of knowing.

"General, you need to arrest this man immediately," said Junior, sticking a finger in his former commander's face. "I have proof that he's working for—"

"Taranis," finished Mezo, "we already know this. Now step aside."

"Ah…right." Junior glanced over his shoulder toward Kano, his orange eyes flicking to the floor. Kano looked down around his feet but saw nothing. "I'm afraid I can't let you take Kano. I'm under strict orders to deliver him to my father."

"Your father's orders are irrelevant," said Mezo. "Now *stand aside.*"

Two troopers stepped forward. Junior stepped back, again checking over his shoulder. Once again, Kano saw nothing.

"Stop," said Junior, but the troopers kept marching toward him. "Just let me explain what's going on. There's more that you don't know."

"We know quite enough," said Mezo. "Now let us take you in so we can treat those burns. You can tell us everything you witnessed once this situation is handled."

"But…but…"

He was stalling, Kano realized, but for what?

Junior glanced back, except not at the floor this time. His orange eyes were set on Novak, and they were wide with horror.

Kano saw it too, out of the corner of his eye – the shiny blade driving for his neck.

The next moment went by in a blur. A flash of orange burst from Junior's hand. The knife skated away across the platform, its metal glowing red. Vapor steamed from Novak's hand as he fell to his knees.

Time stood still for Kano. *That's impossible*. He wouldn't have believed it, if not for the collective gasp running its way up the Crossing.

The cadet stood frozen, one hand still outstretched, smoke rising from it. Thousands of eyes were on him now. By the horrified look on his face, Kano could tell that Junior felt every single one of them.

"Get behind me," whispered Junior.

"What?" Kano shook his head, still in shock.

Junior's palms erupted in flames, tall and bright, incredible and terrifying all at the same time.

"All of you stand back!" he screamed. The troopers stood their ground. "I said *get back*!" The flames climbed higher, crackling over his head.

"*Enough*, Junior." Mezo stepped forward. Her troopers kept their weapons aimed, but none dared come any closer. "You're coming with us."

The Crossing erupted in screams. The crowd pressed itself against the railings, fists pounding on the metal.

They're booing.

"GET OUT OF OUR CITY!" one of them shouted.

"GIVE THEM TO TARANIS!" cried another.

Kano inched back, away from the flames, away from the screaming. He knew these people. Maybe not by name, but he knew the faces. He had seen them day after day, many for most of his life, but he had never seen them like this. Never outraged, least of all at *him*.

Something crunched under his foot. He froze. He had only heard that sound once before. And only an hour ago. But how did one of those follow him all the way down here?

He felt something twist around his leg.

"Li!" was the only word he could get out before the vine tugged his legs out from under him and dragged him over the edge. He felt the sudden rush of the fall, but only for a second before his feet struck something metal. He tried to get his bearings, but Li had him wrapped in her arms the moment he landed.

"Oh thank goodness!" she cried.

"You're alive!" Joy swept through him like a lightning bolt. *They're okay. She's okay.* He desperately wanted to hug her back, but the cuffs made it impossible.

Amidst all the emotion, though, one thought did occur to him. "What are we standing on?"

He saw a familiar blond head peeking up at him out of the passenger's seat. "He's here!" called Jaden. *"Go, go, go!"*

The hovertruck lurched beneath his feet. He and Li both fell to their knees, the wind whipping at their faces as they sped away.

"Hurry!" Li grabbed him by the arm and led him toward the back of the truck. He felt a vine wrap around his waist and suddenly he was airborne, lowering slowly over the edge and into the cabin.

Two blue arms reached up and pulled him inside. "Package secure!" called the Jakari.

Kano looked around the familiar cabin. He couldn't believe how relieved he was to have the slimy meat hooks hanging over his head again. Through the slit in the wall, he spotted Makoto nervously at the wheel while Jaden sat beside him, typing away at his datapad. Li climbed in through the open backdoors, the Trampoline shrinking behind her as the hovertruck climbed along the side of the Crossing.

"What's going on?!" he exclaimed.

"Sandra led us through another passage and away from the fighting," answered Li. "We thought it was all over, that we had lost you, when suddenly Jaden got a call from Junior."

"The bastard hung up on me the first time," Jaden called back. "But now *apparently* he needs our help."

"Doing what?"

"Rescuing you, of course!" said Li.

Just like he tried to do the first time. Kano had been too stubborn to realize it then, but now he understood just what everyone here was sacrificing. He looked around at all the smiling faces…but someone was missing. "Where's Yuchi?"

"Your false mother fainted in the tunnel," hissed the Jakari.

"I'm not sure 'false' is the word I would choose," said Jaden.

"Sandra's taking care of her," assured Li.

"And what about Sandra's sister?" asked Kano. "The Zoboros?"

Li rubbed her shoulder. "We don't know. We saw gunships hovering over the house when we came to get the truck. There was no way to reach her."

"By now they have taken her," muttered Akio.

Kano felt a weight drop into the pit of his stomach. *Because of me*. So many had already been hurt, even killed since this whole thing started. No more.

"And what about Junior?" he asked. "We forgot to pick him up from the Trampoline!"

"The big guy can take care of himself," said Jaden, pointing over his shoulder. Out the back, Kano saw the black speeder racing after them, its phantom engines roaring.

Whatever relief Kano felt was short-lived, though. The gunship emerged behind the speeder, its rotary cannons aimed and spinning, its blue wings angling up in pursuit.

"We can't outrun that, can we?" he asked.

Everyone turned to the Jakari. His only reply was, "Shut the doors."

Kano rushed to the back, only to realize that he still had no use of his hands. One of Li's vines whipped past him, wrapped around the door on the left, and tugged it shut.

Through the open door on the right, Kano saw the rotary cannons starting to glow blue.

"MOVE!" screamed Akio. He grabbed Kano by the cuffs and threw him against the wall. Li scooped up Akio and dove beside Kano as blue bolts pounded across the open half of the cabin into hundreds of little pulses of electricity.

"SHIT!" screamed Jaden, before the peephole slid shut.

"What do we do now?!" Kano shouted, unsure if anyone could hear him over the barrage of stun bolts.

Li snapped up her communicator. "Makoto! Take us *inside* the Crossing!"

"Aye…captain?" came Makoto's uncertain voice. The hovertruck hooked right. Kano felt the floor slip from under him. He slid across the cabin, Li and Akio sliding beside him, as the stun bolts pounded the wall behind them.

"Why the Crossing?" asked Kano. "We'll be trapped!"

The slit opened again. "Because it's the rendezvous point," said Jaden, waving his datapad.

"Rendezvous with who?!"

The truck lurched again. Kano felt the floor level out beneath them as they slowed to a stop.

"The hell was that?!" shouted Jaden.

"Oh no," mumbled Li.

"The pedal, it's not working!" cried Makoto.

"It's called an *accelerator*!" hissed Jaden.

"I've never driven before!"

"No, no, no…" Li scrambled to the open backdoor and peeked over the edge.

"What's going on?" Kano raced up beside her, staring over the edge at the walkway spiraling beneath them. Hordes of people were shoving their way down it, screaming.

"It's locked in hover mode again. *Dammit!*" She pounded her fist on the bumper. Suddenly, Kano felt a blast of hot air, and for a split-second he thought she had got it working.

He was wrong. The gunship rose up before his eyes like a hawk swooping in over its prey, steam venting from its rotary cannons as they zeroed in on him.

"You guys shouldn't have come," said Kano.

"We're not going anywhere without you," said Li. Her hand started to glow. She raised it and her vines rose with it, readying to strike. They looked like no more than paper against the metal beast.

The cannons started to spin, faster and faster, glowing blue as the stun bolts readied to fire. Kano braced himself.

A fireball exploded against one of the wings. The whole gunship tipped to one side and careened away while a speeder zoomed by in its place, its rider ready with another fireball in hand.

"Now that's what I'm talking about!" cheered Jaden.

"Okay, did anybody else know he could do that?" asked Kano.

Li turned to Jaden, ignoring the question. "Where is he?" she asked.

"We're too early," said Jaden.

"Early for *what*?" pressed Kano. "Who are you talking about?"

Li started lowering a vine toward the walkway. "Everyone out! We'll use the crowd to lose them."

Kano took one look at the people clawing their way down the Crossing and shook his head. "There's gotta be a better way than that!"

"Nope!" Li spun him around and kissed him on the cheek. He stood there on the edge, flustered. He felt the vine wrap around his waist and the Jakari clamber up onto his shoulder. *No, no, no...* She shoved him, and suddenly he was falling, quickly at first, but then the vine tightened, squeezing his insides together. He gasped, watching the hovertruck slowly shrink as he lowered.

"I like her," Akio hissed in his ear.

"Oh shut up."

The screams grew louder. Off in the distance, the gunship was leveling out. Ropes lowered from its sides and troopers began sliding down them like drops of water onto the walkway above them.

"There will be more below," hissed Akio in his ear. "Soon, we will be trapped."

"I can see that." The walkway was coming up fast, though he couldn't even see its surface beneath all the people. He stretched out his feet, but the crowd swept him away before he could touch down.

"What do you suggest?!" he shouted, fighting for footing as the current of people pushed him into a run.

"Find Junior. He can take you the rest of the way."

Kano scanned the skies, but all he saw were more gunships descending on the Crossing. Right and left, people kept crashing into him: Humans, Braimen, Galanads. The cuffs left him with no hands to keep balance, so he focused on his footing. If he tripped, he was as good as dead.

"*Railing!*" barked Akio, pointing a long finger.

Junior hovered on the other side of it, hand outstretched. Just a few more feet. Kano reached out, when suddenly a blue bolt whistled over his shoulder and struck a runner in front of him. The poor Nurrano collapsed, sending everyone around them into an even greater frenzy.

Kano glanced over his shoulder. He spotted the troopers on the loop above them firing at Junior. The cadet had no choice but to dive out of sight.

No, no, no! Kano picked up the pace, slamming his cuffs into anyone that dared slow him down.

"*Put your head down!*" cried Akio, shoving Kano by the neck until he was practically at a ninety-degree angle to the floor. He could still hear the bolts whistling, still see the bodies hitting the floor, stunned.

Suddenly, all the feet in front of him were skidding to a stop. He lifted himself upright just in time to crash into someone's back. People mashed up behind him, but that did nothing to push him forward. He was up against a wall of people, trapped like cattle ready for slaughter. The stun bolts had stopped firing, but the people continued to scream.

"They have us right where they want us," muttered Akio.

A gunship swooped in, its spotlights sweeping through the frightened faces, searching for just the right one.

"It's over Kano," boomed a woman's voice. It was coming from the gunship. Kano noticed the speakers folding out just beneath the cockpit. "Hold your hands up so we can get you out before anyone else gets hurt."

Kano started to lift his cuffed hands. Akio slapped them back down.

"No you *fool*," it hissed.

That seemed to get the attention of the man next to them. His eyes widened at the sight of the cuffs. "HERE!" he screamed. "Over here! We have the Zoboros!"

All eyes turned to Kano. Everyone started shouting, pointing, waving, all trying to help seal his doom. He felt the heat of the spotlight as it blinded him. All the shouts and jeers echoed in his ears. In that moment, he wanted to melt away, to disappear to some far-off world and never return to Famora again.

A wail blared through the loudspeakers. Everyone screamed and covered their ears; everyone except Kano, who wished his hands were free to do the same.

"Hello, is this thing on?" came a nasally voice as the wailing died away.

"JADEN?!" blurted Kano. Everyone around him began to lower their hands. They all looked as confused as he was.

"There's our white knight!" boomed Jaden's voice over the loudspeakers. "Turns out the protocols on their sound system are even worse than the ones at the Archives. Speaking of archives: Kano, do you remember in history class, how the Nurranos fought back the Gorvs in the Battle of Andor?"

All eyes turned to Kano. He just stood there, dumbfounded. *Like I remember that.* There were clearly more pressing things to worry about than one of the hundred battles that Jaden liked to recite.

Something struck the gunship, the ping of metal on metal echoing up the Crossing. Kano heard it again and again. People started shouting, pointing, ducking as screws and bits of wire rained down on them. A large piece crashed at Kano's feet, its red light fading away as it died.

A bot?

Hundreds of them rose up through the Crossing and swarmed the gunship, coating its damaged wing and tilting it back down and away.

"CAVALRY!" boomed Jaden's voice as the gunship sank down the center of the Crossing. "THE ANSWER WAS CAVALRY!"

Kano couldn't help but smile. For once, his friend's crazy plan had actually worked out.

He felt two wiry arms clamp onto his shoulders. He was hoisted into the air, his legs flailing over the crowd, the Jakari still perched on his shoulder.

"Put me down!" he screamed, but the bot just kept lifting him higher. It felt far less secure than the bubble; he worried the arms would snap off at any moment. What was worse, its glowing eye had drowned him in red light. The whole Crossing could see him now. Flashes of blue lit up the night, whistling over and under him as he floated up. *Faster*, he kept pleading, *go faster*.

It wasn't fast enough. Kano heard the thwoom and the red eye went dark. The wiry arms loosened their grip and he was falling again.

No please, no more falling, was all he could think as the wind howled in his ears. His back felt lighter. *Akio.* He saw the blue guy spinning away toward the abyss. Kano's trajectory was not so fortunate. The Launchpad was closing in fast, and there was no time to thread the needle like Novak had. He readied another shockwave, when a great roar filled his ears. He felt a giant hand snag onto the back of his shirt and pluck him from his fall.

"Junior!" he cheered.

"You're not gonna fall on me this time, are you?" asked Junior, setting Kano down on the seat behind him.

"It seems to be the theme today," said Kano.

"Here." Junior pressed a button on his center console. Kano felt a force pulling at his hands. The cuffs slammed against the frame of the speeder with a clank.

Magnetized. Kano came to appreciate the gesture as Junior steepened their climb up the center of the

Crossing. Without hands, he would've never been able to hold on.

"Where are we going?" he asked.

"My dad's meeting us at the top."

"In what, his parachute?"

"No, his *ship*." Junior tapped on his communicator.

Linked. Just like Junior and the speeder. Kano never imagined something as large as a stealth ship could be connected to a communicator, but if there was anyone who could get their hands on technology like that, it was Hendricks.

"Thanks for the save," said Kano.

"Don't thank me yet," said Junior, pivoting the speeder as more stun bolts whistled by. Kano felt his rear lifting off the seat, but the cuffs kept him locked in place.

"Take a deep breath," said Junior.

"Why?"

There was a crack. Suddenly, the speeder was surging up at triple the speed it had been going before. The wind smacked Kano's cheeks back and stung his eyes while the loops of the walkway whooshed by. He turned his head away and found the phantom engines now glowed green instead of their normal blue.

"GET READY!" Junior shouted back.

Kano looked up, squinting against the wind. The stealth ship was hovering high above them now, its rear liftgate lowering for the reception.

This was it, he realized. The end. No more Taranis. No more troopers. And no more Famora…

Everything flashed through his mind at once. One moment, he was taking Makoto for his first speeder ride. The next, he was helping Jaden put up a new painting. He was on a trip to the Dockyards to visit Li, then racing back home for Yuchi's famous stew. He could still smell the bay leaves and aivin soaking in broth. That was all gone now. Once he entered that ship, he was stepping into the unknown, never to return.

His eyes began to water. As he blinked tears away, he noticed something odd. Amidst all the people scrambling out of the Crossing, there was one near the top standing completely still, its cloak flapping in the breeze, its face shrouded beneath a hood. Slowly, it reached a hand toward the ship.

A metal hand.

"JUNIOR, PULL UP!" he screamed, but it was too late. A lightning bolt struck the wing of the stealth ship with a deafening crack. Sparks exploded as it snapped in half, the broken chunk plummeting toward their speeder in a fiery blaze.

"DAD!" screamed Junior. He veered out of the way of the burning debris. Kano felt the heat as it passed. It was enough to choke the air around him. When he looked back, the stealth ship was gone. He searched the sky, only to realize that it had already fallen beneath them, spiraling down past the Crossing while smoke billowed out the broken wing. It was heading for Lower Downtown, straight for…

Oh no…

The ship smashed through the dome. The crash of glass rang up through the Crossing as the dome crumbled and the ship disappeared in a cloud of smoke.

Kano felt the heat once again, only this time it was coming from one of Junior's fists. With the other, Junior was jamming on the accelerator, keeping them stubbornly, *stupidly*, on a collision course with the masked maniac.

"*JUNIOR, DON'T!*" Kano screamed.

It was too late. More lightning bolts raced from Taranis's fingertips, these ones much smaller than the last. They caught Junior in the chest. He screamed and convulsed as the electricity wrapped around his torso in a terrifying dance. The speeder slowed, but their target was still closing in fast.

Taranis stepped lazily to the side and caught the speeder in his gauntlet, leaving Kano to watch helplessly as he vaulted on board. Taranis scooped the stunned cadet up by the shirt and hoisted him over the side of the speeder.

"Strong," he said, his voice like ice, "but reckless." He let Junior fall back down through the Crossing.

"NOOO!" screamed Kano. He pulled with all his might, trying to rip the cuffs from the speeder, but they wouldn't budge. All he could do was sit there and watch as the Crossing disappeared in the distance, and all his friends with it.

"You killed him!" he screamed. A thousand terrible thoughts swam through his head all at once, but one echoed over all the others.

I failed.

He got the sick feeling in the pit of his stomach again. *The rest of them will go to prison for this – and all so I could end up Taranis's prisoner anyway…*

He stared at the maniac's cloaked back. He had only one question on his lips, one that had haunted him the moment he saw that mask on TV.

"Who are you?"

"The only friend you have right now." The engine rumbled and the speeder raced off into the shadows of the night.

Chapter 20

The Secret of Famora

All the blood was rushing to his head. The vine had him by his legs; he could feel it twisting down past his knees as it slowly raised him up. Everything had gone fuzzy, but if he squinted, he could just make out the girl standing over him. Li, that was her name. His father had told him about her, and the lightning girl at Providence Circle, too. He shuddered thinking what the IDF would do to them now that their secret was out.

Or what they'd do to him.

Everyone had seen him. Thousands were still pouring out of the Crossing, each one with a story to tell. Soon the whole galaxy would know what he was.

He looked to the Archives. The remains of the glass dome twinkled with orange firelight. Smoke plumed from the gaping hole in its center. Emergency hovercraft kept raining water and formula into it, but that did little to douse the flames.

Only I can save him…if he's even still alive. If he was, then he wouldn't be for much longer. This vine was too slow. Li was trying her best, but her face had turned as pink as the clouds. It had been a feat in itself to catch him before he could smash against the Launchpad; he owed her for that. For now, though, she had to let him go.

"Swing me over there!" he called up, pointing to the nearest loop in the Crossing.

"Are you crazy? You can't take the troopers alone. They'll kill you!"

"I'd like to see them try."

He saw Li's gaze shift over to the Archives. Her eyes lit up with the fire's glow; there was pity in them.

"If he's hurt, I may not be able to save him," she said.

"I'm not asking you to. Get the others and get out."

Li held him there for a moment, the strain still written on her face. "Don't let them catch you," she said.

"I won't."

The vine lowered. He could feel his momentum gaining as he shifted from side to side, the cries from the walkway growing louder with every swing. He reached out and clenched the railing between his fists. The vine loosened. He slipped right out of it and dove into the crowd. It was even more chaotic than he had anticipated, with bodies packed from railing to railing – and everyone was so *slow*. He tapped his communicator, only to remember that nothing would come. He was grounded, trapped in a crowd that kept pushing him, bumping him, tripping him, cutting him off. It was infuriating, and his father was running out of time.

"Out of the way!" he shouted.

Flames erupted from his palms. Everybody screamed as the fire coated his hands. They scrambled toward the railings, clearing a path down the middle. He charged on, loop after loop, all the way to the bottom. Just as he suspected, there was a trooper waiting at the exit.

"Freeze!" she shouted. A fireball sent her skating across the floor. Junior hadn't even realized he'd thrown it; it had just come out of instinct.

I don't have to hide it anymore. He ran through Lower Downtown, hurling fireballs at any trooper that stepped in his way, his adrenaline spiking with every throw. *They can't stop me now.*

He raced up the stone steps of the Archives. Two troopers were charging down at him, their rifles aimed.

Junior pointed his hands straight down and two fireballs exploded at his feet. He felt the rush, like a bungie yanking him into the air. The troopers shrank beneath his feet, and suddenly he was touching down at the top of the stairs, continuing his run as if it had never stopped.

Another fireball and the glass-paned doors exploded out of his way. He rushed inside and felt a tickle in his throat. Thick and black, the smoke had consumed the room, choking the air and sending him into a coughing fit.

"Use the suit," Carmichael's voice echoed in his head. It had been the captain's parting advice when he sent Junior back to Famora. He had never worn one before; they were meant for space travel, not terrestrial combat like he had trained for. The only thing he knew about them was that they always had a special button beneath the left wrist.

He pressed it. The nylons leaped up at his face and squeezed around his mouth. He stumbled back, trying to pry them away, when suddenly he felt cool, clean air soothe his throat. He stopped his struggling, running his hand along his new, silky apparatus.

Maybe Carmichael isn't as useless as I pegged him for.

Yesterday morning, the Archives had been a peaceful little getaway. Now, they were a horror scene. Flames licked up the walls and shelves – or at least the shelves that were still standing. Most had been smashed to pieces, their datacubes spilled out over the floor. He climbed over the debris, squinting through the smoke. Just ahead, a path had been dredged through the shelving, just wide enough for a ship to pass along.

Dad. He followed the path and found the ship lying at the center of the room like a crumpled wad of paper, its fine metal bent in almost every possible place. One wing was gone, the other dug into the ground while smoke billowed out its doomed engine. He ran up the wing to the windscreen at the ship's center, a round eye atop a metal bird, its glass so pulverized it was impossible to see inside.

"Dad!" he shouted, pounding on the glass. No answer. He ignited his hand, ready to blast through it, when he heard the groaning of metal on metal.

The liftgate. He slid back down the wing to find more smoke pouring out the back as it opened. He rushed through the opening, near blind, and slammed into something wooden. A crate? He noticed several others nearby; one of them was open. A figure emerged from it, slow, limping.

"DAD!" He rushed to his father's side. The man was leading a speeder out the crate, though by the way he leaned on it, it seemed more like the speeder was leading him. His face was pale and stained with ash, his long overcoat torn in at least a dozen places.

But he was alive. Junior wasn't sure what to do. They never really hugged, so he settled for an awkward clasp on the shoulder. "Where are you hurt?"

"Nowhere. Now help me move this thing."

Well at least he's still himself. Junior grabbed the speeder and led it out of the ship. It was an older model than his own, and bulkier, but it could get them where they needed to go.

"I'm taking you to the hospital," said Junior, assuming the controls.

"Where's Kano?"

Junior felt that name weighing down on him. *I failed again.* He clutched the handlebars, his arms shaking. It was all the answer he needed to give. He felt his father's hands wrap around his own and pull them from the controls.

"Taranis took my speeder," Junior finally said, scooting back. "They could be anywhere by now."

"No," said Hendricks, wincing as he settled into the driver's seat.

The realization hit Junior. "Where are they going? What do you have that he's looking for?"

"A way out of Famora." The phantom engines roared to life.

Junior noticed the machine gun slung over his father's shoulder for the first time. "You're in no condition to fight Taranis. You would need an army to beat him. Mezo's army."

"I trust Mezo to help the other Zoboros, but *not* Kano. This is something I have to—"

"Do alone?" finished Junior. "If you hadn't noticed, Taranis has powers. Mine were barely a match for his. And while we're on the subject, can you at least *acknowledge* that I managed to escape from that maniac?"

"I know. That's why you're coming, too."

"Oh," Junior trailed off. He hadn't expected that one. A part of him was thrilled about being selected, but the other part was absolutely terrified. "Whe…where are we heading?" he asked.

"Down," said Hendricks. "Way down."

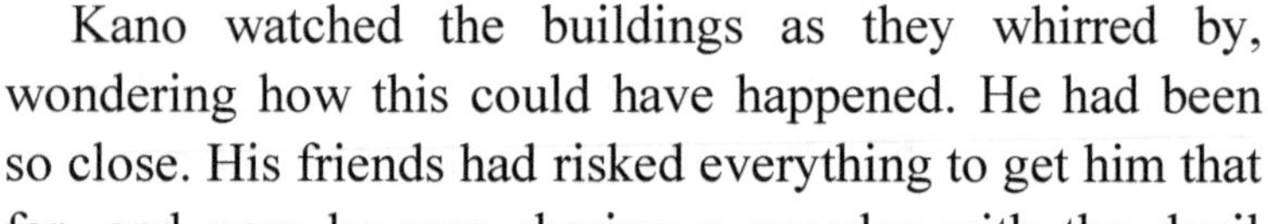

Kano watched the buildings as they whirred by, wondering how this could have happened. He had been so close. His friends had risked everything to get him that far, and now he was sharing a speeder with the devil himself.

Taranis was silent. Kano had thought of plenty of things to say, insults to throw, questions to ask, but every time he tried to speak, he imagined that gauntlet wrapping around his face, shooting electricity until the metal fingers had melted into his skin, and so he stayed silent. He wanted to jump off, to fall through the clouds and into the safe embrace of a blue bubble, but instead his hands were cuffed and magnetized to a speeder that was steering toward an unknown destination.

He searched the skies for a gunship, a police cruiser, even a passing witness would do, but there was no one to be found. The police were gone, the troopers held up at the Crossing, and everyone else was either hiding in their homes or trying to escape from Downtown. Kano looked over his shoulder. He could still see it, the plume of smoke rising from the Archives to blot the stars from the sky. Sirens blared and spotlights sliced through the streets and alleys between the towers as everyone searched for Taranis.

But they won't find him there. Downtown was far behind them now, shrinking as they passed over the wreckage that had once been the Dockyards. With the streetlights all destroyed he could hardly see the rubble, only flashes of it in the headlights – a collapsed warehouse here, a hollowed shell of a transport there. And the man who had done it all was sitting right in front of him.

The speeder steadily descended. Before long, Taranis had them flying inside the rifts between the platforms. The space was tight; Kano could reach out and touch the bases floating on either side of him. Looking down, each one must have been at least a hundred feet tall, thick enough to support the starships and transports coming in through the atmosphere. Green gas hissed out of vents on either side of him, its strange energy somehow keeping all this afloat.

Up ahead, a platform loomed over them. Kano felt the speeder slowing. *What could he possibly be stopping here for?* In the headlights, he spotted a crack in the base. No, not a crack. An entrance. It was so small and insignificant that a passing eye would never notice, but as Taranis steered them closer, the indent began to take shape. It was just wide enough to fit the speeder through.

Taranis stopped once inside. A hydraulic door stood just a few feet away, a control console blinking beside it. Grappling gear hung from the narrow walls on either side of them. *For the engineers.* They were the only ones allowed down here, though few people even knew who they were, and even fewer knew what they did. In fact, Kano didn't even know what the inside of a hoverpad looked like, save for that tunnel beneath Providence Circle. The city kept the hoverpads under lock and key for fear that someone would tamper with one and send it plummeting to oblivion.

Apparently, they hadn't done a very good job.

Taranis struck a button on the center console. Kano felt the pull of the magnet evaporate. He hadn't realized how much he had been leaning on the cuffs during their journey; they slid under his weight and he hit the ground with a clang.

Taranis ignored his fall, marching down the narrow walkway to the door. He drew a card from his sleeve and swiped it through the console. The door whooshed open.

Kano rolled his eyes. *What else did Novak give him access to?* Then again, Novak had been so eager to ditch Taranis that he may not have been the one to give away that swipe card. That thought gave Kano a chill.

"Who else is helping you?!" he blurted, his voice finally returning to him.

Taranis didn't answer.

"Was it the Poterians?" Kano found himself firing off faster than he could think, shouting all the things he had been holding in on the ride over. "They planted operatives in Famora, didn't they? They gave you everything you needed to tear the city apart...just so you could find me..." His knees shook as he tried to stand. "*Why?*"

"Come. You'll find your answers here...if you ask the right questions." Taranis waved his gauntlet toward the darkness looming beyond the door. It seemed to grow deeper the longer Kano stared at it. Taranis stepped forward, his metal boots echoing on and on through the innards of the hoverpad. With a deep breath, Kano followed.

Lights began to flicker on. Dim, yellow, not of much use. What truly illuminated their path were the long glass pipes weaving through the room. They climbed high over their heads, interwoven in some elaborate maze, each filled with the same green, glowing substance. At first glance, Kano thought it was liquid, but it didn't flow like a liquid. It pulsed, inching forward as if some force was pushing it.

The room proved much wider and taller than Kano had anticipated, with steps carrying them up and back down again between the pipes. *No wonder they need grappling gear.* Soon he lost track of how many turns they had taken. If he tried to escape now, he doubted he would be able to find the door they had entered through.

The green substance continued to ooze alongside them. Kano felt something pulling him toward it. The cuffs. He raised them and they snapped to the glass with a click. He had to press his foot against a lower pipe just to pry himself free.

"You don't know what that is, do you?" asked Taranis.

Kano jumped as if he had just been called on in class. The calmness in Taranis's voice made the question somehow more frightening. He shook his head.

"Levithium," said Taranis, "though some call it 'gravity jelly' because of its strange properties." He raised his gauntlet and it stuck to the glass with a thud. "Highly powerful, highly unstable. Many of our greatest minds still don't understand it."

"Then how did they build a whole city with it?" asked Kano.

"They didn't. The Poterians did."

Kano felt the room shrink around him. *That's impossible.* He stepped back without looking and let his cuffs bump against the glass. "There are no Poterians here," he said, trying to pry his cuffs free again.

"Not anymore," said Taranis. He reached over and yanked Kano's cuffs off the glass. "About a hundred cycles ago, the Poterians tried to make peace with your government. They had been raiding along the borders of the Rift for generations, stealing cargo and sacking trading outposts before slipping back to their Empire. Naturally, the Republic was hesitant to accept a peace offering, so the Poterians offered some of their technology as an act of goodwill. They worked with IDF scientists to build this city as a symbol of peace between the two governments. A place where all peoples could live safely, happily." He knelt down so his mask was level with Kano's face. "That was what your Shantima was created for."

Kano shook as he stared into the grooves of the mask, though he sensed no danger from Taranis – only the words frightened him. "What happened?" he asked.

"A new emperor rose to power." Taranis turned away to the shadows. "The Unlikely Heir, they called him. Though the next in line by birthright, he had no powers and therefore no claim to the Poterian throne. The royal family had bred itself to be a symbol of unchallenged power, so they cast him out as a failure. Little did they know that he was Zoboros too, his powers were just latent, and by the time he discovered them the damage had been done. He returned to the palace and destroyed his family. With no one to stop him, he seized the throne and led his people to build the greatest army the galaxy had ever seen.

"It had become tradition at that point for the leaders on both sides of the Rift to meet here at Shantima once every few cycles. When the emperor arrived, however, he was…disappointed. He found the people and their leaders weak and divided, but worst of all, he saw that they were trying to cast out their own Zoboros just like his family had done to him. He knew he could fix things if only the Zoboros lived under his rule, and so, on the next Shantima, he arrived on the other side of the Rift with an armada. He didn't attack Famora, though. No, the emperor wanted to save it for last, when he could truly say that the two sides had been united. Until then, he would settle for every other planet on his march toward Vasilia."

Kano looked away from Taranis. *He's not a Poterian, but he worships them.* No one had ever told him much about the Poterians, only that they were savages that destroyed everything they touched. "What was his name, the emperor's?"

"Palorex."

Something about that name chilled Kano right down to his bones. "Why didn't anyone tell me that the Poterians came to Famora?"

"Your government would prefer that everyone remember the Poterians only as killers. Despite what you might have been told, they are not an evil people."

"Says the murderer who blew up half a city."

Taranis turned, his shadow falling over Kano. "You defend these people as if they deserve it. You saw what they did at the Crossing: they abandoned you the moment they discovered what you were."

"Not all of them," mumbled Kano.

"And now your friends will suffer at their hands. There's no place for people like us here, but there is with the Poterians. They understand what true power is." Taranis raised his gauntlet, and sparks began to jump between his fingers. Kano wasn't watching the electricity, though. He was watching the pipe beside it, how the jelly inside began changing direction, smashing against the glass as if it wanted to leap into the gauntlet.

Taranis snapped his powers away and the jelly settled once more. He spun around, his cloak sweeping behind him as he marched on.

Kano followed. The path was beginning to brighten. More pipes. They were all moving in the same direction now, one on top of the other, all arcing in a wide circle. There was something inside that circle, he realized. Something the pipes had to go around.

Taranis led him through a gap in the pipes, and he nearly lost his footing at the sight of what laid beyond. A ship towered over them, its wings arcing so high they almost touched the ceiling. Black as night, it could have stayed hidden in the shadows if not for the pipes glowing around it. Its face was that of a great beast, rounded with two rudders pointed down like fangs on either side. Kano knew that face. He had seen it on TV.

"Used by the emperor himself," said Taranis. "He named it—"

"The *Derelict*," finished Kano.

Chapter 21

The Pin

He saw Kano in the distance, hands cuffed, the shadow lingering over him.

The shadow that burned my face.

Junior clenched his fist, feeling the heat rising from within it. He had to be careful in a dark room like this: the faintest flicker could give away their position. His father was crouched beside him, surveying the scene through a seam in the pipes. They lined either side of the narrow walkway that his father had chosen as their vantage point, each one pulsing with glowing goop. Junior and Hendricks were too far away to hear anything Taranis might have been saying beneath his mask, but not far enough to risk raising their voices.

"A crew of seven…and they have a Gorv," whispered Hendricks.

Junior had seen it too. It kept dipping out of sight as it paced the other side of the ship, but now that Taranis was here it had emerged. It stood guard at the entrance ramp to the ship, seven feet of pure muscle with a machine gun in one hand and a bandolier slung over its shoulder. Scars marked half its pale face, all interwoven into a sickening jigsaw puzzle. Junior preferred not to think about how they had got there.

"Can they fly a ship that size with just seven?" he whispered.

"Yes, but that's where you come in." Hendricks paused, watching as Taranis led his prisoner up the ramp, the Gorv falling in behind. "Once we take off, I want you to melt through the coolant system."

Junior shook his head in disbelief. "*Take off?* Why not blast the engines from here and get away on the speeder?" The thought of being trapped on a ship with Taranis made him sick.

"No. If we strike now, we'll never get to Kano. Once the ship takes off, though, Mezo's interceptors will be on it. We'll give them a chance to catch up, and while both sides get caught up in the fight, we'll grab Kano and take an escape pod."

"And go where? Those interceptors will catch us long before we're out of the planet's atmosphere."

"In a Republic-made escape pod, sure, but not a Poterian one. I can guarantee that."

Junior didn't like the sound of that. He didn't like the sound of any of it. Getting caught in a fight between Taranis and Mezo, relying on Poterian tech to escape, and all the while his father too weak to fight. Hendricks had played down his injuries on the way here, but Junior knew him too well. He could see the gritted teeth hidden behind tight lips, the constant adjustment of the torn overcoat. There was something wrong with his father's chest, something broken, and the pain was getting worse.

Thunder rumbled through the hoverpad. The engines ignited, filling the room with flickering blue and orange light.

"Dad, we don't have to do this."

"I told you, we *cannot* lose Kano."

"What's so important about Kano?!" he shouted, not caring to hide his voice beneath the roar of the engines. He could barely hear himself at this point. "I'd like to help him too, but I don't understand why everyone is so eager to tear this city apart just to find him!"

"It's not him that Taranis wants, it's his—" Hendricks keeled forward, clutching his chest.

"Dad!" He reached out to help. Hendricks shook his head, but Junior persisted, grabbing the overcoat and tearing it away button by button. His father tried to push him off, but his arms felt like noodles. There was no weight behind them, no strength.

When the coat finally fell away, Junior's heart sank. *He shouldn't have worn a white flight suit.* A patch of dried blood marked the lower part of his father's abdomen, and there, at the center of it, Junior saw a shard of shrapnel the size of his forefinger staring back at him.

"I told you we should've gone to a hospital," he said, trying to sound calm as his heart pounded inside his chest.

"Well I guess you'll have to improvise," said Hendricks, wincing.

Junior gulped. He knew what he had to do; his father had shown him the technique long ago. It had always been meant as a last resort, something Junior had hoped he would never have to do. For the first time in his life, he truly wished that he didn't have these powers right now.

Carefully, he wrapped his fingers around the shrapnel. His father squirmed at the touch.

"Hold still," he said, trying to keep his own hand steady.

"Wait." Hendricks tore off a corner of the overcoat and stuck the cloth between his teeth, then gave a thumbs-up.

Junior took a deep breath. *Here we go.* He yanked the shrapnel out. He felt the blood instantly ooze between his fingers. Hendricks gave a muffled groan beneath the cloth, his face turning scarlet.

First part done. Now for…part two. Junior pressed his hand against the wound. His father nodded at him beneath beads of sweat. *Make it quick.*

He ignited his hand. Hendricks screamed and Junior stumbled back, smearing his father's blood across the floor. Where the wound had been, he now saw a mangled pile of raw, red flesh. It was done. He exhaled, the weight of the world now easing off his shoulders. His father ripped the cloth out of his mouth, gasping.

"Are you alright?" asked Junior, feeling a little dizzy himself.

Hendricks looked to his son and managed a smile. "Your mother would be proud."

Junior felt something well up inside him. He couldn't explain what, whether it was from saving his father's life or the mention of his mother, but something was choking him. Tears welled up in his eyes, tears he tried to smear away on his sleeve.

"What happened to her?" he heard himself say. He wasn't sure why he had said it. He had asked that question a thousand times before, and a thousand times it was met with the same sad shake of the head. The memory always seemed too painful for his father, but now, knowing how close they were to facing Taranis, it might be his only chance to get an answer.

Hendricks stared at the pipes beside him, sweat still glistening on his face.

"Why did she leave?" pressed Junior.

Hendricks took a deep breath. He sat himself upright against the pipes, wincing with every movement. "Your mother…was the most powerful Zoboros I had ever seen. Too powerful. We tried everything we could to control her powers, but their nature was…unstable. Not even Nobara could help her. Your mother knew it was only a matter of time before she gave herself away, and she knew if they came for her that they would come for you too.

"I told her we would move to the Outer Territories, somewhere our enemies wouldn't find us, but she refused. She said the work I was doing here was too important. She didn't want any of those children, especially her own, to live with that fear."

"Where did she go?"

Hendricks shook his head. "The one place I can't find. The one place that doesn't exist."

Junior knew the name. He had heard it in the old stories. "Iramwerta," he whispered.

Hendricks nodded. "There was a rumor that the displaced Zoboros were gathering there after the war. Your mother went to join them, but I lost contact with her as soon as she reached Mogaddu. I spent cycles searching for her, but I never found a trace."

"Do you think she found it?"

"Or something worse," muttered Hendricks.

Junior shivered. The more he thought about it, though, the more it didn't add up. "If she's as powerful as you say, then she's still out there. She *has* to be. When we get out of here, we can find her. Together."

Hendricks's eyes widened. There was fear in them, fear Junior had never seen on his father's face before.

"Dad what's wrong? Say something, you—"

"Back from the dead, I see," came a voice like ice.

Junior froze. The roar of the engines faded, and all he heard now was the soft breath hissing through the mask.

He turned, slowly. Taranis stood just a few feet away, the glow of the pipes casting shadows across his mask. Kano stood in front of him, shaking, the blade pressed against his neck.

"After all this trouble, you would just kill him?" said Hendricks. He placed a hand on the machine gun laying at his side, but made no move to pick it up.

"If only to see the look on your face while I did it," replied the monster, tugging Kano's scraggly hair back. Kano yelped, a drop of blood trickling down his neck.

"That's enough!" shouted Hendricks. Junior watched the machine gun slide past his feet and clunk against Taranis's boot.

"Do you take me for a fool?" hissed Taranis, tugging Kano's head back a little farther.

A pistol skated past Junior's feet and stopped beside the machine gun.

"Satisfied?" asked Hendricks.

"No."

"Well there's no fixing that."

"There is, Hendricks. I hold half the puzzle in my hand." He shook Kano for effect. "You can give me the other half, and then no one else has to die. Hell, I can leave the boy here with you and go my own way. Just tell me where."

Where what? Junior racked his brain. What else could Taranis want? Another Zoboros? Another Poterian ship? What else could his father possibly be hiding?

"Let's not kid ourselves, Taranis," said Hendricks. "You won't trust anything I tell you, and frankly I wouldn't either. No matter what happens here, you are still going to take the boy, and you are still going to kill me."

Taranis fell silent. Beneath that mask, Junior could practically hear the wheels turning as the maniac planned its next move.

"You are a tough man to break, Hendricks – as is your son."

Junior sensed the threat. "Don't take the bait, Dad," he said, igniting his hands. "I can protect myself."

"So strong," continued Taranis. "Twice I thought I'd killed you, and twice you have survived. There's fire in your eyes. You see it too, don't you Hendricks? You see *her*."

The flames snuffed from Junior's hands, but he didn't even notice it. He just stood there, shocked. "You know nothing about my mother," he said.

"How would you know?" asked Taranis. "Your father sent her away long ago, just like he did all his Zoboros. Reconciling for old sins, no doubt. But your father never told you about his gift, did he? He was quite the prodigy back in his day."

"Don't toy with him, Taranis," said Hendricks, his voice sharp enough to make Junior tense.

Taranis inched forward, keeping Kano out in front of him. "You see, when the war was at its peak, your father was assigned to an elite group, hand-picked by Admiral Carmichael for one very important purpose."

"Junior, do not engage," said Hendricks.

He's scared. Junior looked to Taranis, his heart pounding. "What…what was their purpose?"

Blue light flickered through the mask. "Killing Zoboros."

No. His father had been many things, but he wasn't an assassin – a murderer. He was a pilot, for goodness sake. He flew…top-secret missions.

He turned back and saw the truth written on his father's face.

"I'm sorry," said Hendricks.

"Ironic, isn't it?" said Taranis. "That he would fall in love with the very thing he was supposed to—"

"ENOUGH!" screamed Junior. His hands ignited with flames, blue and hot. There was nothing he wanted more than to watch Taranis burn.

"Junior," came his father's voice, softly. "It's going to be okay. Just close your eyes and take a deep breath."

Deep breath? There was little chance of that. All he could feel was the blood pumping through his veins, the anger swirling through his head, all focused on one central point.

That mask.

"Junior," came Hendricks's voice again, "look at me."

Don't try to stop me, thought Junior, *I can't let Taranis win this time*. He turned, expecting that stern look he always got, the one that said, "You're about to do something stupid," but instead his father was *smiling*. Of all the occasions to finally crack, why now? Why when he was facing down a terrorist, with blood all over his…flight suit.

He saw it: his father's finger hovering over the button on the wrist.

"Son, close your eyes."

Junior nodded. He turned to face Taranis once more, the slits in the mask bearing down on him. He closed his eyes.

The rest happened fast. There was a crack so loud that his ears started ringing, and a flash so bright that his eyes still felt its sting. Through the ringing, he heard someone scream. He opened his eyes but all he saw was a big, white blur. He started forward but stumbled and fell, his body sinking into the metal scaffolding. Slowly, he began to blink away the spots. Kano was lying across from him, struggling blindly to stand back up. Beyond him, two figures began to materialize, one in front of the other, with nothing but a sword between them.

"DAD!" he screamed. He started forward and immediately fell again. The room was spinning, but the blade in his father's chest was clear as anything.

"It's fitting, isn't it?" hissed Taranis, grazing a metal finger down Hendricks's scar. "That the same blade be the one that killed you." He yanked it from Hendricks's chest, and Junior watched his father spill onto the floor.

"NOOO!" he screamed. He leaped to his feet, but not before Taranis shot five bolts from his fingertips. Junior felt all his muscles seize at once and he slammed back down.

Hendricks groaned on the floor. "Please, don't…"

Taranis marched past the dying man and toward Junior. "You should have just enough time to watch this end, Hendricks."

"NOOO!" screamed Kano.

Junior saw the metal boots stop just a few feet from his face. He tried making a spark, but his hands kept twitching. He was just able to tilt his head back and look up into the glowing blue eye slits.

"I'm sorry, boy," said Taranis. "This wasn't your fault."

Junior saw the lightning swell. The lights flickered. This was it. He braced, but when the lightning flashed, something came between them.

"KANO!" he screamed. Lightning danced over the cuffs and across Kano's body. Taranis snapped the bolts away as soon as they started, leaving Kano to collapse beside Junior, smoke rising from his singed clothing.

Taranis raced over and clutched Kano's hair in his gauntlet. Kano barely seemed to register the pain; he looked unconscious. "You *fool!* You almost killed yourself, and for what? To give him a few extra seconds of life?" Taranis dragged him to the pipes and left his limp body to lean against them. "If only you understood how important you were."

Junior saw the boots marching back for him. He felt them reverberate through the floor with every step. His muscles were starting to settle, though. Now was his chance. He raised his fist to summon a fireball, and felt another bolt sting him, throwing him back into more convulsions.

"That's three times he's cheated death!" shouted Taranis. "So I'll make this quick."

Taranis raised the bloodied sword. His father's blood. His blood. Time seemed to stand still. In the corner of his eye he could see his father crawling desperately toward the guns, but he would never reach them in time. He looked to Kano, who was...*standing?* Smoke still rose from his clothing. His body looked ready to collapse again, but there was something in his eyes, some strength that had taken over him. He raised his cuffs and aimed them for Taranis.

Don't do it, thought Junior. *You'll only hurt yourself more*. But then he noticed something. The lights on the cuffs: they had all flickered out. Some had even burst into pieces.

Taranis had made a mistake.

The cuffs exploded off Kano's hands. Junior felt the floor turn into an ocean wave as thunder rolled over him. It lifted the metal boots off the floor and smashed Taranis against the pipes. One burst, dumping green ooze over his body as he sagged to the floor.

Kano did it.

Junior rolled onto his side, his muscles finally coming under his control again. Sirens sounded and lights flashed across the chamber, bathing it in red. Downstairs, he could hear the crew panicking as they raced out of the ship, but they quickly faded from his mind. Only one thing mattered now.

Dad.

The man laid limp a few feet from his weapons, his eyes closed. Junior tried to stand but his legs shook like jelly, so he crawled as fast as he could through the red puddle slowly forming around his father.

"Dad, please…please don't go," he said, nudging feebly at his father's shoulder.

Hendricks's eyes opened. He managed a small smile. He opened his mouth, but no words came out. It looked like the effort was choking him.

"Don't speak," said Junior quickly, frantically. "I'll get you on the speeder. I'll get you to a hospital. I'll make sure Mezo gives you her best medics." He tried to lift his father, but the electricity had sapped the strength from his arms. It was like trying to lift a boulder.

Hendricks shook his head, still smiling, and reached into his pocket. He drew a pin no larger than his fingernail and placed it in Junior's hand.

A golden triangle, Junior saw. Stained with his blood.

When he looked back, the light had faded from his father's eyes.

"No, no, no!" He clutched onto his father's chest, checking for a heartbeat. There was none. *"PLEASE!"* Tears streaked down his face. He didn't know what to do. He didn't want to do anything. He just wanted to lie here and melt into the floor.

He felt a hand wrap around his arm, still warm and sweaty from being trapped in the cuffs. "Junior, I'm sorry," said Kano, his eyes red and puffy, "but we have to go…the Gorv…we have to go *now*."

Junior rose, letting Kano lead him down the walkway. Everything passed by in a whir. Horns began to blare, but he didn't hear them. The lights still flashed, but he didn't see them. All he saw was his father's killer, dripping with green ooze, rising to block their way.

Chapter 22

A Fatal Mistake

Kano stopped in his tracks, blurting the first word that came to his lips.

"*Murderer!*"

The mask just stared back at him, the red lights washing over it. Spots of green ooze sank into its grooves, setting the Mogaddan letters aglow. "Don't make us kill you," Taranis whispered.

Us? Kano heard the click of a magazine. He turned, slowly, to face the barrel of the machine gun that was wrapped in the Gorv's massive paws.

Junior stood beside him, motionless. *Now would be a good time to spark a flame*, thought Kano, but Junior didn't seem to be aware of the present danger. He just kept staring at the body lying across from them.

Don't look at it, Kano reminded himself. Looking would only shatter him, too. He needed to focus on the moment. He needed to focus on beating Taranis.

Kano aimed at Taranis with an open palm. His heart was pounding, but he couldn't let it show. He tried puffing his chest. "Let us *pass*," he croaked, his voice cracking on the last note.

Well, so much for sounding tough.

Taranis shook his head. "Where would you go, Kano? Back to the city? They'll hand you right over to Mezo, and she'll make sure you live the rest of your life in a cage."

"It doesn't sound so different from your plan," said Kano.

Taranis shook his head. "I would've given you freedom, Kano. I still can, if you cooperate." Kano glanced back at the Gorv. Taranis raised his voice, a hint of frustration echoing through. "Face it, you have no other way out. Your last chance died with Hendricks."

Kano suddenly felt warm. He thought it was his own anger at first, but he was wrong. It was Junior's anger, turned to flames that crackled over each hand.

"Do not test me," said Taranis, his sword flickering in the firelight. A drop of ooze hung from its tip, readying to fall. A little jolt of electricity danced across the blade, and then something strange happened. Kano watched the drop retreat back to the metal, sticking to it like glue.

Highly unstable. Kano looked to the break in the pipes. Gravity jelly was drizzling out and pooling onto the walkway. And just a few feet away from Taranis. Kano took a step right; Taranis took a step left. *Good.* Kano kept his hand aimed at the mask, his ears listening for the Gorv.

"You told me to ask the right questions," said Kano, inching in a semi-circle while Taranis did the same. "So tell me, what makes my powers so special? You've never stayed in a place this long, never done this amount of damage, and it wasn't for Junior or any other Zoboros who came through Famora. It was just for me."

Taranis chuckled. "Your *powers?*" he spat back. Kano could sense his smile hidden behind the mask. "Dimitri, it appears no one ever told the poor boy." The Gorv grunted. "Your powers are something to be admired, sure, but they are of little consequence to my mission."

Kano heard the splash of Taranis's boot in the puddle, but he was too stuck on the monster's words to act. "Then what is your mission?"

Taranis pointed toward the leaking pipe. "Didn't you ever wonder what happened to the Poterians? How their entire fleet disappeared in a single battle? Only a few people know the secret of what happened in the Battle of Mogaddu – and your parents are two of them."

"Careful, Kano," said Junior with sudden command in his voice. He had two flaming fists aimed at the Gorv. It seemed his mind was focused back on the moment, though Kano couldn't say the same for himself.

"You're lying," he said. "My parents weren't soldiers. They never killed Poterians."

"I didn't say they killed Poterians," said Taranis. "I said the Poterians *disappeared.*"

"So you're saying they're magicians?" said Kano. "Last I heard they were scientists." He had also heard that they blew up a government facility, but he preferred to leave that part out.

"And you would be correct," said Taranis. "Two of the brightest minds this galaxy has ever seen. And when the enemy was at their doorstep, when all other options had been exhausted, they developed a weapon so powerful that it ended the war the moment it was fired."

"What kind of a weapon?" asked Kano.

"That's the same question I'll ask when I meet them."

Kano froze. All the pieces suddenly snapped together into a horrifying picture. "And I'm the bait."

"No Kano," said Taranis. "You're the solution."

"*Do it now!*" screamed a voice in his head. He threw his open palm at Taranis, but no power came out…

Just like he planned.

Kano hit the floor, praying this would work. He saw the blue glow as the bolts rushed through the gauntlet. Suddenly, the puddle rushed away. It leaped up and smashed Taranis's electrified hand into his own face. He screamed, his mask skating away. Kano tried to get a look at his face as he stumbled back through the break in the pipes, but Taranis fell over the edge and disappeared into darkness.

The Gorv roared. A fireball surged toward it but it dipped out of the way, machine gun still in hand. *He's going to kill us for that one.* Kano summoned the energy into his fist and threw it forward.

"No, Kano, *DON'T!*" screamed Junior.

It was too late. The Gorv hit the floor, letting the shockwave roll over him and smash through the pipes. Four of them shattered and green ooze exploded across the walkway. The alarm lights pulsed faster. Sirens blared across the chamber.

The Gorv rose, trying to wipe the goop from its eyes with its pale hand. In the other it held the machine gun at its hip, spraying bullets in a wide, blind arc.

Junior tackled Kano to the floor. They laid side by side, covering their heads as glass rained down on them.

"Stay down," said Junior. Before Kano could protest, the cadet was up on his feet and charging toward the Gorv, hands ablaze. With one hand he knocked the gun away, with the other he went for the creature's throat. The Gorv dipped out of the way in one seamless motion, its eyes still shut beneath a layer of goop. Junior swung again and again, the Gorv dodging each strike perfectly until Kano finally puzzled it out.

"Junior, the *fire*!" he shouted. Junior seemed to catch his meaning, for all at once the flames snuffed out. *Let him sense your punches now*. One struck the Gorv across the face, then a second. Junior was going for the third when the thing drove its fist forward, catching Junior in the gut and sending him skating back down the walkway.

Kano leaped to his feet, using both hands to throw the biggest shockwave he could muster. The glass pipes shattered as it rolled past them, catching the Gorv and flinging it straight down the aisle and out of sight.

Kano turned to Junior. The cadet was rising on hands and knees, clutching his chest.

"Are you alright?" He held out his hand. Junior grabbed onto a pipe instead and lifted himself up.

"Did you get him?" Junior rasped between short breaths.

"Yeah, but I don't know for how long."

Junior nodded, aiming his palms toward where the Gorv had disappeared. Fire jetted out of them, though it was more smoke than flame. Soon the aisle was filled with a black cloud so thick that even the glowing ooze on the floor faded beneath it.

"Come on," said Junior, tugging Kano in the other direction. Kano kept glancing back at the smoke as Junior forced him into a run, waiting for one of the monsters to emerge. Sirens kept ringing in his ears, but he heard something else, too – the groan of metal.

"What's happening?!"

Junior didn't answer; he just kept running.

The floor felt slippery even though they were well past the ooze. He kept feeling his weight pulling him to the left, little by little, until he was all the way to the pipes, one hand against them for support while the floor tilted beneath his feet.

"What's happening?!" he shouted at Junior. "Did I break the walkway?!"

"No, you idiot!" Junior shouted back. "You broke the damn platform!"

A wave of terror seized him. The walkway kept twisting, the ooze pressing up against the wrong side of the pipes as gravity pulled it there. Soon he had to transfer his feet onto the pipes just to keep running while the walkway rose up beside him.

The ceiling began to open (though now it was to their left instead of over their heads). Stars hovered in the distance, eclipsed as firelight lit up the chamber.

Engine light.

"Hurry!" shouted Junior. He turned toward the stars, ascending the long stack of pipes to reach them. Kano followed, feeling the pipes trembling beneath his feet as the engines rumbled. A pair of huge fangs emerged on the other side of the glass. The whole ship swam past, the repulsors on its belly blazing blue.

Junior kicked up into a sprint, trying to keep up with the ship. *He wants to board it.* A terrible idea, but it was better than falling with the rest of the platform. Kano picked up his pace, his skinny legs bounding over the pipes as fast as he could go. His chest felt tight, his muscles screamed, and the gap between him and Junior kept growing. *I'm not gonna make it.* His foot slipped on the glass and suddenly he was on his back.

It's over. He started to pick himself up, but what was the use? The ship was well past him now, and he had nothing left in the tank. Only bruises and sores from two straight days of abuse. And all just to fall out of the sky.

He felt a burly hand clench onto his shirt and hoist him to his feet.

"The ship," said Kano. He spotted its blazing engines over Junior's shoulder as it charged into the night sky, its cannons flushing red as Mezo's interceptors dove toward it. "You missed the ship."

"*We* missed the ship," said Junior. He turned and marched toward the edge of the pipes. Kano followed, feeling the cool breeze rushing in.

"They won't be able to stop a ship that size," said Junior, the distant cannon fire flashing across his face.

When they reached the edge, Kano fell to his knees, watching Famora shrink as they slowly sank beneath it.

"The hoverpads will try to fight gravity as long as they can, but soon they'll fail," said Junior. He summoned a fireball and hurled it high into the air. It flickered against the night sky for a few moments before fading away. He hurled another, and another, over and over until his arms grew so weak that he fell to his knees beside Kano, his breath heavy.

The lights of Famora were far away now, turning into a single bright star in the night sky.

"You never met your family, did you?" rasped Junior.

Kano glanced over, surprised. "I don't remember them, if that's what you mean." He eyed Junior carefully, trying to understand what he was probing at. "It always seemed unfair, but given everything that's happened the past few days…maybe it was for the best."

Junior clenched his fist, and Kano saw a spark hiss between his fingers. "My father thought a lot of things were 'for the best,' and look where that got us."

Kano felt cold. All around them, the pink mists began to roll in.

"It was a hell of a ride though," said Kano.

Junior's eyes widened. He glanced back at the labyrinth of pipes behind them. "We…we beat Taranis back there, didn't we?"

Kano smiled. "Yeah. I guess we did." He rose, the ache in his muscles finally settled. He should have been panicking, he knew, but as Junior rose beside him at the edge of the world, he felt at peace.

"All this time, I wondered where she had gone," said Junior. "My mother, I mean. I guess my dad kept it from me so I wouldn't go chasing after her."

"And if you could chase her, where would you go?"

"Mogaddu. She went there in search of a place that's never been found." *Iramwerta*. Kano didn't need to ask to know what he was referring to. "I guess it doesn't matter now. She's somewhere out there and we're stuck here."

"With all that firepower you just unleashed, someone's bound to have seen it," said Kano, more for his own reassurance than Junior's. "They'll come."

"They might," conceded Junior, "but if they do, it'll be no better than if we crashed into the rocks. You know what they do to Zoboros, don't you?"

Kano gulped. He had been so focused on escaping Taranis that he had forgotten the fate that still awaited them. "We have Carmichael though. He's helped us before; he'll do it again."

"I wouldn't put your faith in a Carmichael," said Junior. "My father may have been close to the admiral, but he never trusted him. Not that he ever trusted anyone, but I knew by the look on his face anytime that name came up that it meant something personal. Even if

Carmichael pretends to be different than the admiral before him, he's still just as dangerous. Whatever he's done to help you, I'll bet it's part of his own plan."

"I…I don't believe you." Kano thought back to the cellar, to how Carmichael had made a fool of himself in front of the general just to keep them safe. Could it be part of a bigger plan? Everyone else seemed to be playing one: Hendricks, Novak, Taranis. Why not Carmichael? The rocks below were suddenly sounding a lot more inviting. If only his friends were here with the truck – but they were probably prisoners by now, and even if they weren't, Kano would still have no way to contact them in the city…

He saw the communicator glint off Junior's wrist. "Your speeder!" he blurted.

Junior looked to his communicator, his eyes widening. "Do you remember where Taranis parked it?" he asked. "If we get close, I can get a—"

"You don't need to get close. Jaden boosted the signal so you can reach it from anywhere!"

"Well at least he's good for something," mumbled Junior as he pounded on the center button. The screen blipped for a few painful moments, until it finally turned green.

"Did it work?!" asked Kano.

"YES!" Junior scooped Kano up into a bear hug that nearly crushed the boy's back. "WE'RE GONNA LIVE!"

When Junior finally released him, Kano had a sudden, important thought as the air returned to his lungs. "But…where do we go?"

Junior shrugged. "Stow away on a freighter, I guess. Or find some smugglers who don't ask too many questions. Whatever gets us to Mogaddu."

Kano blinked. "You want me to come with you?"

"Well where the hell else are you gonna go? Besides, Mogaddu is a dangerous place. I could use your powers in a pinch."

Kano considered it. A life on Mogaddu. This was his chance to escape the IDF. His chance to chase Iramwerta. He could find answers there. Maybe even find the mountain. But if he did, he would be leaving everyone else behind. Everyone who saved him on the Crossing. He couldn't just leave them to be punished while he walked free.

"I—" He was cut off by a rush of wind and the rumble of engines. A ship floated down before them, one unlike any of Mezo's other toys. This ship was tall and thin, with two wide, slightly arced wings at the very top.

"Oh no," grumbled Junior.

"You know that ship?"

"I was on it."

The bottom opened with a blast of compressed air. It lowered into a ramp that a shiny pair of shoes were strutting down.

"Boys! It's great to see you again!"

The ramp touched down on the pipes. Kano started forward, almost automatically, when Junior stepped in his way.

"Where are you taking us?" asked the cadet.

Carmichael squinted down at him. "Off the falling platform, for a start. Unless you have someplace else to be?" Troopers descended the ramp in two lines on either side of him, stopping at the snap of his finger.

Junior gave Kano a look that could only mean 'I told you so.' "I take it you have cuffs on that ship for us?" Junior called up.

Carmichael nodded. "Ideally, you'll only have to wear them for a short time, just until Mezo gets over the mess you made on Famora."

"*Mess?*" Junior spat back. "You trusted me to help you and I did."

"And you did your job well. Kano is safe and Taranis is on the run, but there's also a city floating up there that's been smashed apart by all this. We need to make sure that never happens again."

"And how do you plan to do that?" asked Junior.

Carmichael glanced around. "I have a few ideas, but we'll talk about them another time. Now get on before this platform starts picking up speed."

It took just a single look from Junior for Kano to know that he wasn't getting on that ship. Kano spotted the speeder in the distance, a silhouette against the stars, waiting for Junior's signal.

"Come on," said Kano, "we have no choice." He started up the ramp, tugging Junior along. The helmets followed them as they passed, intent on their every move. "A long fall from here, isn't it?" muttered Kano, nodding at the abyss beneath them. Junior nodded slowly and pressed a few buttons on his communicator as they came face-to-face with Carmichael.

Carmichael smiled. "I promise you boys, this won't last long."

"No, it won't," said Kano. In the corner of his eye, he saw the speeder slip underneath the ramp. Junior hit the ground. Kano aimed a palm in each direction, one pulse launching the troopers down the ramp, the other launching Carmichael back up into his ship. Junior rolled over the edge and down into the seat cushions, his speeder purring as he grabbed the controls.

"Come on!" he shouted up.

Kano saw the troopers starting to rise. He threw another shockwave down. It was enough to make them stumble over themselves, but at this distance he wouldn't be able to propel them any farther away. "GO!" he shouted.

"Are you crazy?!"

"I can't leave my friends behind!" Kano shouted back. He felt an arm wrap around his neck.

"That's *enough*, Kano," said Carmichael in his ear.

But it wasn't. Junior was still hovering there. Kano threw his hand back at Carmichael and felt it slide into something cold and heavy. It tightened around his hand. He felt his energy drain away in an instant.

He swung the cuffs into Carmichael's gut, and the captain's grip loosened. Kano slipped out and threw his free hand at Carmichael, but all that came out was a little puff, barely enough to blow Carmichael's hair.

Enough to make a ripple, though.

"Kano, jump now!" cried Junior.

For a moment, Kano thought he would. He saw the speeder floating there, his ticket away from whatever punishment awaited him. *But my friends.* He stopped himself. There was a flash of blue. He felt his whole back clench up. Another flash and his legs gave out from under him. A third, and he was flat on his face. Still the flashes kept coming.

"Hold your fire!" screamed Carmichael, rushing to his side. Kano felt the captain's fingers checking his neck for a pulse. He tried to flinch, but he couldn't move his neck. He couldn't move anything.

"We need a medic!" shouted Carmichael, his voice sounding deeper, slower, as if he was drifting farther away. *"You...hit...him...with...toooo...much!"*

The last thing Kano heard was the thunder of engines in the distance.

Chapter 23

The Proposal

Cranes dotted the horizon, silhouettes against the orange and pink sunset. Crews had been working day and night on the reconstruction, many having flown in from across the quadrant. Famora had offered to pay them well for their work, so long as they worked quickly. Junior couldn't help but smile as he watched the new riggings come to life. This city had never given a second thought to the Dockyards; it was only when they were gone that Famorans realized how much they needed them. Judging from all the buzz below, the Dockyards would soon be better than ever, but he wouldn't be here to see it.

His communicator buzzed. It was time. He left the railing and headed down the walkway, pulling his hood in tight as he passed the rows of old brick buildings. Few people hung around these parts, but he could never be sure who was watching.

The tavern door opened with a creak. The stink of spilled booze tickled his nostrils as he stepped quietly between the patrons. Fewer than usual, but still enough to fill most of the seats. Workers needed someplace to take a break, he surmised. He could only be thankful that they were all smoking bareno; someone would need sharp eyes to spot him through the cloud they generated.

He found his seat at the bar, a drink already placed in front of it. Beside it sat his contact, short but plump enough to spill over the edges of the barstool, blotches of grease dotting his gray uniform. Junior sat. The man said nothing.

Do I talk first? Junior drummed his fingers awkwardly on his glass, not daring to drink from it. He trusted Nobara had taken precautions for this meeting, but there was no way of knowing who might be skulking around the tavern at this hour.

"Ya know, a week ago I thought you was some kinda miracle worker," said Cassius, his brown eyes looking anywhere but at Junior. "Then I watched the news and realized, 'Dammit, the kid coulda walked through that fire in his sleep'."

Junior smirked, following Cassius's lead by letting his eyes wander. "Did Nobara tell you the job?"

Cassius nodded and took a sip. "Nobara poured your drink, too. You'd be smart to use it, before these new folks catch on that you're not a regular."

Junior glanced around. No one seemed to be watching, but at the same time it felt like everyone was. He took a sip. Tasted like piss.

"Can you do it?" he asked.

Cassius drew a long, uncertain breath. "It's a long way. The Guild doesn't operate in those territories anymore, on account of our ships don't always come back." He took another sip. "Under normal circumstances I might be able to arrange a detour for one of our light freighters, but Taranis changed everything. Now every checkpoint has extra security and every route is carefully watched. If a ship shows up late, someone's bound to ask why."

Junior tightened his grip on the glass. From what he had heard, Mezo's troops found no sign of Taranis in the wreckage. There was still a chance he may have perished, but Junior knew better. He took another sip. Somehow his drink was much warmer now. He realized his palms were starting to heat up, and shook them out.

"Are there any…less conventional ways of getting there?"

Cassius chuckled. "There's really no talkin' you out of it, is there? Kid, I feel compelled to tell you that there are plenty of *safe* places that I can very easily get you to."

Junior glowered at him with his orange eyes.

"Alright, alright," said Cassius, slapping his hands down on the counter. "I'm only tellin' you this because I owe ya: there is a way. A *dangerous* way. But you'll need more friends than just me to get you there undetected."

Friends. Junior knew the cue. He drew his father's pin from his pocket and placed it on the counter, cupping his hand over it so only his contact would see.

Cassius smiled, his golden teeth twinkling. "The Guild is at your service."

◁◆▷

He had been climbing for days, but he finally reached it. Dark and cold as he remembered, but safe from the rain. The water had carried him down the rocks three times, and three times he had climbed back up. Nothing would stop him now. He was ready.

Kano walked along, following the blue lights as they flashed overhead, though once one disappeared in the distance it would take a minute for the next one to arrive. He wished Junior were here now to spark a flame.

Soon he reached the glowing pool. All was silent. *Come on, come out.* The water just sat there, undisturbed. He stepped up to the water's edge and stared down at the crystal blue, his face staring back at him. The same young face, the same disheveled hair. *But I looked older last time. He made me older.* Kano knelt down and touched the water's surface. Suddenly, the water turned to green where he had touched it, the color spreading through the pool like a virus. *That's not right.* The walls started to glow too, only they weren't made of rocks anymore.

They were made of pipes.

He heard the splash, saw the mask rising from the water. *No, no, no.* He tried to run but the gauntlet grabbed him by the hair and yanked him into the pool. He felt the rush of cold and suddenly he splashed up onto a sandy shore, coughing up water. Waves lashed at his back as the monster dragged him through the sand. There was light here, and in the distance a giant wall of stone, with ancient markings etched into it.

Taranis finally let him go when they reached the wall, using the tip of his boot to roll Kano onto his back.

As Kano stared, he realized something: the markings on the mask matched the stone wall exactly.

"Where are we?"

Taranis said nothing.

"Who…who are you?"

The monster pulled the mask from its face, revealing fire beneath it.

Kano snapped up, gasping for air. He glanced around his bedside. Monitors beeped and little bots wheeled this way and that. He hardly had time to ponder any of it, though, because hovering over his bedside was the face he had missed most of all.

"It's okay," she whispered. "It was just a dream."

"How are you here? What happened to…?"

Everything started to spin. He felt something cold press against his chest. *Cuffs*. Li was using hers to ease him back onto the pillow.

"Everyone's okay," she said. "Carmichael took good care of us."

"For now," said Kano, gazing at the pair covering his own hands. "Where are they?"

"They're on board. They said we could visit you one at a time, so we've been taking turns."

"On board?!" blurted Kano, his heart sinking. "Going where?"

"I don't know, but we've been in hyperspace for about five days now."

"*Five days!*" Kano started to climb out of bed. Pain shot through his head like a hot knife.

"Relax," she whispered, her voice soothing, "don't do anything stupid."

"No promises," muttered Kano, falling back onto his pillow. He suddenly felt exhausted.

She smiled. "Carmichael wants to meet with us in a few hours. Rest until then. I'll have the medic bring you some food." She kissed him on the forehead and headed for the door.

Kano's head still spun as he laid there. *They're okay,* he thought as he nodded off. *They're okay and we're all in space...*

⊲◆⊳

Kano drummed his fingers on the wooden table. To his left sat Li and Makoto. To his right Jaden and Akio. A chandelier hung over their heads, bathing the little room in a yellowish glow. The walls were lined with shelves full of old, worn books, most written in languages Kano had never seen before.

They sat in silence. Kano turned to Jaden, hoping for a joke to lighten the mood, but Jaden just stared miserably at the table. From what Kano had gathered, Jaden had come up with most of the rescue plan at the Crossing, and he was taking their defeat very personally.

Akio kept watching the door with a proud, defiant look on his blue face, even with his arms and legs bound together by chains. Li was focused on the books, scanning over each in silent fascination.

Makoto was the only one to meet Kano's gaze, offering him a reassuring nod, though Kano couldn't help but notice that his brother's hands were shaking.

The door swung open.

"Hello, *hello!*" exclaimed Carmichael as he strolled into the room. Cera and Eines filed in after him. "Good to see the gang all together again."

"Happy to be back," answered Makoto, a hint of truth behind his sarcasm.

Carmichael claimed the seat right across from Kano while his two officers hung back by the door, each preferring to stand. Kano eyed the captain carefully, Junior's warnings echoing through his head.

"So you're all probably wondering where we're going—"

"And what the hell we're doing here," mumbled Jaden, still staring at the table.

"Right, well, my intention is to keep you all safe until we learn more about what happened to Taranis."

"But I thought you were leading the search for Taranis?" said Makoto.

"I am, but—"

"Then how are we going to be safe if you're putting us on the frontlines?" asked Li.

Kano felt a knot tighten in his stomach. Taranis was alive. He had gathered that much around the ship before coming to the meeting. No one could prove it yet, but everyone knew.

"To be fair," began Carmichael, "you're in the company of the only person who's ever sent Taranis packing." His eyes fell on Kano.

"*You* beat Taranis?!" blurted Jaden, looking up from the table for the first time.

Kano realized that all eyes were on him now. "Sorta. I mean, Junior and I held him off long enough to escape, but—"

"Well damn! I wish I had been there!" said Jaden, smiling. The others smiled as well, all except Akio, who gave Kano an approving nod instead. Strangely, Kano found that a bit more touching.

Kano returned his attention to Carmichael. "Do we know where he'll strike next?" he asked.

"No," answered Carmichael, tipping back nervously in his chair.

"So what? Do we just hide out until you find him?" asked Makoto.

"Not necessarily," said Carmichael. By the nervous look on his face, Kano could tell the captain was choosing his next words very carefully. "The fact is…Taranis is one of *many* threats to the galaxy—"

"So we hide until you stop them all?" snapped Li.

"No, I…" he kept tipping back and forth in his chair, trying to find the words. "When we get to our destination, everything will make sense."

"Why wait?" hissed Akio, his bulbous eyes bearing down on Carmichael.

"Yeah, tell us what's going on here!" chimed Jaden.

Carmichael turned to Cera. She nodded. He gulped. "I was hoping you'd get to meet the others before I explained everything. I figured then you'd be a bit comfortable with the whole idea—"

"What others?" asked Makoto, leaning forward.

"*Part of his own plan,*" Junior's voice echoed in Kano's head.

"What I mean is—" Carmichael tipped back too far this time. He started to fall and there was a flash of green. Everyone gasped. From Cera's hands came two glowing beams of energy, coming together beneath the captain to form a transparent cushion.

The energy beams began to tilt, lifting Carmichael up to face them once more. He looked so nervous that the color had drained from his face, but as he looked at their shocked faces, he couldn't help but crack a smile. He cleared his throat and addressed the crowd.

"My friends, I'm building a team."

Michael Ciccarelli-Walsh lives in Tallahassee, Florida, where he attended Florida State University for both his undergraduate and graduate degrees (Go Noles!). He is also the author of *Project Vortex,* the second novel in the Zoboros series.

ciccarelliwalsh.com